Snow

Place for

Murder

Snow Place for Murder

Diane Kelly

St. Martin's Paperbacks

First published in the United States by St. Martin's Paperbacks, an imprint of St. Martin's Publishing Group

SNOW PLACE FOR MURDER

For information, address St. Martin's Publishing Group, 120 Broadway, New York, NY 10271.

www.stmartins.com

ISBN: 978-1-250-81601-6

Our books may be purchased in bulk for promotional, educational, or business use. Please contact your local bookseller or the Macmillan Corporate and Premium Sales Department at 1–800–221–7945, ext. 5442, or by email at MacmillanSpecialMarkets@macmillan.com.

Printed in the United States of America

St. Martin's Paperbacks edition / November 2023

10 9 8 7 6 5 4 3 2 1

ACKNOWLEDGMENTS

As always, there is a slew of people to thank for helping bring this book to life.

Thanks to Linda A. Conte and Anita Learned for suggesting the name Pebble for Rocky's daughter. It's the perfect nickname for her! And thanks to Christine Steckel for suggesting I have characters from my other series visit the Mountaintop Lodge. What a fun idea!

Thanks to the hardworking team at St. Martin's Press who make these books possible. Thanks to my editor, Nettie Finn, for your spot-on suggestions and for being so enjoyable to work with. Oodles of appreciation go to Sara Beth Haring, Sara LaCotti, and Allison Ziegler for all your hard work on marketing and publicity. Thanks to Executive Managing Editor John Rounds for leading the way. Thanks to artists Danielle Christopher and Mary Ann Lasher for creating such cute, eye-catching covers for the books. And ongoing thanks to my agent, Helen Breitwieser, for all you do to keep me doing what I love.

As always, thanks to you readers who chose to spend your time with Misty, Rocky, Brynn, Patty, Yeti, and Molasses at the Mountaintop Lodge. Enjoy your stay!

CHAPTER 1

Misty Murphy

FUTURE SITE OF THE RETREAT ON BLUE
RIDGE—AN ADVENTURE CAPITAL RESORT

The huge sign loomed over the two-lane mountain
road, its colorful paint at odds with the subdued browns
and grays of the surrounding late-fall forest, the mod-
ern luxury hotel depicted thereon an existential threat
to the pines, hemlocks, and ubiquitous beech trees that
gave Beech Mountain its name. A trio of does tiptoed
past us. One glanced at the sign, twitched her tail, and
snorted, as if offended by the project that would require
her and her graceful, brown-eyed friends to find a new
path through the woods to drink at the Elk River.

I felt a twinge of guilt in my gut. I'd soon host the
developer of this project at my lodge, plus more than a
dozen potential investors. Maybe I'd agreed too quickly.
But I'd been flattered a venture capitalist from London had discovered my humble lodge and wanted to fill
every room for five nights with guests. Midweek, too,
Sunday through Thursday—nights that usually garnered only a few bookings. A hawk swooped overhead,
its *caw-caw-caw* sounding as if it, too, were chastising

me for my part in destroying thirty-five acres of pristine forest.

Biting my lip, I turned to Rockford Crowder, better known as "Rocky," who stood beside me. As of recently, the handsome handyman at my Mountaintop Lodge had become a romantic partner, as well. With his graying sandy hair, the light beard spanning his cheeks, and the well-developed shoulders rounding the fabric of his plaid flannel shirt, he resembled an anthropomorphized mountain lion. "Did I make a mistake allowing Nigel Goodwin to pitch this project at my lodge?"

Rocky's blue-gray eyes, the same color as the distant peaks, locked on mine. His face clouded with conflict. "Hard to say. This resort would be good in some ways, bad in others."

"But mostly bad," came a deep male voice from the woods to our right.

We turned to see a brawny beast emerge from the shadows. If not for the fact that he'd spoken, I might think the big, burly man with the bushy brown beard was a sasquatch. He wore boots with toes covered in dried mud, nylon hiking pants with an abundance of zippered pockets, and a puffer vest over a long-sleeved T-shirt. Atop a head of unruly hair sat a khaki camping hat, its chin string disappearing into the man's beard. He carried a fancy camera with a long lens attached. A camera bag was slung over his shoulder. He headed our way, offering a pleasant, gap-toothed smile and stretching out a meaty hand when he reached us. "Hi, folks. I'm Gus."

"Misty," I said, taking his hand and giving it a shake.

He repeated the routine with Rocky. When introductions were finished, he cocked his head and eyed me. "Did I hear you say Nigel Goodwin is coming to your lodge?"

No sense denying it. "That's right. He'll be pitching this project to potential investors." In fact, Goodwin would be footing the entire bill for their five-night stay.

"You own the Mountaintop Lodge, right? I believe I saw you out front a while back." He chuckled. "You were engaged in battle with a scarecrow."

I cringed. *How many others had witnessed me wrangling that straw-filled rascal?* "Yep. That was me." With the recent high winds that had battered the mountain, keeping the decorative scarecrows in place had been challenging. Fortunately, when Thanksgiving was over a week from now, I'd be able to take the autumn adornments down and replace them with winter and Christmas-themed decorations.

The man's fuzzy, friendly face turned serious. "Take a look at this." He turned his camera so we could see the images displayed on a small screen on the back. He scrolled through them. There were deer galore, mostly does and fawns but a few antlered bucks among them. Several lone groundhogs. A pair of playful skunks. A frolicking fox. Many of the photos depicted the animals coming to the bank of the Elk River to drink.

When he stopped scrolling, I looked up at him. "Are you a wildlife photographer?"

"Photographer. Researcher. Rescuer. Rehabilitator. If it's got anything to do with the animals around here, I'm involved in it—other than hunting that is. I believe we should live and let live." He removed the lens and slid the camera and attachment into its case. The equipment secured, he pulled his cell phone from a pocket on his hiking pants and showed us a series of videos. Many were grainy and dark, taken at night. "All of these videos were captured right here." He gestured around us.

"With this acreage being on the river, the wildlife is very active."

I pointed to the screen, which played footage of a black bear ambling along the riverbank in the dark, his eyes shining like flashlights. "How long did you have to wait to spot that bear?"

"I didn't have to wait at all," Gus said. "My trail cam caught this footage. I've got cameras situated all around this area. There's one right there." He pointed to a nearby tree. The camera's camouflage cover was designed to make it blend in with the foliage, and it took me a few seconds to make out the device attached to the trunk. A sad frown claimed his face. "Lots of animals cross the road here. If that resort is built, there will be untold amounts of carnage."

My stomach tied itself in tight knots. Collisions with deer were common in the mountains, and accidents involving bears happened frequently, too. The incidents weren't only dangerous for the animals, they also posed risks to the vehicle's passengers. Adult bears could weigh three hundred pounds or more. I made a mental note to suggest that Nigel Goodwin include wildlife warnings on his resort's website, maybe even install signs around the resort to remind guests to drive slowly. And wondered again if it was a good idea to be hosting these people at all.

The rumble of a diesel engine drew our attention to the road, where a mud-splattered black pickup eased to a stop behind my Subaru Crosstrek. A man sat at the wheel, a baseball cap shading his face. He cut the engine and climbed out. Now that he was outside, I could see that his cap bore the image of a deer skull with an impressive rack of antlers, a symbol for trophy hunters. A gun rack was mounted inside the back window of his truck. Though the rack currently held no hunting rifles, the man wore a handgun holstered at his waist. He was clean-shaven, with eyes as flinty as stone. He slammed the door behind him and strode our way, wordlessly but with purpose. He jabbed a finger in the air to indicate the sign. "Y'all involved in this bullshit?"

"The proposed resort?" Gus shook his head. "No way, man. I'm hoping to stop it."

Rocky's gaze met mine, flicked to the gun at the man's waist, then traveled to his face. "We're not involved, either. Just curious and stopped to take a look."

Gus looked askance at Rocky. He probably thought Rocky was being insincere, but he probably also realized why. The man in the hunting cap seemed to be looking for a fight. No sense adding fuel to the fire, especially when he had a firearm in easy reach. Besides, other than hosting the developer at my lodge, it was true that Rocky and I had nothing to do with the resort itself. We weren't investors or contractors, and we didn't work for Goodwin.

Gus cocked his head, eying the man. "You're not in favor of the resort, either?"

"You got that right," the guy snapped. "Come hell or high water, I'll put a stop to this abomination." He didn't elaborate on this hell-or-high-water plan. Rather, he strode back to his truck, slamming the door again after he climbed in. He drove only a short distance before turning into a gravel driveway on the other side of the road. Through the trees, we caught glimpses of his truck as he ascended the steep drive of a rustic cabin on a slope above us. Though we could see the cabin now, it would be fully obscured once the trees leafed out again in late spring. The truck stopped in front of a detached prefab garage and the door rolled up, revealing a wide deep freezer and the largest gun cabinet I'd ever seen against the back wall. The man pulled the truck inside, slid out, and pushed a button on an exterior keypad to close the garage door. As he approached the cabin, two dogs came down from the porch, a black Labrador retriever and an orange and white Brittany spaniel, both hunting breeds. Given the location of the man's home, his aversion to the resort made sense. The development would put an end to his peaceful refuge.

We bade Gus goodbye and returned to my car. As we wound our way back up the road to the lodge, we passed a herd of deer who stood on the side of the road, staring accusingly at us as they chewed their cuds. I groaned. "I'm getting a bad feeling about hosting Goodwin's group. I wish I'd done more digging before I agreed to let him use the lodge."

Rocky released a long exhale. "If you had said no, he'd have just found another place. You can't stop *progress*." He made air quotes with his fingers as he said the word. He gave my knee a supportive pat. "Focus on the positive, Misty. You've got lots to look forward to."

I certainly did. My two sons would arrive from college on Wednesday to spend the Thanksgiving holiday with me. My ex-husband would be coming, too. We'd had a rare, truly amicable split, and were determined to remain a family, albeit a somewhat nontraditional one.

The smell of pancakes and fried foods greeted us as I turned into the parking lot that my lodge shared with the Greasy Griddle Diner. The old-fashioned diner was owned by Patty, who'd become not only a business associate but also one of my dearest friends. I parked in my usual spot at the far end of the lot to allow my guests to use the more convenient spots. As Rocky and I headed inside, we passed a couple from Texas who'd just checked out. The Pratts both worked for the IRS. They'd given me free tax advice over biscuits and gravy at breakfast. Their two young children were quite a handful but, despite their high levels of energy, the kids were also well-mannered and absolutely adorable.

I raised my hand in goodbye. "Safe travels back to Dallas. Hope to see y'all again soon!"

Mrs. Pratt gave me a smile. "You can count on it. Our daughter has already insisted we come back next summer to see the fawns while they still have their spots."

Their inquisitive little girl had peppered Rocky and me with questions about the deer, and we'd told her that the babies kept their spots only for three or four months. Most deer were born in May or June, so they'd lost their spots by this time of year.

"Wonderful!" I put my hands on my knees and bent down to look the little girl in the eye. "I'll make sure we've got plenty of fresh blueberries for your pancakes."

Her eyes widened in delight and she clapped her itty-bitty hands. "Yay!"

As our departing guests aimed for their car, Rocky and I headed into the lodge. My assistant manager, Brynn O'Reilly, looked up from the reception desk. Brynn was tall and thin, with wavy red hair and a bohemian sense of style. Brynn embraced New Age philosophies and practices, and regularly burned sage in the lodge to banish bad juju. The ritual might not help, but it didn't hurt, either. Besides, I wasn't about to lose a reliable and hardworking assistant by questioning her beliefs.

She pointed to the computer. "Three more reservations came in for Thanksgiving weekend. All the rooms are booked."

With my prior innkeeping experience at a zero and Mother Nature's tendency to be very fickle with the weather, buying a lodge in the Blue Ridge Mountains had been a risky endeavor. But, so far, things were going remarkably well. Of course, the success of the lodge didn't come without a price. I worked 24/7 in an attempt to keep the rooms full and the bottom line in the black. When I wasn't cleaning or attending to guests, I was online, promoting the lodge on Facebook or Instagram, posting photos to show off the area's natural beauty, abundant wildlife, and variety of activities.

"We're full? Woo-hoo!" I performed a happy dance right there in the lobby, borrowing moves from the "Cha Cha Slide" and getting funky. Rocky and Brynn joined in the happy dance, each performing their own moves. Rocky imitated a Russian dancer by crossing his arms and bouncing up and down, kicking out one leg and then the other in the traditional Dance of the Cossacks. Brynn's happy dance involved turning in a circle while snaking her arms and shaking her hips like a belly dancer. Not only were my staff reliable and hardworking, they were fun, too. We made a great team.

With the last of the non-returning guests having departed, I placed the bell at the desk along with the small placard directing anyone needing assistance to ring it. While Brynn and I rounded up our housekeeping carts, Rocky set off to add weatherstripping around the windows. My guests' comfort was my number-one priority, but ensuring there were no drafts would also keep the lodge's electric bills in check. It was going to get very cold very soon in the mountains.

CHAPTER 2

Yeti

Misty stood at the front windows of the lodge, staring out into the dark night and holding the cat so tight in her arms the poor beast could barely breathe. Baroness Blizzard, aka Yeti, could sense Misty was excited about something. She just didn't know what, exactly, the excitement was about. But whatever it was, she didn't want to be left out.

Headlights flashed as a vehicle turned into the parking lot. It was too dark to make it out clearly, but when it rolled up in front of the doors, Misty squealed in delight. Yeti recognized the Jeep. She also recognized the man at the wheel and the boy in the front seat. She and Misty used to live together with them in a big house. The other boy who used to live in the house with them was in the back seat. Yeti's purr ignited automatically. She knew the man and boys were good for a never-ending supply of ear rubs and chin scratches. She'd even let them stroke her beautiful white fur, so long as they scratched at the sweet spot where her tail rose from her backside.

Misty carried the cat out the door and into the cold night, hanging on tight so she couldn't escape her arms. The boys emerged from the car, simultaneously exploding in happy shouts. "Yeti!"

CHAPTER 3

Misty

Guests often asked to use a computer to make dinner reservations or to print airline boarding passes or other documents. Though I'd previously been allowing them to use a computer at the registration desk, that practice had often tied up the devices at critical times. So, to make things easier on everyone, I'd recently installed a couple of cheap desktop computers on a narrow table in the lobby, along with a printer, creating a rudimentary business center for the guests. When the computers were not in use, I had one of them set to play the feed from the webcam positioned near the town's visitor center on Beech Mountain Parkway, the primary thoroughfare. The other screen displayed the feeds from the lodge's security cameras. The indoor cameras hung from the bottom of the truss in the center of the lodge, where they captured images throughout the public areas. The outdoor cameras showed feeds from the parking lot and from each side of the building.

Jack had texted when he and our sons left what used to be *our* house, but was now only his. The boys, Jack, and I shared our phone locations, so I could tell exactly where they were. Nonetheless, for the last quarter hour, I'd had an eagle eye on the parkway feed, too. When I saw Jack's Jeep drive by, I knew my ex-husband and boys would be arriving at my lodge in mere minutes. I'd scooped up my cat to watch for them. Now, they were here! "Hi, boys! Hey, Jack!"

Both Jack Jr. and Mitch were tall and lean, like their father, but they had my dark hair, hazel eyes, and pale, freckled skin. J.J. rushed over and reached for Yeti. I tried not to be jealous that my boys seemed more excited to see the cat than they were to see their mother, but I wasn't successful. "What am I? Chopped liver?"

J.J. barked a laugh and gave me a hug, crushing the purring kitty between us. As he pulled back, he took Yeti out of my arms. "Hi, girl!"

She looked up at him and batted her eyes. *Feline flirt.*

My ex-husband came over and gave me a hug and a peck on the cheek. He stepped back and assessed me. "You look good, Misty. Mountain life agrees with you."

It certainly did. For the first time in my life, I felt that I was truly home, that I was where I was meant to be. But there was nothing to be gained by telling my ex how happy I was here in the mountains without him. Besides, he'd already figured that out for himself. I decided to go with, "You're looking good, too, Jack."

"Liar," he said, though his words were without malice. "I've gained eight pounds eating junk food and I can't iron to save my life."

Now that he'd said it, I noticed the collar of his shirt was slightly cockeyed. He was still in his work clothes, the standard white dress shirt and navy chinos he wore as a dental supply salesman. At least he'd removed his tie. "Take your dress shirts to the cleaners," I suggested. "It's worth the splurge. Ask them to go light on the starch or

your shirts will stand up on their own." Before buying the
lodge, I'd been primarily a housewife and had taken care
of the family's laundry. Virtually every other detail of our
lives, too. Come to think of it, I probably should have left
the guy a set of instructions when I'd moved out.

Once they'd unloaded their luggage and Jack had
moved his Jeep to the parking lot, I waved for them to
follow me to their room. "Come on in and get settled."
I'd given my ex and sons the royal treatment, loading
their minifridge with juices, sodas, and energy drinks,
and stocking their coffee bar with fresh fruit and snacks.
I stopped in the hallway outside the room as they carried their luggage inside, then followed them in. "Y'all
hungry?" I asked. It was a stupid question. Boys their age
were always hungry.

"Can we get pizza?" Mitch flashed one of those big,
phony smiles kids use to get their way.

As if I needed any convincing. I'd give my two boys
the moon if I could. "Sure. I'll order from the Brick
Oven." Of course, I couldn't leave the lodge to get the
food. I turned to Jack.

He was one step ahead of me. "I'll pick up the pizzas
when they're ready."

A half hour later, my boys, Jack, and I gathered at a
table in the lodge's great room. Brynn had already left
for the day and Rocky had driven down to Boone to pick
up his youngest daughter from Appalachian State Uni-
versity. Like my boys, she wanted to spend the holiday
snowboarding on the mountain. The four of us caught
up over slices of pizza. While my life was totally different now than it had been before our recent split, little
had changed for Jack since the divorce except that he had
to cook his own meals and no longer had me sitting on
the couch beside him when he watched television in the

evenings. With me gone, he was working more hours and had been the top salesman last month. He seemed happy enough, if a little lonely.

"Have you considered getting a dog?" I asked. Like the boys, he'd enjoyed Yeti's antics and company when we'd lived together. Maybe a pet would lift his spirits.

"I have," he said. "But with the long hours I've been putting in, I'd hate for it to be home by itself all day."

"Get two, then," I suggested. "They'd keep each other company." Besides, the shelters were full of dogs that needed homes.

"I just might do that." He cast a glance at our sons. "A couple of dogs might encourage the boys to come to the house more often."

"So, it's not just me they're ignoring, huh?"

He chuckled. "Not at all."

Of course, I knew the boys would come back around as they grew up and settled down. Maybe I'd host my sons and their own families at the lodge one day. I certainly hoped so.

While the boys finished their pizza, Jack came out back with me to help me get a fire going in the fire pit. It was a clear, crisp night, just cold enough that a fire would bring welcome warmth, but not so cold your toes would go numb. Once the fire was roaring, I rounded up skewers, marshmallows, graham crackers, and dark chocolate bars from my bedroom and carried them back to the great room. "Who wants s'mores?"

Despite having just eaten half his body weight in pizza, Mitch leaped to his feet. "Me!"

J.J. stood, too. "Sounds good."

We went out the back door of the lodge and headed down the deck stairs to the stone patio, taking seats around the fire. As the boys roasted their marshmallows,

I issued a contented sigh and turned to my ex. "They're good kids. We're lucky, aren't we?"

Jack reached over from his chair and gave my hand a squeeze, just like old times. "We sure are."

When he released my hand, I glanced at my watch. It was nearly ten o'clock, but Rocky had yet to return. I supposed he'd stopped in to visit his oldest daughter, her husband, and their baby, who occupied his house in Boone. Who could blame him? Between his duties at the lodge and his work as a freelance handyman, he made it down the mountain only every two weeks or so to see his family.

A few minutes later, Jack and I left the boys to their s'mores and headed inside to our rooms. I'd put my ex and our sons in the room next to mine so I could have them close by. Jack stopped and turned to unlock his door, raising a hand in farewell. I continued on to my room, which sat at the end of the hall. When I'd moved into the lodge, I'd chosen one at the end of the building because it had a window along the side wall as well as the back, giving the room more natural light and Yeti a larger view of the outdoors. I stepped inside to find Yeti lying on the back windowsill, watching my sons at the fire pit. Her tail swished. Clearly, she was annoyed the boys had chosen to spend their time outdoors rather than inside giving her the attention she deserved. I picked her up and placed her on the bed, turning back to close the interior shutters.

With tomorrow being Thanksgiving, it would be a hectic day. I decided to take a few minutes to relax before getting ready for bed. I settled on the convertible sofa with a mystery novel in my hands and my cat on my lap. A few pages later, a soft knock came on the door. *Rap-rap-rap.* I set the book and my pet aside and walked to the door. I put an eye to the peephole to see Rocky standing in the hallway, a bouquet of fall flowers in one hand and a bottle of Beaujolais in the other. I opened the door.

"For you." He held out the flowers. Once I'd taken them, he raised the bottle. "For us."

I stuck my head out, looking down the hall. "Where's your daughter?"

"In our room. She was bushed. Pulled an all-nighter studying for an exam she had today."

I frowned. "What kind of professor gives an exam the day before Thanksgiving?"

"I know, right?" He came inside, closing the door behind him.

I arranged the flowers in an ice bucket. It was the closest thing I had to a vase here. Meanwhile, Rocky set the wine bottle down on my coffee bar and fished around in the drawer for my corkscrew. He'd just managed to get the cork free—*pop!*—when another soft knock sounded, this one coming from the door between my room and the one next door.

Rocky eyed the door first, then me. I felt my face heat with a blush. Before I could move, Rocky walked to the door and opened it.

Jack stood on the other side, a bottle of red wine in his hand. The smile on his face faded when he found himself face-to-face with Rocky instead of me. His confused gaze shifted from my handyman to me. "Sorry. I didn't realize you had company."

So much for not being awkward. I introduced the two of them, and they shook hands.

Rocky pointed down at the bottle in Jack's hand, then at the one standing open on my coffee bar. "Looks like you and I had the same idea."

"Guess so." Jack shrugged. "You can't blame a guy for trying."

The two men shared a chuckle, and now my entire body was aflame in embarrassment. This wasn't how I'd wanted my ex-husband to learn I was dating a new guy, but there was no turning back now. I grabbed Jack's arm and pulled him into the room. "Come on in. You can have a glass with us." *They'd have to meet sometime. Might as well be now.*

They took seats at the table. I only had two wine glasses, but one of us could make do with a coffee mug. I set the glasses and the mug on the table, and Rocky poured generous amounts of vino into each vessel, emptying the bottle. After setting the bottle down, he grabbed the coffee mug and raised it into the air in toast. "To our gracious and gorgeous host."

Jack tapped his wine glass against Rocky's mug. "Hear, hear."

We made small talk over the wine. As we chatted, Yeti wound figure eights around Jack's ankles while he reached down to scratch her ears with his free hand. The men discussed their work, I gave Jack a summary of a day in the life of an innkeeper, and we discussed the dismal weather report. There was no snow in sight, and temperatures were forecasted to be in the fifties on Thanksgiving. The mountain wouldn't exactly be a winter wonderland. Thank goodness the ski resort had snowmaking equipment. In fact, the faint roar of the blowers could be heard even here, a half mile away, as white noise. With any luck, we'd get a snowstorm or two in December, giving folks fresh powder for skiing and a traditional white Christmas.

We finished our wine, deciding to hang on to Jack's bottle of pinot noir to enjoy with our Thanksgiving meal the following day. Jack retreated through the adjoining door into his guest room. Rocky and I left my room and performed a final sweep of the lodge, making sure everything was as it should be before parting ways at the reception desk.

"Sweet dreams." He wagged a finger at me. "And keep that adjoining door locked tonight. You don't want any more surprise visitors."

CHAPTER 4

Misty

Rocky, Jack, and I ended up around another table the following morning with beverages in front of us, this time in the great room and the beverages were coffee rather than wine. And rather than Yeti at our feet, we had Molasses, Rocky's enormous black, white, and tan Bernese mountain dog. He'd adopted the fluffy fella from the pound a few years back. Molasses was the mellowest dog I'd ever seen. Nothing seemed to rattle him. He was also exceptionally intelligent, something I'd learned was a trait of his breed.

I'd purposely not placed a television in the great room, hoping to make it a place where people would unplug and interact with each other rather than stare at screens. As a lifelong fan of the Macy's Thanksgiving Day Parade, though, I'd made an exception this morning. I streamed the parade live on a pull-down video screen Rocky had installed after Nigel Goodwin had inquired about the lodge's audiovisual equipment. Not wanting to lose his business, and realizing the equipment would be useful for later events, I'd purchased a screen, projector, microphone, and speaker, and Rocky had used some spare wood to craft a podium. He'd added wheels so it could be easily moved about.

Once the Radio City Rockettes had finished their performance on Manhattan's 34th Street, I checked my watch. It was nearing 10:00. There'd been no sign yet of my boys. There'd been no sign of Rocky's daughter yet, either. With no classes to attend today, the kids were sleeping in. Who could blame them? But the staff from the Greasy Griddle would be by soon to pick up the serving trays from the breakfast buffet. If the kids were going to get something to eat before Thanksgiving dinner later in the day, I'd better pack up the remaining items for them.

"I'll be right back." Leaving the men at the table, I hustled to my room, passing by the laundry where Brynn was washing towels, the machines rhythmically sloshing. When I returned to the great room with a stack of Tupperware, Rocky met me at the buffet table and took two of them off my hands. While he scooped grits into one container, I ladled gravy into another. I was packing up pancakes when Jack Jr. materialized beside me in flannel pajamas and socks, feeling very much at home. I supposed this *was* his mountain home, so I didn't scold him for the casual dress.

I introduced him to Rocky. While my son's clothing might lack decorum, at least J.J. remembered his manners. "Nice to meet you, Rocky." After they shook hands, his gazed shifted to the hall behind my handyman. A young woman headed our way, also wearing pajamas. Her dark hair was pulled up into an adorably messy pile atop her head. J.J. lifted his chin to indicate the girl. "Whoa. Here comes a smoke show."

Rocky turned and cast a look down the hall before

turning back to J.J., his expression stern. "That 'smoke show' is my daughter."

J.J. raised his palms, taking a step backward. "Sorry, dude."

The girl broke into a short sprint then turned sideways to slide across the wood floor in her fluffy socks until she collided softly with Rocky, hip checking her father.

"About time you got up," Rocky said. "You almost missed the pancakes."

"That would have been tragic." She turned to me, her eyes as deep brown as the coffee in my mug. "Are you Misty?"

"I sure am."

"Cool-cool-cool. I'm Pebble."

"Pebble?" *Had Rocky really named his child after a small stone?*

Seeming to read my expression, she said, "My given name's Phoebe, but my grammy started calling me Pebble when I was little. She said I was a teeny version of my father." Pebble held out a fist.

Thankfully, I knew what to do. I made a fist and bumped my knuckles against hers.

"Hey, Pebble." J.J. stuck out his fist for a bump, too. "I'm J.J., Misty's older son. The smarter and better-looking one."

Pebble's brows arched. "I'll make my own judgment once I meet your brother."

"Ooh," I said. "Sick burn."

J.J. cast me the same look of disgust he did every time I used any of the younger generation's lingo.

Pebble bumped my son's fist in greeting, then turned to eye the remaining food in the trays. "Home fries! Yessss!" She pumped her fist.

After the kids filled their plates, Rocky and I finished transferring the food to the containers. Just in time, too. Patty arrived to collect the trays as I removed the final biscuit.

"Good morning!" she called cheerily as she came through the front door of the lodge. Patty had dark skin and hair, bright eyes, and a smile as warm as the pancakes she served. The padded oven mitts on her hands made her look like a boxer. She wore ankle boots, jeans, and a sweater, as well as an apron bearing the Greasy Griddle logo—the diner's name in red lettering beneath a cast-iron skillet in which a square of melting butter formed the letter G.

I introduced Patty to J.J., Pebble, and Jack, who'd come over from the table to meet her.

As they shook hands, Jack said, "Misty says you've given her lots of business advice."

Patty shrugged. "I've run my diner for years. Learned a few things along the way."

Fortunately for me, she'd been willing to share those lessons so that I wouldn't have to learn them the hard way. She shared her know-how because she was a kind and giving person, and I was happy to know that when my lodge succeeded it meant more customers for her diner, an indirect return of the favor.

Rocky rubbed his belly. "I can't wait for a big slice of your walnut pumpkin pie."

"Got a dozen of 'em in the oven right now," she said. "Thanksgiving is one of our busiest days of the year."

Jack pointed to the windows, where we could see a crowd waiting outside the diner. "I've seen a line at your place all morning. Glad we got personal service here without the wait." He wrapped his arms around himself. "I can't imagine standing out in that cold."

Rocky, Patty, and I exchanged subtle smiles. The temperature was in the mid-forties, what we mountain folks considered downright balmy for this time of year. Jack, however, had thin blood. If he ventured outside today, it would be in a knit cap, parka, and fleece-lined boots.

After helping Patty stack the metal serving trays and the plastic bussing bins, I held the door for her as she left with them cradled in her arms. How she could carry so many things at once without dropping them I'd never know. She'd clearly built some major muscles over her years at the diner. I returned to our table to find that J.J. and Pebble had pushed another one over so that we could all sit together comfortably. The kids talked about their schools and classes, while Rocky, Jack, and I listened in. Pebble reached down occasionally to offer Molasses a small chunk of biscuit or a cube of fried potato. The dog waited patiently between bites, though he kept his eyes on her plate, watching the food disappear with a slight look of concern.

I got up to attend to a thirtyish couple who'd come to the front desk with questions about local hiking trails. There were miles of them in the area, with a trailhead just behind the lodge. I handed them a printed map and advised them that they could also download the Explore Beech Mountain app to have maps and information easily accessible on their cell phones.

"Thanks!" said the woman. "We've got to get our steps in to earn some pie later."

Brynn, who'd been folding towels in the laundry room, appeared with her housekeeping cart. I supposed I had better get to work, too. I let Jack and J.J. know they were on their own for the time being, grabbed my cart, and started my rounds. Rocky, too, set to work, heading outside to the storage shed for the Christmas lights he planned to hang around the lodge.

As I went about my work, Mitchell finally emerged from their room. Jack offered him the leftovers from breakfast, which he warmed up in the microwave. He devoured the food as if he hadn't eaten in weeks, even though he'd ingested impressive amounts of pizza late yesterday evening. *Oh, to have that teenage metabolism again.*

Like the guests I'd spoken to earlier, the boys decided to take a hike before lunch, including both Pebble and Molasses in their plans. I was happy to see them all getting along, and the dog would enjoy the exercise and change of scenery. Rather than brave what he considered an arctic outdoor temperature, Jack opted to return to his room to watch a football game.

As I wiped down a mirror in a room along the front of the lodge, Rocky scooted his ladder over outside the window to continue hanging icicle lights from the eaves. When he spotted me through the glass, he wagged his brows then pulled his cell phone from his pocket. His thumbs moved over the screen. A few seconds later, my phone pinged in my cart with an incoming message. I picked it up to find his note: *You sure know how to work a spray bottle.*

I walked over to the window where he was looking in now, hands cupped around his eyes. I held up the bottle and spritzed the glass in front of his face. He pulled back, grinning. I wiped the window until it gleamed.

Before I knew it, I'd finished cleaning the rooms and was back at the reception desk with Brynn. She had no family in the area, and had graciously agreed to work the Thanksgiving holiday. She planned to take two weeks off in late December to celebrate the winter solstice with fellow Wiccans at a site in New Hampshire known as "America's Stonehenge." I hadn't been familiar with the place, but Brynn had filled me in. Ancient peoples had arranged stones at the site more than four thousand years ago, though who those people were and precisely why they'd assembled the rocks were a mystery. My sons would fill in for Brynn to earn spending money for their spring semester. We all had our holiday plans lined up and ready to go, and I couldn't wait.

Rocky came inside with two strings of colored lights that had twisted themselves into a hopelessly tangled tumbleweed.

He placed it on the countertop in front of me. "Help! I've been working on this darn mess for ten minutes and it's only gotten worse."

"I'll see what I can do." As he went back outside, I spent a few minutes threading an end back through the jumble but, like him, I seemed to be making little, if any, progress. I set the ball aside on the counter to deal with later.

Four o'clock arrived as did one of Patty's servers with a cart loaded down with a Thanksgiving feast. Jack was right. We were being seriously spoiled. The delicious aromas of savory gravy and cornbread dressing made my mouth water as I helped the young man set up the warming trays on the buffet tables. The bowl of cranberry sauce was put on ice and the pies were lined up like beauty contestants hoping to be chosen. Patty had given each double-crust pie a unique design, ranging from a snowflake design on the cherry pie to a moon-and-stars design atop the blueberry. She wasn't just a great cook and baker, she was an artist whose medium was delicious, down-home food. The enticing scents lured Jack from his game. He assisted Brynn and me in putting tablecloths on the tables. For centerpieces, we set out votive candles in holders adorned with pine cones. Between the gorgeous view from the back windows, the enticing aromas of the food, and—if I did say so myself—the charmingly decorated tables, I was certain this would be a Thanksgiving to remember.

The sun had already begun its descent, and I dimmed the lights in the great room to give it an elegant feel. Rocky came inside and tossed a couple more logs on the fire, stoking the embers until the fire burned bright and warm. I brought up an orchestra playing Vivaldi's "Autumn" on a computer at the reception desk, connected the computer to the wireless speaker, and set the music to repeat at low volume, providing a nice auditory backdrop for the feast.

A family of five came in the door, ready to check in. The children exclaimed when they saw the food and ran over to the buffet tables to check out the feast. Fortunately, they kept their hands to themselves and didn't touch the hot trays. Their mother said, "That food smells so good! Looks like we arrived at just the right time."

I finished processing their reservation and handed them the keys to their rooms. "Help yourselves whenever you'd like. The buffet will be open until nine o'clock."

A half hour later, chatter and laughter outside announced the kids' return. J.J., Mitch, and Pebble came in the front door and, much like the younger children who'd recently checked in, exclaimed when they smelled the food. Molasses lifted his snout and sniffed the air. He smacked his jowls, clearly hoping he'd get a bite or two.

Mitch put a hand on his belly. "I'm starving!"

"I doubt that. You ate enough earlier to feed an army."

He'd put away four biscuits smothered in gravy at his late breakfast, along with a stack of pancakes covered in bananas, walnuts, and maple syrup. Carb-loading. "Wash up!" I called as the hikers rushed to their rooms to change. "Then we can all eat together."

The promise of a feast must have given them wings since, just minutes later, we reconvened at a long table in the great room. I waved Brynn over from the desk. "Join us." To give her incentive, I raised the bottle of pinot noir Jack had brought. "We'll pour you a glass."

She sat down with us at the table and we all spent the next hour filling our stomachs with food and the room with laughter and conversation. The kids discussed the horrors of dorm food, pop quizzes, and their upcoming final exams before switching the subject to the ski slopes.

Mitch said, "The lifts open at nine tomorrow morning. I want to be on the first chair up."

Jack held a forkful of stuffing aloft. "That's awfully bold talk for someone who didn't drag himself out of bed until noon today." He turned to me. "Remember when he was a baby and he'd wake us up before dawn babbling from the crib?"

Mitch's eyes cut to Pebble before they returned to his father. "Stop embarrassing me," he said in a stage whisper.

"We're parents," I said. "Embarrassing our children is in our job description."

Rocky nodded. "Besides, it's fun." In one quick motion, he reached around the chair beside him, hooked an arm around Pebble's shoulders, and pulled her down into a headlock. He rubbed his knuckles over her head. "Noogies!"

"Daaaad!" She squirmed and pushed him away, giggling. "You're such a dork!"

He smiled, not a bit insulted.

"I've got some news." I ran my gaze around the table. "There may soon be a fancy new resort on the mountain."

"Oh, yeah?" Jack topped off his wine glass. "Where?"

I told him a developer had bought a plot of land on the backside of the mountain. "Thirty-five acres on the Elk River. I'll host him here in December, along with a group of potential investors."

Brynn tossed back her remaining wine and frowned. "I hope it doesn't go through. I'd hate to see Beech Mountain become another Pigeon Forge."

Jack cocked his head. "What's wrong with Pigeon Forge? We went there on vacation once and it was a lot of fun. Right, boys?"

Mitch and J.J. murmured in agreement. I, too, had fond memories of our family trip to Pigeon Forge, Tennessee, a decade earlier, when the boys were younger. We'd visited Dollywood, where we'd heard some great music and I'd ridden a colorful carousel rooster. We'd attended a Hatfield and McCoy dinner show complete with folksy music and traditional clog dancing and visited WonderWorks, an interactive attraction housed in a building that appeared to have been turned upside down. The town was also home to a *Titanic* museum in a building shaped like a sinking boat, as well as a wax museum. Though we'd had a fantastic time, admittedly the town's vibe leaned toward gimmicky attractions. Of course, we'd also ventured a few miles farther south through Gatlinburg, and toured the Great Smoky Mountains National Park. *Such a beautiful, awe-inspiring place.* There had been something for everyone.

Brynn said, "Pigeon Forge is too built up. There's crowds everywhere and the traffic is terrible."

She'd raised a valid point, but just because a big new resort was in the works here, tourist traps and unfettered commercial development wouldn't necessarily follow, would they? The mere thought made me feel heavy. Then again, maybe it was the three servings of stuffing I'd eaten that was weighing me down. A glance at my sons' faces said they, too, felt concerned.

J.J. mused aloud. "It gets crowded here during ski season, too, but in summer when there's not so many people around, we can hike the trails and hardly run across anyone."

"And it's quiet and dark at night," Mitch added. "The stars are easier to see without all the light pollution."

"Peaceful," I agreed.

Brynn exhaled sharply. "Let's hope it stays that way."

We turned back to our meal and turned the conversation to lighter topics. After we finished the main course and topped it off with pieces of scrumptious pie, Brynn gathered up her purse and left for the day. The rest of us cleared the table and I broke out a one-thousand-piece jigsaw puzzle of a snow-covered Mount Everest. The kids spent the next hour or so putting it together while Rocky, Jack, and I enjoyed hot toddies in front of the fireplace. Molasses lounged on the rug in front of the hearth, enjoying the warmth. When Patty came over to get the warming trays after the diner closed at nine o'clock, I suggested she take a load off. "You've been on your feet all day. Why don't you sit for a bit? I'll pour you a drink."

"That's not a bad idea." She flopped down in a chair

and lifted her feet to rest them on an ottoman. Molasses rose to his feet and moseyed over to greet her and collect a pat or two. Meanwhile, I poured her a drink from the thermal pitcher, adding a cinnamon stick and lemon slice in the classic style. As I handed Patty the warm mug, she issued a contented sigh. "It's nice to have someone serve me for a change."

"Is Eli home for Thanksgiving?" I asked. Patty's husband was a long-haul trucker who was often gone for days at a time.

"He got home yesterday. Just in time for me to put him to work in the diner today." She raised her mug in salute and took a sip. "He'll be home through the long weekend, and he's taking off Christmas Eve through New Year's."

I was glad to hear the two would get some time together.

When she finished her drink, I helped her gather up the warming trays and dirty dishes and load them onto her cart. "Y'all enjoy the rest of the evening," she said, giving us a nod as she pushed her cart out the door.

I went to bed that night feeling truly grateful. Though we'd had an unusual holiday, spending it with a mix of people rather than just family, I realized that the people here felt like family to me even if we shared no DNA. I couldn't imagine my life without Rocky, Brynn, or Patty any more than I could imagine it without Jack or our boys. I was one lucky woman to have so many wonderful people in my world.

Clearly, the call of the slopes could work wonders since the kids had no problem getting out of bed Friday morning. In fact, they were among the first guests to show up for the breakfast buffet. Again, we pushed tables together so we could gather for our meal.

My sons once again put away enough food to feed an army. When they stood to go, I pointed to the lobby. "There's a little something for you two behind the front desk."

After exchanging a curious glance, they scurried over to the counter, where Brynn sat ordering shampoo, conditioner, and small bars of soap to replenish our stock. While Mitch used the gate to circle behind the counter, J.J. hopped up onto the counter and swiveled on his back like a break-dancer, putting his feet down on the other side. They shouted in delight when they found the brand-new snowboards, boots, goggles, and helmets I'd hidden there, along with season passes for the Beech Mountain Resort. Christmas had come early for them: they'd no longer have to wait in line to rent gear.

They rushed back over, giving me hugs. Mitch said, "You're the best mom ever!"

J.J. said, "The coolest, too!"

I knew they were sucking up, but I'd take what I could get.

A few minutes later, as the kids and Rocky gathered to set off for the slopes, I issued a heavy sigh. "Y'all have fun. I'll look for you on the webcams." In addition to the webcam along Beech Mountain Parkway, there were two webcams at the ski resort, one at the base of the slopes and one at the summit. A live stream was broadcast online.

Jack eyed me across the table. "You want to go with them, don't you?"

"Of course I do," I said on a sigh. "But this lodge doesn't run itself."

"The only thing I planned to do today was stay inside and keep warm, maybe watch a little television. I can make a bed and scrub a sink. I'd be happy to cover for you."

Brynn looked our way from behind the desk. "I'll show Jack the ropes." She flung her hands dismissively. "Get ready and go. Shoo!"

I stood up and beamed in delight. "Thanks, you two!"

Rocky and I had a wonderful day on the slopes, but by the middle of the afternoon, my knees, thighs, and glutes were screaming in agony. Gone were the days when I could ski from dawn to dusk and get up the next day to do it again. These days, I had to pace myself. Rocky did, too.

While our children remained at the resort, we headed back to the lodge. We carried our gear inside to find Jack finishing up his housekeeping rounds. "I couldn't fold the towels to look like a bear," he said, "but I managed to make them look like skis."

I glanced into one of the rooms he'd cleaned, taking in the bath towels lying at an angle at the bottom corner of the bed. He'd merely folded the towels into narrow strips lengthwise and turned back the ends, but the simplicity of the design made it no less fun. "You earn an A-plus for your improvising skills."

Once Jack had headed up the hall with the housekeeping cart and was out of earshot, Rocky slid a look my way. "It was nice of your ex to cover for you."

"Jack's a good guy. I wouldn't have married him otherwise." Besides, I hadn't divorced him because we didn't get along. We ended our marriage simply because the romance had waned and we now wanted different, incompatible lifestyles.

"What if I hadn't been in your room when he knocked last night?" It was a rare, vulnerable question from a man more given to flirtatious banter.

I looked Rocky straight in the eye. "Then Jack and I would have shared some memories and a glass of wine."

"That's all?"

"That's *definitely* all."

Rocky's lips curved up in a small smile. "Good to hear."

Rocky, Jack, Brynn, and I spent Saturday decorating the inside of the lodge for Christmas. We put up a real tree, a six-foot potted spruce pine that I could move out front and use again next year. Rocky wound a long string of colorful twinkle lights around the tree, and we hung cute ornaments that I'd purchased at local souvenir shops on the branches. Bears on skis. Santa on skis. A buff buck standing on its hind legs on a snowboard. Rather than the traditional star or angel, Jack plunked our family's abominable snowman tree topper atop the pine. Silly, sure, but fun. After I spread the gold tree skirt around its base, Rocky installed a circular train track for the model train I'd ordered online. We strung a garland along the fireplace mantle and the reception desk, adorning them with red velvet bows. We hung real pine wreaths on each guest-room door, the boughs giving the lodge a lovely fresh scent. I created a Christmas playlist to add to the festive feel. The only thing left to do was dream of a white Christmas.

Sunday came much too soon, and I found myself again standing out in front of the lodge, hugging my ex and sons—this time to say goodbye. It made it easier to see my boys off, knowing they'd be back in two weeks once they'd completed their finals. Nevertheless, I held them each in a tight bear hug as they squirmed in a vain attempt free themselves. *A mother's love is powerful.* They climbed into the Jeep and I stood, waving, until they disappeared from sight.

CHAPTER 5

Misty

Climate change made temperatures and snowfall uncertain, and the last few years had been drier and warmer than the preceding winter seasons. If this trend continued, white Christmases would be rare here and the area's ski resorts could find themselves unable to maintain the manmade snow. But luck was with us, at least for now. In early December, a days-long storm dropped two feet of snow on Beech Mountain, creating a soft shush and transforming our town into a winter wonderland. No doubt we'd have a slew of tourists heading our way for the weekend.

Late Friday morning, Rocky attached a plow blade to the front of his pickup truck and cleared the lodge's side of the parking lot, piling the snow up on the lawn to the left of the building. Meanwhile, I used an electric snowblower to clear the walkways.

When Patty came out of the diner with a bag of garbage, Rocky unrolled the window on his pickup and called to her across the lot. "Hey, Patty! Want me to plow your side, too?"

She angled her head, considering. "What's your going rate?"

Rocky offered snowplowing as part of his freelance handyman services, and charged local homeowners a fair fee depending on the size of their driveway. But Patty wasn't a typical client, she was also a good friend. "It'll cost you one apple streusel pie!"

She raised a finger in the air. "You got yourself a deal!"

Rocky plowed her part of our shared lot, adding the snow to the massive mound beside the lodge. When he finished, Patty came over with a fresh-baked pie wrapped in foil, steam rising from the top into the frigid air. After handing the pie to Rocky and thanking him for the discount, she eyed the towering pile of snow. "Y'all've got your own mountain over here."

We certainly did. The mound stood six feet tall. "The guests will have fun playing in it."

"I will, too," Rocky said. "I'm gonna build a snow fort."

My mind went to the stack of sleds in our storage closet. Some were the old-fashioned wood-and-metal style, and had likely been around the lodge for decades. Others were cheap, lightweight plastic ones that had been purchased more recently. I'd planned to offer them to guests to use at the town's sledding hill. But they could have fun with the sleds right here at the lodge, too, sliding down the snow pile. When I suggested the idea to Rocky, he agreed.

"I'll smooth the pile out a bit," he said. "I'll make a small wall of snow at the edge of the woods, too. Don't want anyone going out of control and crashing into a tree."

"Good idea." There had already been one death at the

lodge, and another guest had died while taking a motor-cycle ride on the Blue Ridge Parkway. The last thing we needed was another life lost, or even a minor injury.

Patty bade us goodbye. While Rocky used a snow shovel to form the pile into a smooth slide, I went inside and retrieved several of the sleds, leaning them up against the side of the lodge where guests could easily find them. After smoothing out the sledding hill, Rocky piled a line of snow a few feet before the edge of the woods to stop sleds from careening into the trees.

When he finished, he leaned a wooden ladder against the near side of the hill to help stabilize the snow and to serve as a makeshift staircase so sledders could find footholds. Eyes twinkling with mischief, he pointed to the sleds. "We should take a trial run, make sure everything's in working order."

I grabbed two sleds and handed one to him. He held out a hand, inviting me to be the first to try the hill. Climbing the angled ladder on all fours, I lugged my sled up to the ledge he'd flattened out at the top, set it down, and climbed aboard. "Here I go!" With that, I pushed off. I slid down the slope, all the way hollering "Wheee!" My sled slowed when I reached the flat area at the bottom, and stopped just short of the safety wall he'd formed.

I turned to watch Rocky, who'd climbed up behind me. He set off down the hill like a rodeo rider on a bucking bronc, one hand grasping the rope, the other in the air. He called out a PG version of the phrase made famous by *Die Hard*. "Yippee kai yay, mountain climber!"

He slid until his sled softly impacted mine, like slow-motion bumper cars. "Oops." He leaned over and pressed his lips against mine, grinning when he pulled back. "Oops, again."

"Careful," I warned. "Any more heat and we might melt this snow."

The roar of a motor drew our attention to the parkway, where one of the town's snowplows rumbled past, clearing the road. The plows made regular passes along the main thoroughfare to ensure residents and vacationers could get up and down the mountain as safely as possible. The wall of snow on each side of the road was growing higher and thicker with each pass of the plow. I hoped Nigel Goodwin and the guests he'd invited to the lodge would be able to make it here without any problems. Goodwin was due to arrive tomorrow. So were my boys—I could hardly wait! The potential investors would arrive on Sunday.

I was turning away from the road when a mud-and-snow-splattered black pickup caught my eye. It cruised slowly past in the plow's wake. The face of the man at the wheel was lost in the shadow created by his ballcap, but the rifle rack mounted in the back window told me he was the same man we'd encountered at the resort property a while back, the same day we'd met Gus, the affable wildlife photographer. My first thought was that the hunter might be casing my lodge, watching for the developer to arrive so he could give the man his two cents about the proposed resort. But I was being paranoid, wasn't I? After all, Beech Mountain Parkway was the only public road that came up this side of the mountain. Everyone who lived in the area drove it. In fact, it would be more suspicious if the man didn't come this way on occasion and stuck to sneaking around the mountain on minor back roads. I shook myself mentally as Rocky and I returned the sleds to the side of the lodge and turned our attention from each other to our tasks.

* * *

Saturday morning, I repeatedly pulled out my cell phone to track my boys' progress from Raleigh to Beech Mountain. As they drew close, I took a seat at the reception desk and kept a close eye on the computer monitor that displayed the parkway feed, eager to catch a glimpse of Jack's Jeep. Several cars and SUVs rolled by, many with skis in racks atop their roofs. One held a fresh-cut Christmas tree. A blue Subaru Outback drove past, towing a small teardrop camper. I recognized the model of the car because it resembled the station wagons of my youth. The plow went past again, followed by a rattle-trap bus that served as a shuttle from the remote parking lot to the ski resort. Jack's Jeep was next. *They're almost here!*

I circled around the desk and waited by the front window, rushing outside as they pulled up. We repeated the process from Thanksgiving. Hugs all around, especially for Yeti. Carrying their luggage inside and setting them up in the room next to mine. More hugs from me. More groans from the boys.

I turned to Jack. "Will you be staying the night before heading back to Raleigh?"

His expression became sheepish. Before he could answer, Mitch said, "He's driving back. He's got a date tonight."

I looked from my son to my ex. "You do? That's great! Who is it? Anyone I know?" *Please don't let it be someone I know!* Although we'd had an amicable split and there were no lingering romantic feelings, it would still feel awkward if he went out with a woman I knew.

"No," Jack said. "It's someone I met online. She lives in Durham."

Close enough to be convenient but far enough that she wasn't likely to run in the same social circles I used to.

Good. Even if I wasn't there any longer, I didn't want my life to be fodder for the gossip mill. "I hope it goes well."

Jack said, "I'm nervous. I don't remember how to flirt."

"It'll come back to you," I said. "Flirting is like riding a bike."

"You mean if I go too fast and I might flip over and break my neck?"

Jack hadn't lost the sense of humor that attracted me all those years ago. "Exactly."

I saw Jack to the door and bade him goodbye. "See you at Christmas!"

I returned to the boys' room, where I found them pulling out their snowboarding gear. I raised my palms. "Whoa, whoa, whoa. You two are supposed to be in training here today."

"Can we do it tomorrow?" J.J. begged, putting his hands together as if in prayer.

"Pleeeeease?" Mitch pointed out the window. "There's fresh powder."

While I hadn't expected my new employees to engage in collective bargaining before they'd even started their jobs, my sons had a point. Who knew if the cold would last or when we'd have another snowfall? Besides, as brothers they shared a special bond and, despite the usual sibling squabbles, enjoyed spending time together. It warmed my heart that the two had a close relationship. "All right. You can train tomorrow. But you'd better pay good attention. It'll be Brynn's last day until January. I'm counting on you."

I rounded up my car keys, handed them over, and sent them off with another hug.

* * *

With Nigel Goodwin spending a small fortune to host his investment group here, I wanted to make a good impression. Whatever I might personally think of his plans, I had a business to run. To that end, I'd assembled a gift bag for him and his wife filled with local treasures. Soaps and candles from the shop down in Banner Elk, a bottle each of white and red from the winery, two knit beanies I'd purchased from Fred's General Mercantile. I'd put Nigel and his wife in the room at the opposite end of the hall from mine, where they'd have a gorgeous long-range view of the mountains through the bare trees. I'd just come back from putting the gift bag in their room later that afternoon when two vehicles pulled up out front. The first was a black Chevy Tahoe. The extra-large SUV had three rows of seats. A basic white fifteen-passenger van followed it.

I used my cell phone to call Rocky. "The Goodwins have arrived."

"On my way."

Rocky came out of his room, gathered one of the rolling luggage trolleys, and met me at the desk. We walked outside as the drivers emerged from their vehicles. From photos I'd found online, I recognized the driver of the Tahoe as Nigel Goodwin. He was fair-skinned, lean, and lanky, his brown hair cut short. He reminded me of Dick Van Dyke from the *Mary Poppins* film of my childhood. Goodwin's nose was longer and more pointed than the chimney sweep's, though—at least until the very tip, which flattened out as if pressed against unseen glass. The driver of the van was an athletic, dark-haired guy who appeared to be in his mid to late twenties, only a few years older than my boys.

"Welcome to the Mountaintop Lodge!" I extended

my hand first to Nigel, then to the younger man. "I'm Misty."

Rocky gave his name and extended a hand, as well.

"Nigel Goodwin," said Dick Van Dyke's doppel-ganger, offering a pleasant smile. He held out a hand to indicate his associate. "This is my assistant."

"I'm called Rayan Gandapur." The younger man's accent, name, and brown skin told me he could be of Pakistani descent, like many in England. While Rayan had offered his name, he offered no smile.

The passenger door opened on the SUV and a thin middle-aged woman slid out. Her skin and hair were so pale she appeared nearly translucent, like the fog for which London was famous. Her clothing, though well-fitting and well made, was equally drab, all of it in shades of light gray. Her mouth hung open slightly, as if she suffered a stuffy nose, and a cloud formed in the frigid air as she exhaled. Despite being delivered in a British accent, which I normally found cheery, her greeting was as dreary as her appearance. "We've finally arrived," she said on a sigh. She glanced around with a sour expression as if she'd rather be anywhere but here. She shuddered and wrapped her arms around herself. "Oh, my giddy aunt! It's arctic out here!"

Her demeanor and words bordered on rude, and were somewhat ridiculous. After all, it was no secret that high altitudes were cold in winter. But, again, I chalked up the behavior to jet lag and forced a smile at her. "You must be Mrs. Goodwin." I knew her name was Aileen from the registration information her hus-band had provided, but decided it best to stay on more formal terms. "Why don't you head on inside where it's warm? There's tea, if you'd like some." I'd been sure to order some fancy flavored teas to have on hand for the group. I turned to her husband. "May we help with your bags?"

"That would be grand," Goodwin said. "Many thanks."

While Aileen scurried into the lodge, Rocky and I loaded the Goodwins' suitcases onto the trolley and Rayan proceeded to unpack the van. The cargo bay was full, holding a suitcase, two pairs of skis in travel bags, and several large, hard-sided storage cases that likely contained business items. We carried everything into the lobby where I proceeded to check them in, handing over their keys on our kitschy pine-cone-shaped key rings.

Goodwin held up the key ring, chuckling. "An actual key? Haven't seen one of these in years. It's . . . charming."

Hmm. I got the impression he'd used *charming* to mean *outdated,* but I wasn't going to let this man's opinion bother me. My old-fashioned keys worked just fine and went with the retro vibe of the lodge much better than plastic keycards would have.

Rocky and I showed our guests to their rooms. I put Rayan in the room that adjoined the Goodwins' in case they needed to tend to business privately. Aileen immediately flopped down backward on the bed, closing her eyes and throwing her arm back over her face as if she were swooning. Her husband ignored her, apparently accustomed to his wife being a negative Nellie.

Once Rocky and I had finished unloading their bags from the cart, I said, "We'll leave you to get settled. Let us know if you need anything."

We closed the door behind us and returned to the registration desk. Rocky frowned, then leaned in, whispering in a fake cockney accent, "The missus is a right dour one, I'll say."

He wasn't wrong. Still, I hoped she'd come around. How could she not be happy in a beautiful place like Beech Mountain? "Maybe she just makes a bad first impression. She could be a completely different person once she gets some rest." The flight from London to Charlotte had been several hours long, and the drive from Charlotte to Beech Mountain took another two and half hours. And that didn't even count the time they'd spent going through customs, waiting on baggage, and collecting their rental car. They'd been on the go for twelve hours or more.

Rocky set off to sprinkle sand on the sidewalks for improved traction in the inclement weather. Though the former owner of the lodge had left two fifty-pound bags of rock salt in the tool shed, we had no intention of using it. Sand was a more environmentally conscious choice than rock salt, which could flow into waterways and harm fish and other aquatic life. Meanwhile, Brynn came out of the guest laundry and vending room, where she'd been sweeping and mopping the tile floor and restocking the machines with bags of trail mix, protein bars, and the like. I informed her that the Goodwins and Nigel's assistant were unpacking in their rooms.

No sooner had the words left my mouth than Rayan reappeared at the desk with the large, hard-sided cases. "Where should I set up the model?"

"Over here." Brynn took a few steps toward the great room and held out an arm to indicate the six-foot portable table we'd set up at the front of the space. She'd covered it with a tablecloth in red and black buffalo plaid, the lodge's signature fabric.

Rayan thanked her—still without a smile—and wheeled the cases over to the table. He lay them on the rug in front of the fireplace, released the latches, and knelt down beside them, carefully removing pieces. His shoulders sagged, as if they bore the weight of some unseen burden. The guest rooms having all been cleaned, Brynn and I puttered around the lobby, straightening the sightseeing brochures in the display, dusting the bookshelves, and rearranging the books, games, and knickknacks on the shelves. Soon, Rayan had the model assembled. He added faux foliage and miniature human figures around the outside of the building, and stepped back to survey the display.

Having finished sanding the walks, Rocky came back inside. He joined me and Brynn as we stepped over to take a look at the model of the resort.

"That sure is something," I said. The proposed resort stood three stories tall, and featured an attractive mix of rustic and contemporary elements, including copper awnings and accents. The exterior walls were of stone and wood—represented by miniature faux plastic pieces—and in the center of the resort was a large clear dome, which resembled a snow globe. Through the transparent surface, we could see small waterslides, turquoise blue pools, and a faux waterfall.

Rocky bent over to gaze into the dome. "The resort will have an indoor waterpark?"

"Among other things," Rayan said. Seeming to realize his vague response could be taken as impolite, he straightened and turned to address us more directly. He gestured to the model. "What you see here is only the main lodge. The resort will have outdoor activities, too, some on-site and others off-site."

Before Rayan could elaborate, Nigel ventured into the great room, a laptop tucked under his arm. He smiled when he spotted us and came over. "I see you're admiring the resort."

"It's beautiful." It was true, though I still wasn't sure I was in favor of it being built. "It's much fancier than most places up here."

"Including *this* place." He pointed down at the floor to indicate my lodge. "This inn was the only place up here big enough to host my pitch meeting, but it doesn't even have a hot tub. Once my resort is built, maybe the three of you should come work for me."

My lodge might not have a hot tub, but after his insulting comments my core temperature didn't need hot water to rise. "I don't just work here, Mr. Goodwin. I own this lodge."

He put a hand to his lips, as if he could force his words back down his throat. "I beg your pardon." He offered a contrite cringe. "I really put my foot in my mouth, didn't I?"

Guess where I'd like to put my *foot?* "No offense taken," I lied. "Your resort and my lodge will cater to different types of guests. Some guests will prefer the luxury you'll offer, while others will like the simplicity and affordability of places like mine."

Nigel gave me a nod. "May I test the audiovisual equipment? I want to ensure everything is in order for tomorrow's presentation."

"Of course." While Brynn pulled down on the cord to lower the video screen into place, Rocky and I rounded up the podium, projector, microphone, and speaker from the storage room and set them up. Once they were situated, Rocky showed Nigel and Rayan how to run the equipment, then stepped back to the reception desk to let them test things on their own.

Rocky sidled up next to me, speaking low. "He may have a point about the hot tub. Nothing feels better after a day on the slopes than soaking your sore muscles. I could install one here, put in the two-twenty volt outlet it would need, and run a water line outside."

I mulled the idea over for a moment, realizing Rocky and I would enjoy the tub as much as my guests. With him on my staff, I'd save an installation fee and only have to pay for the parts and the spa. Still, I had no idea what a hot tub would cost. "Can you price one for me?"

He shot me a wink. "Anything for you, boss."

CHAPTER 6

Misty

My boys had snowboarded until the resort closed on Saturday night, but they roused themselves bright and early on Sunday as directed, sporting the matching buffalo plaid shirts I'd bought for them. They'd be employees of my lodge for the next four weeks and were ready to learn the ropes. Jack Junior got the coffee pots percolating while Mitch helped me unload the warming trays from Patty's cart. She'd remembered that my boys liked their pancakes covered in bananas and pecans, and brought a big bowl of the toppings along with her. I felt lucky to have such a thoughtful friend. Rocky joined us as we were filling our plates. He piled a few logs in the fireplace and got them burning before fixing himself a plate. The four of us took seats at a table near the hearth where we could enjoy the warmth of the flames.

A few early risers came to get in a morning meal before making a few final runs down the ski slopes and heading home. Everyone but the Goodwins and Rayan would be checking out today, and the potential investors would arrive later this afternoon. Aileen, who hadn't shown her face since they'd arrived yesterday, was among the early risers. Her internal clock was probably still on London time, which was five hours ahead of North Carolina. If she were back home, she'd be sitting down for lunch rather than breakfast. As she had the day before, she wore a drab outfit in varying shades of gray, reminding me of how the mountains devolved into grayscale when viewed from a distance. She seemed distant herself, not bothering to look at those around her, as if mentally somewhere else. She fixed a cup of tea and proceeded to the buffet. Although we didn't serve scones or beans for breakfast like they did in Britain, at least she seemed to find the Greasy Griddle's Southern fare to her liking. She put a little of everything on her plate.

I caught her eye, gave her a smile, and called, "Good morning, Mrs. Goodwin!"

She returned the sentiment, but without the smile or enthusiasm. Rather than taking a seat at one of the empty tables in the great room, she turned and carried her food back down the hall to eat in their room. Maybe she still wasn't over the jet lag. *Or maybe she's just a wet blanket.*

When we finished breakfast, I led my boys to the reception desk and gave them a tutorial on the lodge's reservation system. I showed them where the guest-room keys were kept, as well as the inventory of toothbrushes, toothpaste, razors, shaving cream, and nail clippers for forgetful guests. A few of the guests came to the desk to check out, and I supervised as my sons collected the payments and room keys, and issued receipts. They'd caught on fast and did an excellent job.

We'd finished reviewing phone etiquette when Brynn arrived for the day. All that was left was to train the boys in housekeeping. To that end, one would shadow me while I went on my rounds, and the other would shadow Brynn. She locked her purse in the desk, then crossed her arms over her chest and looked from J.J. to Mitch. "Which of you is less annoying?"

J.J. hiked a thumb at his chest, while Mitch and I simultaneously said, "J.J."

She gave Mitch a pat on the shoulder. "You might be the more annoying one, but honesty and self-awareness count for something." She turned to J.J. and motioned for him to follow her. "Come on, kid. I'll teach you to work magic with a toilet brush."

Mitch came along with me, pushing the housekeeping cart. As young boys, my sons had rarely cleaned up after themselves—at least not without whining or an argument. It felt like poetic justice for them now to be helping me clean up after others. We tackled the guest rooms along the east wing, switching duties with each room so he'd get practice in all aspects. Bedmaking. Vacuuming. Dusting. Disinfecting the bath. Refilling the soap, shampoo, and conditioner dispensers. Ensuring the room was supplied with adequate toilet and facial tissue. Checking the drawers and closets for items guests might have left behind. Sure enough, we found a single snow boot under a bed. I'd contact the guest and arrange to ship the footwear to them.

As I dusted the shutters on the window in one of the front-facing rooms, a black mud-encrusted pickup turned into the parking lot and slowly circled. When the truck cruised past the window, the driver looked over at me, the long barrels of the rifles in the rack forming horizontal stripes behind him. My heart bounced in my chest. The man at the wheel was the one I'd met the day Rocky and I had visited the resort site. *What's he doing here?* Rather than pretend he hadn't noticed me, he tipped his ball cap before gunning his engine and continuing on. I had a feeling he'd be back. Whatever business he had here had yet to be completed.

By the early afternoon, we'd finished cleaning the empty guest rooms. From the hallway, I could see Rayan and Nigel setting up the great room for the evening reception. Aileen wasn't helping them. From what I'd witnessed so far, she didn't seem to be much involved in her husband's resort business. I wondered if she had a career of her own. Maybe she was working in their room right now. If she wasn't involved in her husband's resort business and despised cold weather, though, why had she bothered to come here at all? Why not stay back home in London?

Mitchell and I cleaned Rayan's room in record time. Goodwin's assistant was exceptionally tidy, which made it easy for us to wipe down the surfaces and vacuum. When we finished with Rayan's space, we knocked lightly on the door to the Goodwins' room. "Housekeeping!" I called cheerily.

A few seconds later, the door opened. Aileen walked out wearing a heavy hooded coat—in gray, of course. She tugged her purse strap up over her padded shoulder. "I'll get out of your way." She raised her other hand, which held the key fob to the rental SUV, and circled a finger in the air. "Where's the closest city? Maybe somewhere with an art or history museum?"

She'd paid little attention to anything other than the breakfast since she'd arrived, so it was both surprising and pleasing to know she took some interest in the local scene. "Visit the BRAHM." With new exhibits every few weeks, the Blowing Rock Art & History Museum was always a treat. I also suggested she consider touring downtown Boone, which included markers and statues dedicated to explorer Daniel Boone, the small city's namesake. "Proper is a great place for dinner." The restaurant was housed in the former Watauga County Jail building. She'd get her fill of both Southern culture and Southern fare.

She thanked me for the suggestions and aimed for the lobby. She didn't bother telling her husband where she was going or when she'd return. Jack and I had functioned independently in our marriage, too, but it seemed odd she didn't at least touch base with Nigel before heading off.

Mitch and I entered the Goodwins' guest room. You could tell a lot about people by the way they left their space. This room told me there might be trouble in paradise. Though all of the bed pillows rested against the headboard and the convertible sofa was not currently folded out into a bed, the corner of a sheet poked out between two of the couch cushions. Brynn and I never would have left the linens that sloppy. *Someone slept on the foldout.* What's more, it seemed that the Goodwins didn't want this fact to be obvious. Otherwise, they would have left the sofa converted so the housekeeping staff could remake it. Ironically, I wouldn't have thought much of it had they left the bed open. Couples sometimes slept in separate beds if one of them was active at night or snored. A CPAP machine on the night table between the bed and couch told me one of them suffered sleep apnea. Though I knew little about the devices, I'd seen them in my guests' rooms before. This particular model came with a full-face mask that covered both the nose and mouth. Sleeping separately under these circumstances was no big deal.

I debated what to do, but decided to err on the side of

thoroughness. After all, a guest couldn't complain that I'd been too fastidious, right? To that end, I converted the sofa to a bed and smoothed out the linens, tucking them tightly under the thin mattress before folding the sofa back up. As I went to vacuum the closet, I noticed that Nigel and Aileen's clothing hung at either end of the rod, as if their garments had turned their backs on each other. Their toiletries, too, sat in distinct zones on either side of the bathroom sink rather than side by side or intermingled.

Mitch could be a typical clueless kid sometimes, but even he seemed to sense something was awry. "They might as well have put a piece of tape down the center of the room."

"Like you and J.J. did before you got your own rooms?"

"He kept playing with my Legos!"

On the bright side, whichever of the Goodwins had slept in the bed left a ten-dollar tip on the pillow. I held it up. "Speaking of splitting things down the middle, while Brynn is off on vacation, you and J.J. can share the tips fifty-fifty."

Mitch whooped. "Sweet!"

At the end of her shift, I handed the day's tips over to Brynn. "Enjoy your vacation and the solstice celebration."

She thanked me and tucked the cash into her wallet. "See you next year!"

She'd just headed out the door and climbed into her Prius when a sporty red Dodge Challenger coupe with a black stripe over the hood roared up to the lodge. The Challenger was one of the few muscle cars with all-wheel drive, an alternative for sporty types who didn't want an SUV. The car screeched to a stop. A thirty-something shaggy-haired white guy sat at the wheel. Mitch and J.J. rolled the trolley out front to help the guest with his luggage. As they approached, the driver climbed out of his car. "Heads up!" He tossed his key fob to J.J. My son caught it and looked back up, confused. We hadn't covered this situation in our training.

I scurried outside. "Hello, Mister . . . ?"

"Cochrane," the guy said. "Sebastian Cochrane."

I took the keys from J.J.'s hand and held them out to the guest. "I'm sorry, Mr. Cochrane. We don't have valet service."

He pointed at J.J. "He know how to drive?"

"Yes, sir," I said. "But—"

"Then you've got a valet." He snatched the fob from my fingers and forced it on J.J.

Entitled jerk. I felt myself heat with frustration, burning as hot as the embers in the great room's fireplace. "The lodge's insurance policy doesn't cover the staff driving guest vehicles."

"No problem." He shrugged a shoulder. "I've got plenty of insurance." He pulled out his wallet, whipped out a bill, and tucked it into J.J.'s breast pocket. "You work for me now." He swung his arm. "Park my car, please, valet sir." He performed a dramatic bow.

J.J. looked my way. *What could I do?* Releasing a huff, I addressed my son. "Be careful. Park in the closest spot." As he climbed into the car, I sent up a prayer I wouldn't be sued.

As J.J. eased the car away from the door, I noticed it bore a North Carolina vanity plate that read HCANES. Sebastian must be a Carolina Hurricanes hockey fan. Once J.J. had parked the car, he and Mitch pulled Sebastian's luggage and snowboarding equipment from the trunk, along with a large plastic cooler. J.J. returned the key fob to our guest. We strode inside where I checked the man in.

Sebastian drummed his fingers on the counter. "I forgot my shaving case. You got a razor? Toothbrush? Toothpaste? That kind of stuff?"

"Sure." I pulled the basket of complimentary toiletries out from under the counter, noticing the supply of toothbrushes was running low. "What do you need?"

He reached in and grabbed a handful willy-nilly, like a greedy kid reaching into a bowl of candy on Halloween. He shoved the items into his pocket. "That'll get me through the week."

His arrogant and obnoxious behavior earned him a stay in our worst room, the one next to the guest laundry. After checking him into the system and running his credit card, I called out "Heads up!" and tossed him the key to his room.

Sebastian grabbed the keys out of the air, chuckled, and pointed at me. "I like you."

The feeling was certainly not mutual.

When Sebastian turned away from the desk, he spotted Rayan and Nigel in the great room. "This where the party's at tonight?"

"The *reception*," Nigel corrected with a smile. "We'll convene here at eight p.m."

"That gives me time for a disco nap." Sebastian began backing down the hall, but not before pointing two finger guns at Goodwin. "You'd better be serving top-shelf liquor tonight. I don't drink the cheap stuff."

Goodwin's smile and patience didn't falter. "Of course. Only the best for my investors."

"That's what I like to hear." Sebastian pretended to fire his two finger guns in quick succession, then tucked them into invisible holsters. He turned and set off down the hall, beatboxing and dancing some hip-hop moves, my boys dutifully following with the luggage cart.

My sons returned to the lobby a few minutes later. After rolling the trolley into position by the front door, they came to the desk. Mitch pulled no punches. "That guy's an A-hole."

I bit my lip. "I should probably tell you to watch your language, but you're not wrong."

J.J. pulled the bill from his shirt pocket. It was a single. "He's a lousy tipper, too."

I'd had a handful of guests like Sebastian Cochrane before, ones who thought any unreasonable demand or disrespectful act could be rectified by tossing a bit of cash at hotel staff. Little did they know I flagged them in my system. Should they attempt to book a room at my lodge again, they'd get an automated response informing them no rooms were available. I'd rather lose some business than my self-respect.

Fortunately, the next guests who checked in were much more polite. A blue Subaru Outback pulled into a spot outside. It looked like the one I'd seen pulling the teardrop camper on the webcam the day before, but the relatively affordable four-wheel-drive vehicles were everywhere in the mountains.

A man and woman in their late forties climbed out of the car as Mitch and J.J. rolled the luggage cart outside to assist them. Both wore heavy winter coats and knit caps, so I couldn't tell much about them until they came inside. As they entered the heated space, they stamped their feet on the mat to rid their boots of snow and pulled off their beanies. With their heads uncovered now, I could see they were both blond-haired and blue-eyed. They were squarely built, of sturdy stock. The man wore a traditional plaid scarf around his neck, while the

woman had donned one of the more contemporary infinity scarves in salmon pink. She'd doubled the loop
around her neck. I owned an infinity scarf, too, and who-
ever had invented the design had my eternal gratitude.
Unlike regular scarves, they didn't come untied and fall
off.

I greeted the couple with a smile. "Welcome to the
Mountaintop Lodge."

"Hey, there," the man said in a Midwestern accent.
The two stepped up to the counter. "We're with the Adventure Capital group. Kyle and Laurie Jensen."

I logged into the system and found the Jensens' registration. "I'll just need to see an I.D. and get a credit
card for incidentals."

"Okey-dokey." The man pulled his driver's license
and a credit card from his wallet, and lay them atop the
counter facing me.

I picked up the license first, noting it was issued by
the state of South Dakota and that their home address
was in Rapid City. "You've come a long way. I hope you
had a good flight."

"Oh, we didn't fly," Laurie said. "We drove. We enjoy road trips."

"Passed lots of cattle," Kyle said. "Three hundred and
eighty-two to be precise. Guess how I know." Before I
could even attempt an answer, he said, "I added them up
on my cowculator. Get it? *Cow*culator?"

"Good one."

Laurie groaned. "Don't encourage him. Kyle is the
king of bad dad jokes." The look she cut him told me she
adored the man, bad jokes or not. She cupped a hand
around her mouth, as if to share a secret. "If he wasn't a
doctor, I wouldn't put up with him."

If they hadn't arrived in an economical car and

budget-friendly clothing, I'd think the woman was bragging. Instead, she simply seemed proud of the man she'd married. I turned to her husband. "A doctor, huh?" It was reassuring to know we'd have someone with medical training on-site in the event of an injury or health issue. I finished with his license, slid it back over the counter, then picked up the credit card. "What type of medicine do you practice?"

"Brace yourself." He raised his palms and splayed his fingers in a bracing gesture. "I'm an orthodontist. Get it? *Brace* yourself?"

"Another good one." I sent up a prayer. *Please don't let there be five days of this schtick.* I liked jokes—even corny ones—as much as the next person, but some guests treated hotel staff as their captive audience and would tie us up at our busiest moments, oblivious that they weren't the only guest in need of our attention.

Laurie said, "For a dirt-poor farmer's kid, he's done well."

"Pulled myself up by my bootstraps," Kyle said.

His childhood likely explained the sensible car. Surely, the couple could have afforded a more expensive vehicle on an orthodontist's income, but he'd probably been raised to count his pennies. It had been the same in my middle-class household growing up. I'd never wanted for any necessities, but my parents weren't wealthy and had to keep a careful eye on their spending.

"My former husband works in dental supply sales." I ordered the toothbrushes, small tubes of toothpaste, and floss I kept on hand at the lodge from Jack, who sold them to me at cost.

"Dental sales? What a coincidence. It'll give us something to *jaw* about."

We had no more time for jokes, thank goodness, as another couple arrived and strode into the lobby. I handed the Jensens their room keys, and informed them of the breakfast hours. "Let me know if there's anything you need. Enjoy your stay."

As Mitch helped them to their room, J.J. relieved our latest arrivals of their baggage. Like the Jensens, these two appeared to be around forty, though their dress was far more fashionable. The woman had flaming red hair, probably not natural but eye-catching and attractive nonetheless. She was tall and trim, in skintight white nylon winter pants and a fitted neon green puffer jacket. She wore tan shearling snow boots, though hers had a high, blocky heel rather than the more utilitarian flat sole. Her companion had olive skin and shiny, jet-black hair he couldn't seem to leave alone. He'd run his long fingers through it, slicking it back from his forehead, only for an impertinent lock to fall back over his face a second or two later. He, too, wore fitted skinny ski pants, the tight black fabric doing little to hide his, shall we say, snowballs? He'd topped the pants with a bright striped sweater. As they stepped up to the counter, the smell of cigarette smoke and a musky men's cologne met my nose, the scents competing for dominance.

The woman did the talking for the two. "Daphne and Jean-Paul Fournier."

The woman's heavy French accent took me back to the charming rom-com *Amélie* I'd forced Jack to watch with me years back. He'd pretended to suffer through it, but I could tell he'd enjoyed it as much as I had.

"Welcome." I'd never seen a French driver's license before. I was surprised to see it was pink but, then again, the French were known for their style. The name on the license was Daphne Moreau, but her reservation and credit card were in the last name Fournier. Maybe she hadn't had time to visit the French equivalent of the DMV and update the license. I wondered if the French DMVs were the same horrid hellscapes they were here in the U.S. "I noticed the surnames are different on your driver's license and credit card. Did you two marry recently?"

They exchanged a glance, and said something to one another in French, before Daphne turned back to me. "In France, the license is in your birth name."

Their system made sense. One of the reasons I'd decided to keep my married name after my divorce was to avoid the headache of having to get a new driver's license and social security card. I ran her credit card through the machine. As I handed it back to her, I offered my standard spiel about the breakfast buffet, et cetera.

"Merci." Daphne turned to her husband, who ran his fingers through his hair yet again. She said something in French and they began to walk to their room. J.J. took off after them with their luggage and skis.

Shortly after J.J. returned to the desk, an orange Ford van pulled up in front of the lodge. It wasn't quite a minivan, but not a cargo van, either. The blue handicap tag hanging from the rearview mirror told me these latest arrivals must be Celeste and Emilio Salazar. By the time Mitch and I got outside, the two had their doors open and were assembling their wheelchairs in the space beside their seats. The couple were in their mid to late thirties and, like everyone else who'd arrived so far, very fit. Celeste wore her dark-brown hair in a short, sporty, carefree cut, while Emilio sported a salt-and-pepper beard and ponytail.

Celeste greeted me and my son, then glanced around

at all the snow, her eyes bright with excitement. "The skiing is going to be epic! I can't wait to conquer those runs."

"You came at the perfect time," I said. "It's the best snow up here in years."

Mitch grabbed their bags and loaded them onto the trolley. Their specialized wheelchairs had knobby all-terrain tires on either side and a third, smaller wheel that extended out in front, designed for off-roading. Two long levers stuck up on either side of the seat. They maneuvered the chairs by pumping the handles. We followed after them as they rolled into the lodge.

Though I'd intended to convert one of the guest rooms to an accessible room since I'd bought the lodge, Goodwin's inquiry about the accommodations had moved the item to the top of my—or rather Rocky's—to-do list. The lodge's entrance had no steps, the existing doors throughout the lodge were wide enough for a wheelchair to pass through, and the lodge comprised only one floor, so only the guest room needed modifications. Rocky lowered the countertop in the bathroom and on the coffee bar, as well as the rod in the closet. He'd removed the porcelain tub and converted the space into a contemporary shower with a fold-down seat, grab bars, and an adjustable, handheld showerhead.

I'd just finished checking in the Salazars when a green Range Rover pulled up to the lodge. I wasn't familiar with the models in the company's lineup, but I knew none of them came cheap. Rocky was busy, J.J. was assisting the Fourniers, and Mitchell hadn't returned from helping the Jensens. I feared Kyle had sucked my son into being an unwitting listener for a long comedic bit. It would be up to me to help this guest.

I slid into my coat and hustled outside, where a thir-tyish Black man stood at the open cargo bay. He was short and slight, and wore round eyeglasses rimmed in plastic tortoiseshell, sneakers, ripped jeans, and a short-sleeved T-shirt with a cartoon character printed on it—a tough-looking orange and black monarch butterfly with tattoos on his wings, a menacing scowl on his face, and a gold hoop piercing his left antennae. The man's light attire was inappropriate for the weather, but he seemed immune to the cold.

"Hello, there!" I called as I approached, my words leaving visible puffs in the air. "May I help you with your bags?"

He threw up a hand, like a crossing guard stopping oncoming traffic. "No, no, no!"

I stopped in my tracks, the sudden loss of momentum making me slide on the slushy asphalt. Fortunately, I didn't end up on my rear end.

My confusion must have been written on my face, because he said, "Some of my property is . . . sensitive. It's better if I take care of it."

Sensitive? What, exactly, did he mean by that? The term could apply equally to dynamite or an explicit personal journal. Then again, maybe he'd been trying to find a synonym for the word *valuable* without being obvious. I didn't know much about private equity other than that the investors were wealthy individuals. Everyone who'd checked in so far appeared to meet that criterion, though the Jensens' wealth wasn't conspicuous like the others. From what I'd heard, Midwesterners tended to be humble and practical, not showoffs, and the Jensens seemed to be living up to the stereotype. I gestured to the doors. "When you're ready to check in, I'll be at the desk."

"Great. Thanks." He didn't move until I'd turned to head back into the lodge. *Odd.*

A few minutes later, he rolled two large, hard-sided suitcases into the lobby. They were a standard black style, similar to the ones that Rayan had used to transport the pieces of the model. He had a death grip on the handles, as if afraid someone would try to rip them out of his hands. One looked especially heavy. Even though it had wheels, he strained to move it.

As I was registering the man, my sons returned from helping the other guests. J.J. spotted the suitcases the guest had rolled inside. Before my son could attempt to take them, I looked down at the man's license. The name on it was Amari Lott. I looked back up. "Mr. Lott prefers to handle his luggage himself."

J.J. looked from me to our guest. Spotting the character on the man's shirt, my son exclaimed, "Hey! That's Papillon from Butterfly Brawl. You play that game?"

The man's eyes sparked and he seemed to stiffen. "Every now and then."

J.J. said, "I wonder if we've ever battled each other. My screen name is JX2."

Before my son could ask the guest for his screen name, which I feared might offend the enigmatic man, I pointed down the hall to the laundry room. "J.J., could you check on the sheets in the dryer, please?"

"Sure."

As J.J. strode off, I handed Mr. Lott his room key. "The Wi-Fi password is—"

"That's okay." The man put up a hand again. "I won't need it."

He plans to go the next five days without internet access? Everything was online these days. Seemed it would be hard to function without it. "Enjoy your stay, Mr. Lott."

As he walked away, I found myself wondering if the contents of his luggage was the only secret he was hiding.

CHAPTER 7

Yeti

Yeti could hear music and the murmur of conversation from down the hall, along with an occasional laugh and clink of ice in a glass. But she didn't care what the lodge guests were up to. In her experience, humans were a mixed bag. Some were kind, others ambivalent. A few could even be cruel. She recalled a little boy who'd come to their house once, a kid from the neighborhood. He'd yanked on her tail. It hurt like the dickens! Thankfully, Misty had caught the little booger and never allowed him back in their home. But Yeti wasn't going to think of that now. She was in absolute bliss sandwiched between two of her favorite humans on the sofa in their room. Misty had left the door between her room and the boys' room open so Yeti could venture back and forth unfettered. She was glad to have another space to explore, another window from which to watch the world, and especially to get attention from J.J. and Mitch.

She flipped shamelessly onto her back. J.J. scratched under her chin while Mitch tended to her belly. *Aaaaaah* . . . When she'd had enough, she let them know in her standard feline style—with a nip of their fingers.

It's been nice, but we're all done here. Mitch cried out and whipped his hand out of her reach. J.J. merely laughed. Yeti slid off the sofa and sauntered back into her and Misty's room to see what treats had been left for her. *Salmon! Hooray!*

CHAPTER 8

Misty

Sunday evening, I helped Nigel and Rayan set up a make-shift cocktail bar on a table in the great room. Along with several varieties of red and white wine, they offered mixers and top-shelf spirits. I went to fill a couple of spare ice buckets and returned to find that Aileen had joined her husband and his assistant in the great room. The Salazars had arrived as well, as had Amari.

Though Nigel hadn't explicitly asked me to play bar-tender, I didn't mind stepping into the role. The man had filled my lodge, after all. Besides, it would give me an opportunity to get to know my guests better. I lifted a glass and addressed Amari. "May I pour you a drink, Mr. Lott?"

"Gin and tonic," he said. As I filled the glass with ice, he asked, "Is there a path or trail from the lodge to the ski resort?"

While sections of some trails ran through town, there was no direct shortcut from my lodge to the ski resort, paved or otherwise. The road between was steep and curvy with no shoulder. Vacationers sometimes walked along the narrow roadside, but it was much safer to take a vehicle. "You'll have to drive," I said, "but it's not far. Just a mile or so."

I added a finger of gin to his glass, then filled the rest with tonic water. Were I an authentic bartender, I would've added a lime wedge and served it along with some witty banter, but I had no garnishments or quips to offer at the moment. I handed him the drink. "Enjoy."

As Amari walked off and joined Rayan in conversation with another relatively young male investor, the Salazars pulled their wheelchairs up to the table. Emilio requested a bourbon neat, while Celeste asked for a whiskey sour. Rather than joining the other investors right away, they remained by the bar after I served them.

Celeste sipped her drink, then rested the glass on her thigh and eyed me. "This is a cozy place. Do you stay booked up year-round?"

Though she was purportedly making a mere casual inquiry about my inn, I suspected her question was more intended to gauge the town's need for additional lodging rather than any real interest in my business. Still, I couldn't blame her for wanting to get the inside scoop from a local before deciding whether it was a good idea to invest in Goodwin's resort.

"I've only owned the place since August," I said, "but the lodge is in the black." *Thank goodness.* I'd invested most of my divorce settlement in the place, taken a risk. But already I'd reaped so many rewards, the best of which were not financial. I'd met Rocky, Patty, and Brynn, forming meaningful personal and professional relationships. What's more, I'd been able to spend my days in a beautiful place that brought peace and serenity to my soul. But that's not what the Salazars wanted to know. "Occupancy rates vary. The lodge is usually at or near full capacity on weekends. We're about to enter peak season, and bookings are solid through February." If the snow held up, we'd be full of families and college students during the school spring breaks in March, too.

Emilio swirled the liquid in his glass, his face thoughtful. "Is it hard to get help? It says online that the population is less than a thousand up here. I noticed a lot of open job listings."

The question made me a little uncomfortable, but I wouldn't lie. "I'm lucky to have two reliable staff. My maintenance director lives on site, which makes things easier for both of us." I'd been thrilled when Rocky asked if he could move into the lodge. It was as much a benefit to me as it had been for him. "But, yes, I've heard from other local business owners that they've had trouble filling positions due to the long commute from larger towns in the area."

Emilio and Celeste exchanged glances, as if both were making a mental note. They turned back to me, thanked me for the drinks, and set off to mingle with the other investors. I hoped they wouldn't share what I'd just told them with Nigel. I didn't want him to think I was working against him.

Kyle and Laurie stepped up to the table. Both asked for a simple glass of white wine.

"Just a little." Laurie demonstrated by holding up her thumb and index finger in a near pinch. "We're lightweights."

I poured them each a couple of ounces, enough to get a taste of the expensive vintage without feeling its effects. They thanked me and set off to mingle.

As more of the guests arrived for the meet and greet, a smiling Nigel worked the room, making them all feel welcome, seen, and important. He had a knack for small talk, and was able to pull information from them like a magician pulling quarters from ears. Eavesdropping, I learned that a remarkable percentage of Dr. Jensen's orthodontic patients were adults, a growing trend. I also learned that Daphne and Jean-Paul's favorite place to ski was in Zermatt, Switzerland, home to the world-famous Matterhorn peak. The Salazars had three kids back home in Greenville, where Celeste was an executive in a manufacturing facility and Emilio worked in a regional advertising agency. One of their favorite family activities was kayaking the paddle trails in the Alligator River National Wildlife Refuge.

When traffic at the drink table slowed, I returned to the registration desk to take care of some administrative matters. I was looking at my computer screen when, in my peripheral vision, I saw Aileen attempt to slink away from the party. Nigel excused himself from a conversation with Sebastian Cochrane and strode quickly after his wife. Though the two were out of sight down the hall, they were close enough that I could hear their angry whispers.

"You can't leave now!" Nigel insisted. "In a few days, I'll be asking these investors to hand over a small fortune. It's critical we earn their trust."

Aileen scoffed. "Always the salesman. You only give people attention until you've closed the sale. Then the thrill of the chase is over and you're done with them. I know that better than anyone."

Uh-oh. Looked like my earlier suspicions were correct. There was indeed trouble in paradise. I might not be the only one who realized it, either. Amari had quietly wandered into the lobby with his drink to check out the display of brochures from local tourist sites. He glanced down the hall where the Goodwins stood arguing, watching for a beat or two before turning back to the pamphlets. Meanwhile, the marital spat went on.

"That's not true!" Nigel hissed.

"It is!" Aileen said. "You've treated our marriage like one of your deals. Ever since we walked down the aisle all those years ago, you've hardly looked my way. Yet you expected me to drop everything, to give up a job I loved, to further your business. When's the last time you did something for me?"

"Adventure Capital isn't just *my* business, it's our livelihood." His tone was slightly patronizing now. "It's how we can afford our flat in London and food and clothing, not to mention all that art you're intent on collecting. But this is not the time or place for a debate. Come back to the party and we'll continue this conversation later."

"No!" Aileen snapped. "I'm tired and I'm going to bed." Her declaration was followed by the sound of her footsteps retreating down the hall.

I continued to stare at my computer screen, pretending I hadn't overheard the exchange, when Nigel came back up the hall and returned to the meet and greet. He seamlessly resumed his role of charming host. "Well, we've lost Aileen, poor thing," he said cheerily to the group. "Jet lag caught up to her. She bids you all a good night."

It was an outright lie, but I couldn't blame him for wanting to keep their troubles under wraps.

He circled behind the drink table and waved Rayan over to assume bartending duty. "Would anyone like another drink?"

Sebastian raised his glass in the air for what had to be his fourth cocktail, at least. "Fill me up!"

* * *

Four inches of fresh snow had fallen overnight, blanketing the guests' cars in white. Several more inches were expected today. Workers in Raleigh, Durham, and Charlotte were probably calling in sick to come up here and sneak in some time on the slopes during the week, when the resort was less crowded. Work would always be there, but fresh powder was a gift from the gods.

Rocky had cleared our parking lot once again, and left the lodge to perform snowplow services for private clients on the mountain. His phone had been ringing and pinging since sunup with people wanting to hire him. He'd be gone most of the day. I'd miss having him around, but since his only compensation for his work at the lodge was free rent, the man had to make a living.

The breakfast buffet wrapped up at 9:30, giving me and my boys just a half hour to clean up and arrange the great room for Goodwin's investor pitch session at 10:00. We wiped down the tables and situated them in wide rows with chairs on one side only, classroom-style, facing the podium and screen. Meanwhile, Rayan readied the projector and microphone and placed a pen and folder with the Adventure Capital logo on the table in front of each seat.

Kyle and Laurie were the first to arrive. While Laurie fixed them cups of coffee, Kyle cornered me as I refilled a bin with sugar and sweetener packets. "Nothing against Beech Mountain, but I wish Nigel Goodwin was building this resort in Ireland because then our *capital* would be *Dublin*." He snickered. "Get it? Our capital would be doublin'? *Dublin doublin'*?"

On the other side of me, Mitch whispered, "Kill me now."

I gave my son a discreet elbow to the ribs. "You're hilarious, Dr. Jensen."

Kyle rejoined his wife and they took seats in the front row. Over the next few minutes, the others filtered into the room. Celeste and Emilio Salazar sat next to the Jensens. Daphne and Jean-Paul Fournier sat in the row behind them. Amari Lott secured a discreet seat in the back corner by a window. As others arrived, the guests slid over or rearranged themselves to accommodate one another.

At 10:00, my boys were in the housekeeping closet loading the carts with fresh sheets and towels, I was in place behind the reception desk, and, in the great room, a single seat remained empty. Goodwin checked his watch and walked over to Rayan. The two bent their heads together for a moment before Rayan set off down the hall to Sebastian's room. He'd just raised his hand to knock when the door swung open in front of him. The cocky young man emerged and threw an arm around Rayan's shoulders. "Let's get this party started!" Sebastian dragged Goodwin's assistant back up the hall to the great room, where he released his unwitting prisoner and dropped into the open seat in the back row.

His audience complete, Goodwin welcomed the potential investors. "Now that you've had the chance to chat at last night's mixer, you've probably realized you are an elite, exclusive group. I believe Americans use the term *one percenters*?" He paused to give the group a smile. "Congratulations on your financial achievements."

He went on to state why investing in a private resort was a wiser choice than investing in publicly traded companies, rental real estate, certificates of deposit, and other forms of investments. Per Goodwin, the stock market had become too volatile, rental real estate came with never-ending hassles, CDs paid too little, and other investments were unacceptably insecure or offered low returns. All valid points. My retirement fund was invested in stocks, and it had recently taken a nosedive. I'd heard from some who owned rental homes on the mountain that last-minute cancellations could leave their places unexpectedly vacant, and that some renters trashed the places or thoughtlessly ran up the electric and water bills.

Goodwin continued. "Adventure Capital Corporation doesn't offer interests in its resorts to just anyone. We ensure our investors are capable of committing substantial funds for the length of the development phase for the resorts. Once the resorts are up and running, you may choose to remain invested and reap a percentage of the profits, or request a return of your capital plus any growth in value." He picked up a folder from the podium and held it up. "The details are explained in the prospectus provided in your folders."

With the guests gathered here, the rooms would be empty. I texted my boys and gave them the go-ahead to begin their housekeeping rounds. With the two of them tackling the west wing together, they'd finish in time to spend the afternoon snowboarding. Meanwhile, Goodwin gave a nod to Rayan, who pushed a button on the projector to turn it on. The screen behind Goodwin lit up with the Adventure Capital Corporation logo. The oversized *A* in *Adventure* was a snow-topped mountain. The *T*s in the words *Capital* and *Corporation* below formed supports for ski lifts running up the side of the *A*. The image was clever and eye-catching. I supposed I should be starting my rounds, but I was curious about the resort. I decided to stay at my desk for a bit and see what Goodwin had to say about the proposed project.

He rubbed his hands together. "Let's start with the

basics. Why are we here in Beech Mountain, North Carolina?" He paused and ran his gaze over the crowd. "It's because I've got the perfect nose for sniffing out great opportunities." He tapped the flat end of his long, pointed nose. The group burst into laughter. If Nigel Goodwin could laugh at himself, why shouldn't they? More businesslike now, Goodwin continued. "We are here because history tells us that hundreds of thousands of people are willing to come to Beech Mountain each year if there's something to draw them here."

Goodwin used a remote control to advance to the next slide. It showed images of the Land of Oz theme park, an immersive theater experience based on *The Wizard of Oz*. The park operated on the mountain from 1970 to 1980, suffering many ups and downs during the decade. Although it closed for some time, former employees and parkgoers nostalgic for the magical place eventually brought the park back to life for annual limited-run events, including "Autumn at Oz" weekends each fall. My parents had taken me and my siblings to the park during its original heyday on a family vacation, and Jack and I had brought the boys up many times over the years to enjoy the special events. I even owned a pair of red glittery sneakers and a blue-and-white gingham top I'd bought to wear to the park, my comfy version of Dorothy Gale.

"The first season that Land of Oz was open," Goodwin said, "over four-hundred-thousand visitors came up to the theme park. That's a lot of people who need places to stay and eat and who need to be entertained." He circled a finger in the air. "Beech Mountain is within easy driving distance of major population centers not only in North Carolina, but also South Carolina, Georgia, Virginia, West Virginia, Tennessee, and Kentucky."

He pointed out the front windows. "Take a look at the license plates while you're here. You'll see large numbers from Florida, too."

It was true. As one of the southernmost ski areas, Beech Mountain attracted people from areas farther south who could travel here by car.

He continued to point out the window. "Guess which national park was the most-visited in 2021?" He paused for effect. "It was the Blue Ridge Parkway, which sits a short half-hour drive from here. The second-most visited national park? Great Smoky Mountains, only a two-and-a-half-hour drive to the southeast." He turned his pointed finger downward. "We are sitting in a prime location for year-round tourism, yet there's no year-round attraction here."

Again, he had a point. The area attracted distinct groups of people at particular times of year. Skiers and snowboarders in winter. Hikers and mountain bikers in summer. Leaf peepers in the fall.

"You've seen the model." Goodwin extended a hand to indicate the exhibit. "Yet there will be so much more to the resort than just the beautiful building you see." He went on to detail the proposed resorts' amenities and activities. A spa and gift shop. A tavern with live music and entertainment. Snowmobiling. Mountain biking. Snowshoeing. Snow tubing. Zip-lining. A ropes course. Rock climbing. Wildlife viewing. The indoor water park. Helicopter tours of the Blue Ridge Mountains. Multiple hot tubs, a guest perk my modest lodge was so sorely lacking—but maybe not for long. Rocky was looking into the cost of a suitable tub for the lodge.

Emilio raised a hand. When Goodwin gave him a nod, Emilio said, "Will you ensure that all of your activities are accessible? That everyone can enjoy them?"

Goodwin said, "That's a valid question. I'll have to look into it, but I'll certainly do my best to see that everyone can participate in all of the activities, or that alternatives are offered."

Celeste and Emilio exchanged a glance. Neither looked happy that Goodwin hadn't thought of the accessibility issue already himself.

Sebastian raised his hand but, unlike Emilio, didn't wait to be called on. "What about Great Wolf Lodge? Why would people drive all the way up here when there's an indoor water park in Charlotte?"

I'd expected Goodwin to be annoyed, but the developer kept his tone upbeat even as he put off Sebastian. "That's a smart question. I plan to fully cover the potential competition in tomorrow's pitch segment. You'll see there's little cause for concern."

Sebastian issued a skeptical grunt. "You'd better have done your homework. I'm going to need a lot of convincing before I drop a quarter mil in your pocket."

"Rightfully so," Goodwin replied graciously. "You can trust I've performed a thorough analysis, for your sake as well as my own. I, too, have 'skin in the game,' as you Americans say. As you'll see, there is no true competition for the Retreat on Blue Ridge."

Goodwin had taken Sebastian's questions in stride, but Daphne backed him up nevertheless. She cast a glance over her shoulder. "Jean-Paul and I have invested in all of the Adventure Capital Resorts. We have been very pleased with our returns. Nigel knows what he is doing." She pulled out her cell phone. "In fact, I will authorize the wire transfer for our investment right now. That is how confident I am in the resort planned here."

Everyone in the front row turned back now, including

Kyle and Laurie. Laurie's brow furrowed as her focus shifted between Sebastian in the back row, Daphne Fournier working her cell phone in the seat behind her, and Goodwin at the podium. "So, all of the resorts have been profitable? There haven't been any problems?"

Before Goodwin could answer, Sebastian responded for him. "The Alberta Adventure Resort has been a total disaster."

Amari Lott, who'd been silent up until now, leaned forward to look past the others in the back row to Sebastian. "A disaster? What do you mean?"

Goodwin raised his palms in a halt motion, attempting to regain control of the meeting. "There have been minor delays with the Alberta project, all of which are being handled. I'll address the matter in full detail later. In fact, every question you have will be answered, most of them by what is already included in my prepared presentation. This isn't my first experience developing a resort, as you know, and I have anticipated many of your concerns. But I know you all want to hit the slopes this afternoon." He pointed out the window at the falling snow, white woods, and distant snow-covered ridges. "There's so much fresh powder on the runs!" He whooped and raised happy fists like a man half his age would, before lowering them to grip the sides of the podium. "Let's move ahead now, visit the site, and, on Friday, if my presentation hasn't alleviated all of your concerns, we can discuss them in detail." He ran his gaze over the group. "Sound good?"

Most of those seated murmured or nodded in agreement. Sebastian simply shrugged.

I'd delayed as long as I could. As Goodwin resumed his presentation, I rolled my housekeeping cart down the east wing. Rocky's room was at the far end on the front of the lodge. The Goodwins occupied the room directly across from him. I hadn't seen Aileen since she'd grabbed a cup of hot tea and a plate of food at breakfast and carried them off to her room. Though I hated to interrupt her if she was relaxing in their space, I didn't want her to think I was neglectful, either. I raised a hand and knocked softly on their door. "Housekeeping," I called quietly, hoping Aileen would hear me and that I wouldn't interrupt Goodwin down the hall.

Aileen opened the door. Rather than gray, she was dressed in equally drab shades of green today. If she weren't so thin, she might resemble a gin-soaked olive. Her coat hung over her arm, her purse was slung over her shoulder, and the key fob for the rental SUV was in her hand. She said the same thing she had the day before. "I'll get out of your way." With that, she swept off down the hall, a silent specter.

I moved with practiced efficiency as I cleaned the Goodwins' room. The sofa bed had been slept in again, but this time the bed had been left open. I straightened the bed linens and tucked them in tight before folding the mattress back into the frame and replacing the faux-leather cushions. Their belongings remained separated in designated corners on the bathroom countertop, their electric toothbrushes facing off like boxers preparing for a fight. Even their towels were spread apart on the bar, inches of space between them. Though I'd sensed no strong animosity between Nigel and Aileen, I'd sensed no great connection, either. Maybe they were like me and my ex-husband, and had simply drifted apart over the years. If so, I was glad Jack and I called it quits before things got to this point. Thank goodness we could still be friends.

I finished the room, locked it back up, and proceeded

to clean Rayan's space. As before, it was tidy and easy to clean. I then moved on to the Jensens' room across the hall. As I vacuumed the closet, a lift ticket hanging from a basic black ladies' ski jacket caught my eye. The self-adhesive tag was similar to those issued by airlines to be placed on luggage, though this tag was attached to a thin metal frame and designed to be hung from a zipper. The tag was crinkled and torn, but I could make out the image of snowcapped mountains, similar to the one on the Adventure Capital Logo. These mountains, however, were superimposed over a large sun, with the upper part of what was either a letter *E* or *F* below the graphic. With it being early in the season and the print appearing slightly faded, the tag was likely one from last season that Laurie had yet to remove. I was guilty of leaving expired lift tickets on my jackets, too. Without scissors, they were difficult to detach.

I was dusting the dresser when Nigel's voice came from the doorway. "Excuse me. Do you know where Aileen is?"

"Sorry, no. She left with her coat and the car keys when I went to clean your room."

He glanced back at their door and spoke softly, as if to himself rather than me. "I told her I needed the SUV to take the investors to the site today. Everyone can't fit in the van. I suppose we'll have to postpone the site visit until tomorrow." Seeming to remember my presence, he turned back with a pleasant look on his face. "Aileen can be forgetful, but who isn't, at times?"

Had she forgotten, or had she meant to throw a monkey wrench in her husband's plans?

He stepped away and the hallway filled with chatter as the group dispersed, returning to their rooms to change into ski gear. I parked my housekeeping cart out of the way at the end of the hall and went to the desk. I'd resume my rounds once the guests left. My sons were ready to hit the slopes, too. I handed my keys to J.J., admonishing him to be careful on the slick roads.

As I gazed out the window, watching my boys stow their gear in my car, I noticed a group of people gathering in the lot, midway between the lodge and the Greasy Griddle. I wasn't expecting new guests, so I assumed they were amassing to head to the diner together for lunch. Why they hadn't parked closer to the restaurant was a mystery. It didn't remain a mystery for long, though. The distinctive mud-splattered pickup pulled into the lot and parked, and the hunter slid out of it. He spoke briefly to the others before motioning for the group to follow him. They marched, en masse, toward my lodge. *Uh-oh.*

CHAPTER 9

Misty

Before the mob reached my doors, Goodwin returned to the lobby dressed in a bright blue snow jacket and matching pants. He waved the prepaid ski passes at the guests, like a game-show host passing out prizes. In fact, he had the disposition of a game-show host—congenial, slow to get ruffled, always wearing a smile. I feared his jolly demeanor was about to be tested.

"Get your tickets right here!" he called out, placing one in each outstretched hand.

The doors to my lodge opened and the throng burst in. There were about a dozen people included, and an interesting assortment at that. The hunter led the way with Gus, the wildlife photographer, ambling along behind him, looking just as much like a friendly Bigfoot today as he had before. He carried a large dark nylon backpack with the Nikon logo on it. A petite platinum-haired six-tyish woman in a thick white turtleneck and dark gray blazer walked beside him, a cute white pin in the shape of a snowflake attached to her lapel. Despite her small stature, she looked formidable. I felt certain I'd seen her before, though I couldn't quite place her. A couple of others also appeared to have come from work, as they wore clothing intended for inside wear rather than outdoor gear. Several nondescript middle-aged folks in winter apparel filled out the crowd. Many of them looked familiar, too. I'd likely seen them about town.

Though the hunter led the charge, he stopped a few steps inside the door and let the older woman in the blazer take the lead. She walked over to the reception desk and stared me down. Her ice blue eyes perfectly complemented her silvery-white hair. She resembled what Elsa from *Frozen* might look like in fifty years. "Misty Murphy, right?" She extended a hand that was papery, wrinkled, and dotted with age spots, but nonetheless nicely manicured with a pale polish. "I'm Paulette Frost, president of the Chamber of Commerce."

Her title explained why she looked familiar. I'd attended the chamber's monthly meeting in November. I shook her hand. "I'm Misty, yes. What can I do for you?"

Although she purportedly spoke to me, she turned to eye Goodwin, who stared our way with his well-practiced smile. She spoke loudly enough for everyone in the lobby to hear. "I understand the developer who's proposing to build that new resort is here?"

Nigel raised an index finger. "That would be me! I'll be right with you." He returned his attention to his group of investors, dismissing them. "Have a brilliant day on the slopes, chums! I'll join you soon." He said something to Rayan. His assistant nodded, but when he turned away he had a glower on his face.

The investors streamed out the doors, climbing into their cars to head over to the ski resort. While the others turned right out of the parking lot, Daphne and Jean-Paul turned left. Maybe they planned to drive down to Banner Elk for lunch before hitting the slopes.

Once the guests had gone, Nigel strode up to Paulette. "Hello, folks. I'm Nigel Goodwin. Who might you all be?"

Paulette introduced herself again, and many of the others followed suit. There were several local business owners among the group, as well as residents who lived near the proposed resort site. All gave their names, including the hunter. "Tyson Pell." He almost spat the words out. He didn't offer Goodwin his hand, even when Goodwin reached out with his own for a shake.

Goodwin took the behavior in stride, simply shifting his hand to Gus. "And you are?"

"Gus," the burly man said. "I photograph and rehabilitate wildlife."

"Worthwhile endeavors," Goodwin replied. He ran his gaze over the group. "What can I do for you?"

Paulette said, "Your resort would affect all of us. We want details."

"Naturally," Goodwin said without skipping a beat. "If I were in your shoes, I'd want details, too." He held out an arm, indicating the chairs his investors had recently vacated. "Have a seat. I'd be happy to fill you in. I'm sure I can put your worries to rest."

The group moved into the great room, several stopping to help themselves to coffee or tea. I didn't mind. We were a small community up here and I wanted to be neighborly.

Pell walked over to the model and looked it over. "What's this circle on the roof with the *H* in it? You better tell me it's not a helicopter pad."

"It is," Goodwin said. "We plan to offer aerial tours of the mountains. But tours will be scheduled just once per hour from nine a.m. until sunset."

Pell's jaw clenched. "That racket's gonna go on all day long?"

I didn't like that idea, either. The noise would disrupt the peace of this place, as we'd learned from actual experience. Only a few weeks earlier, a police helicopter had flown over Beech Mountain in search of an escaped criminal. The noise had frightened Yeti to pieces. She'd cowered under my bed. I could only imagine how frightened the bears and deer had been.

Goodwin countered with, "The choppers will get into the air and out of the area quickly. They'll be brand-new models with the latest noise-reduction technology. The manufacturer redesigned the tail rotors. You'd be amazed how quiet they are."

The man grunted. "I'll believe it when I see it."

I fought the urge to say *Don't you mean 'I'll believe it when I don't hear it?'* Oh, no. Kyle Jensen's dad jokes were rubbing off on me.

Once the group had taken their seats, Nigel continued. "I've developed several resorts in areas like this, so I'm familiar with your concerns. You want to know how your businesses, properties, and lives will be affected." He quickly ran through the slides he'd shown the investors earlier with an abbreviated pitch. "The resort will draw tourists to the area year-round and help local businesses thrive." He pointed to Paulette. "Ms. Frost. What kind of business do you operate?"

"Property management," she replied. "I handle over a hundred units in the area."

"Then you'll be glad to know the Retreat on Blue Ridge will offer a day pass for folks who want to enjoy the resort's activities but aren't willing or able to pay the resort's room rates. Some will be families or groups looking for lodging that offers kitchens and multiple bedrooms. Those people will be interested in your rental properties. You all are familiar with the Great Wolf Lodge and the Gaylord resorts, I assume?" When the group murmured in the affirmative, he said, "A significant number of visitors to those resorts do not spend the night there. It will be the same for my resort."

A man said, "But you'll be directly competing with many of us. I run a mountain biking and snow tubing facility just eight miles northeast of here."

"Between here and Boone, then." Goodwin looked up as he calculated. "Eight miles is roughly thirteen kilometers. At best, that's a half-hour drive on these roads. It'll take much longer in wintry conditions. There's plenty of folks who won't want to drive to higher elevations, especially to a place with shorter trails and runs. You're sure to get a good deal of business from the students at Appalachian State, too. They'll choose your location over mine nearly every time."

The man really has done his homework.

He proceeded to address the others who offered similar services and activities to what the resort would offer. Restaurant owners. A day spa. A souvenir and T-shirt shop. "The bottom line is, with the resort bringing more tourists to the area, we'll all benefit. A rising tide lifts all boats."

Paulette Frost pursed her lips. "But an avalanche buries everyone."

There's a scary thought.

Goodwin chuckled. "Let's pray that doesn't happen." He turned to his assistant. "Rayan, will you grab a prospectus for each of these folks?"

Rayan gave his boss a nod and headed to his room to round up the materials.

At the podium, Goodwin switched gears. "We've discussed the positive effect the resort will have on local businesses. Let's address the concerns of residents now."

Pell snarled, "I moved here for the peace and quiet and privacy. So did everyone else. The last thing we need is a bunch of noise and traffic jamming our roads."

"And collisions with wildlife," Gus added. "More traffic puts animals at risk."

Though traffic was bumper to bumper heading up the parkway on Friday evenings and Saturday mornings during ski season, the rest of the time the traffic was manageable. That said, with Beech Mountain Parkway being the only road up the mountain, wrecks caused significant delays and headaches. An incident where a truck lost control and crashed into a freestanding garage had closed the road for hours on a Friday night last October. Drivers without an intimate knowledge of the area had a hard time finding alternate routes to town.

Goodwin said, "As I'm sure you know, Highway 105 is already being widened between Boone and Foscoe to help alleviate traffic. We can provide information to our guests so they can avoid harm to wildlife. I'd also be happy to spring for speed bumps or flashing warning signs."

Pell scoffed. "Just what the forest needs. Flashing lights." He muttered under his breath.

Goodwin ignored the man. "As you know, property values have fluctuated here, like they do in many resort towns. Before the pandemic, values were relatively low here and some residences were in disrepair. Prices peaked at three to four times their pre-pandemic values at the height of the market and, although they've declined a bit, values have remained higher than before.

Houses are being remodeled and upgraded. A large, exclusive resort will be a sign that the area is flourishing. The resort will insulate your property values against decline."

Though Goodwin was darn convincing, a few of the residents exchanged unsure glances, conflicted. I could relate. The resort might help fill my rooms. *But would the costs be worth it?*

Goodwin smoothly switched to a different tack—pitting the group against each other. "Homeowners and business owners often disagree. I suspect many of you were at loggerheads in the past, that you residents weren't in favor of expansion or of so many of the area's homes being turned into short-term rentals. You who run businesses might have been frustrated by the pushback from residents, how they were impeding your livelihood."

United we stand. Divided we fall. His tactic worked. The members of the group eyed each other sheepishly. I bit my lip. Though nothing Goodwin had said was incorrect, it felt as if he was artfully manipulating the group.

Goodwin went on. "We'll never get everyone in this room to agree one-hundred percent. But I have no doubt we can come to a reasonable compromise."

Manipulation or not, I couldn't help but be impressed by Goodwin's people skills. The group had clearly come here looking for a fight, and he'd disarmed the crowd by empathizing with them rather than being defensive. He'd also subtly used the tried-and-true tactic of divide and conquer by pointing out that the members of the group had different, and possibly mutually exclusive, interests. They might not be the united front they purported to be. Yet, he also offered them hope that a workable solution could be reached. The man was certainly clever and cunning. But that didn't necessarily make him a bad person, did it?

Rayan returned with a stack of brochures. As he passed them out, Goodwin said, "Give the prospectus a thorough read. I'd be happy to chat with you all again Friday afternoon. I'm sure we'll find common ground. Some of you might even be interested in investing in the resort once you learn more. But I've got to wrap things up now. I have prior plans for this afternoon." Rayan stood dutifully a few feet away as Goodwin left the podium and held out an arm, politely inviting the assembly to depart.

Most stood and walked out the door, talking quietly. Not Paulette Frost, though. "I'm nowhere near sold." She held up the prospectus. "This better be damn convincing or you'll have a battle on your hands." Having delivered her threat, she headed to the door. Her step slowed as she spotted the monitor displaying the lodge's security camera feeds. While the interior feeds were unobstructed, snow had stuck to the lenses on the outdoor cameras and they offered only a crusty white glow. When she caught me watching her, she sped up and sailed out the door. She climbed into a white SUV. Her door bore her company's logo, Frost Property Management, superimposed over a silvery snowflake.

Pell didn't go quietly, either. He returned to the model. Locking eyes with Goodwin, he raised his hand and flicked one of the miniature human figures into the fireplace. A flame shot up, filling the air with the acrid scent of melting plastic as the tiny person turned to toxic goo among the coals. *What an ass.* He wasn't satisfied with cremating the figurine, either. He put two hands under the table that held the model and flipped it onto its side. It hit the floor with a *bang!* The little people, foliage, and cars went flying, and the building broke in two. He punted the plastic roof dome across the lobby. It hit the front door and splintered.

My heart pounded and my body burned with a fury-fueled fever. *How dare this man come into my lodge and act like this!* "You've gone too far! I'm calling the police." I grabbed the receiver from the landline on my desk. As I dialed 911, Pell stormed out of the lodge. I glared at him as he passed the desk, but he didn't bother to look my way. When the dispatcher answered, I told her what happened. "A local resident named Tyson Pell just came to my lodge and harassed one of my guests. He turned a table over and destroyed some of the guest's property." I gave her a description of Pell's pickup. *Too bad I don't have his license plate number.* I didn't have his exact address, either, only the name of the road he lived on, but they could get his license plate and house number from public records.

"Got it," the dispatcher said. "I'll ask all units to keep an eye out for him, and I'll send an officer to your lodge to assess the damage."

I thanked her and we ended the call. At this point, the only one of the group still left at the lodge was Gus. As I hung up the phone, I decided to ask him to leave my lodge. He seemed a reasonable sort, but no good could come from continuing this debate now.

As I walked over, Gus stepped in front of Goodwin, blocking his movement. The photographer held an electronic tablet in his hands. "Take a look at these photos and videos."

I stepped up to the two. "Gus, I think it's best you leave now."

Nigel raised a hand. "Hold on. I'd like to see what he's got here."

I supposed if he was okay with allowing the man to remain, I should be, too. Rayan and I looked on as Gus swiped through the images. The quality of the pictures and videos varied widely. Some were in color and crystal clear, while others were grainy black-and-white images. They'd obviously been taken by multiple cameras with different degrees of resolution.

"See?" Gus insisted. "Groundhogs. Deer. Skunks. Foxes. Coyotes. Pileated woodpeckers. Look at this black bear." He showed a grainy image of a hulky dark beast.

Goodwin cocked his head. "You sure that's a bear? All I see is a black shadow and glowing eyes." He waggled his fingers and chuckled. "Maybe it's the Black Dog of Newgate!"

I wasn't familiar with the reference, but it was clear from the context that he was referring to some questionable legendary creature.

Gus frowned. "This isn't a joke. These animals live on your property. It's not right to destroy their home."

Goodwin cocked his head. "These photos were taken on my property? How?"

Gus lowered the tablet. "I've posted trail cams on trees there."

Goodwin's jaw flexed, though his smile didn't waver. "You've trespassed, then?"

Gus's brows formed a furry V. "It's just woods. I didn't bother anyone."

"That's not the question, though, is it? You knowingly went onto my property to set up cameras. That's illegal. I could have you arrested."

Gus took a step back and slid the tablet into his backpack. "I was only looking out for the wildlife. If it bothers you, I'll take the cameras down."

"Absolutely not!" Goodwin's smile appeared aggressive now. "You are not to set one foot on that property without my prior permission. Do you understand?"

Whoa. It was as if a switch had been thrown. In an instant, Goodwin had turned from friendly to frightening. Although it surprised me, I could understand his position. I wouldn't like people traipsing willy-nilly around my lodge without my knowledge or approval, either, especially if they were doing so with the intent to thwart my plans.

Gus hesitated a beat before acquiescing. "All right. You'll get the cameras for me, then?"

"You expect me to remove them now, when the snow is arse deep?" Goodwin scoffed. "No, sir. I'll remove and return them once the snow melts. I'm going to put in cameras of my own now, though. If you trespass again, you'll be caught on video and I'll prosecute."

Gus bristled, looking more sasquatch-like than ever. "But that equipment cost thousands of dollars!"

"Then you shouldn't have abandoned it on my land."

Gus had seemed like a gentle giant earlier, but no more. His eyes flamed and his hands fisted. For a moment, I feared he might take my guest to the floor. Rayan's eyes went wide and he froze in place, as terrified as I was. I reached under the counter for the canister of bear spray I kept on hand. Luckily, after a brief stare-down, Gus turned and stormed out of the lodge. I returned the bear spray to the shelf and released my breath. *Phew.*

Now that all of the group were gone, Goodwin turned to his assistant. "Remove the trail cameras from the property, then get online and order a dozen of those security cameras we've used on the construction sites, the kind that connect to a wireless network. Pay for overnight shipping to the lodge. Find the nearest hardware store and buy every No Trespassing or Private Property sign in stock. Nail them to trees around the perimeter. Once the police document the damage to the model, pack it up. I don't want the investors to see the mess when they return."

Rayan's shoulders slumped. "But you told me I could ski this afternoon."

"I'm sorry, mate. Things have changed."

Goodwin gave his assistant a pat on the shoulder, but the gesture only seemed to make Rayan angry. He jerked his shoulder away. "This job is nothing like you said it would be. You told me I would have free time when we traveled. I thought I would get to see the world, but all I see is hotels."

Goodwin released a loud huff. "Unexpected things come up, Rayan."

"But they come up every time! Maybe unexpected things should be expected!"

"I'll make it up to you. I promise." Goodwin reached out as if to pat Rayan's shoulder again, but appeared to think better of it and retracted his hand. "Aileen has our rental car. I'll need you to drop me at the ski resort on your way to the property."

Rayan's mouth gaped. "*I* am expected to work, but *you* are still planning to ski?"

"You know how this goes," Goodwin said. "I have to get to know the investors, make them feel comfortable with me. They won't put their money in the resort otherwise."

Rayan stood stock-still for a moment, fury burning so bright in his eyes it wouldn't have surprised me to hear the sizzle of his rage. Then he turned, stomped out of the lodge, and climbed into the driver's seat of the van, slamming the door. I couldn't blame the guy for feeling upset under the circumstances. Still, I was surprised he'd been so openly angry with his boss, especially in front of me. Perhaps Rayan wasn't concerned about the potential consequences?

Goodwin strode up to the desk. "If any of those people return before Friday afternoon, don't allow them into the lodge."

My gut twisted. My lodge was private property, and I had the legal right to deny anyone entry. Still, the thought of bouncing my neighbors and fellow business owners out of my inn didn't sit well with me. But my first obligation was to my guests, and I didn't want anyone getting into an altercation. "You're not going to wait for the officer to come look at the model?"

"You can handle that for me, can't you?" He pointed to the security cameras mounted on the bottom of the truss. "The footage should tell the officer everything they need to know."

I didn't really want to handle the matter, but I also knew Goodwin's time here was limited and valuable. I nodded.

"That's five-star service. Thanks, Misty." Goodwin carried his ski equipment out to the van. Once he'd stowed his gear and climbed into the passenger seat, Rayan started the van and they drove off, leaving a cloud of exhaust in their wake, like a frigid, final gasp of breath.

I donned my coat and snow boots, grabbed a long-handled duster, and carried it outside. Rocky had installed security cameras around the exterior of the lodge, and I made my way around it, running the duster over the lenses to clear them of snow. Some of the snow stubbornly refused to be brushed off, and I had to gently tap the side of the cameras with the pole of the duster to free it. As I circumnavigated the lodge, I ran the duster over the windows, too, so that my guests could enjoy the beautiful view. It was like a Currier and Ives print out here. Some of the guests had left their interior shutters open, and I caught glimpses into their rooms as I cleared the snow. Others, including Amari, had kept their shutters tightly closed.

I'd just finished clearing the snow from the outdoor security cameras when a white male police officer arrived. I'd first met Officer Hardy back in September, when a yoga instructor had been found dead behind my lodge. At around thirty, he seemed young to me, but I realized that was my middle-aged perspective. He'd proven himself smart, hardworking, and more than capable. We went inside, where I played the security camera footage that showed Pell flicking the figure into the fireplace and overturning the table. He asked me to email the video clip to the department and photographed the broken model and overturned table in the great room. "I'll swing by his house. If he's there, I'll book him." With that, Officer Hardy departed.

For safety's sake, I locked the doors to the lodge. Only those with a key—or a battering ram—would be able to enter. I prayed Pell wouldn't return. The glass in the lodge was thick and bullet resistant, but even ballistic glass could eventually give way if enough firepower was used, and Pell seemed to own a personal armory. The thought made my stomach and throat tighten.

I forced my fear aside and continued my housekeeping rounds. Amari Lott had hung the Do Not Disturb sign on his doorknob. He'd left the lodge, so I wouldn't disturb him if I entered his room to clean. However, some

guests used the placard to mean they didn't want anyone coming into their room for any reason. I decided
to wait until he returned to determine if he wanted
housekeeping service.

After cleaning the guest rooms, I spent the rest of the
afternoon dilly-dallying around the lodge. I switched the
camera feed on the monitor in the lobby from the parkway webcam to the webcams at the summit and base
of the ski resort. I mopped the lobby to clean up the
mud and snow the unexpected visitors had tracked in. I
posted photos of my sons snowboarding on the lodge's
social media accounts to build interest. #BeechMoun-
tainNC

On the monitor, I spotted my boys snowboarding
down the Freestyle run. Mitch wiped out swerving
around a child who'd fallen. Luckily, he didn't get hurt.
J.J. stopped to help his brother up. The sight warmed
my heart. It was nice to know my boys had each other's
backs, that they weren't just brothers, but also the closest of friends.

Celeste and Emilio sailed down the slope, each sitting
on a small seat equipped with a ski on the bottom, with
two additional smaller skis affixed to their ski poles.
They moved with speed and style, in full control. With
their standard black ski pants and jackets, and goggles
covering most of their faces, I wouldn't have been able
to identify Kyle and Laurie Jensen on the camera feed
if not for the pink infinity scarf around Laurie's neck.
Though they weren't beginners, they didn't appear to
have the experience of the Salazars, moving much more
tentatively and weaving side to side to slow their pace
down the slope.

Nigel Goodwin was impossible to miss in his bright
blue ski gear. Sebastian Cochrane sported snow gear in

red and black, the same color as his car and the Hurricanes. Rather than goggles, he wore a pair of black sunglasses. He'd foregone a helmet. *Not smart.* He carved the slopes with speed and ease, but even the most talented skier or snowboarder could crash into a tree or pole, have another skier crash into them, or inadvertently go off a small cliff. Then again, I supposed if he wasn't a risk-taker, he wouldn't be interested in Goodwin's proposed resort.

As I wiped smudges off the computer keyboard, I spotted Sebastian sidling up next to Goodwin at the top of the mountain, attempting to goad the older man into a race. Goodwin took the bait, and the two took off, racing down the mountain. I turned my attention to the feed from the base to see how the race would turn out. Sebastian won, but barely. As he raised his poles in victory, Goodwin skied to a quick stop nearby, sending a sheet of snow in the younger man's direction. The two shared a laugh as Sebastian wiped snow from his shoulders.

Daphne's bright red hair hung down her back, making her and Jean-Paul easy to spot as they zipped back and forth, playfully crossing paths. The two certainly embodied the romance the French were known for. Amari appeared to be a beginner. I spotted him on the slopes with an instructor, taking a private lesson. He practiced sliding slowly and stopping, forming his feet into a wedge commonly referred to as a snowplow.

Before long, the afternoon became darker and darker, until the bright overhead lights turned on at the resort. Aileen returned from wherever she'd gone, carrying a take-out bag from an Italian restaurant in Banner Elk, just a few short miles down the mountain. Rayan returned, too. His hair was wet and matted. He carried a jumble of trail cams in his arms, the pile dripping water onto the floor. The fury on his face told me he had not enjoyed his afternoon tramping through the deep snow at the resort site.

After I made another round with the duster outside to clear the security cameras, Rocky and I warmed up leftover vegetable stew and cornbread we'd ordered from the Greasy Griddle a few nights back. We enjoyed our dinner in front of the fire, following it with glasses of red wine. I filled him in on Goodwin's pitch, how he'd promised big returns to the investors.

Rocky was a philosophy buff and had a quote at the ready. "Socrates said, 'He who is not contented with what he has, would not be contented with what he would like to have.'"

He had a point. It was one thing to want financial security, another to chase wealth. When was enough *enough*?

Amari Lott returned shortly thereafter. I called to him as he came in the door. "I saw the Do Not Disturb sign on your door, so I didn't clean your room earlier. But I'd be happy to clean it now if you'd like."

"No need," he said, unzipping his jacket. "Please wait to clean until I check out on Friday."

It was an unusual request, but one I'd received before. Some people were exceptionally private. Standards had changed, too. Guests no longer expected daily housekeeping service, though I continued to provide it. "All right. If you need fresh towels, just call or come to the desk."

As Amari walked off, I noticed he moved with a slight limp. Maybe he'd developed a blister from the ski boots, or twisted or strained a knee. Skiing could be challenging, especially for beginners. I hoped he wouldn't let one difficult day put him off the activity. Many people gave up on the sport when they didn't catch on right away, but skiing was like riding a bike. It took some time to learn how to maneuver properly and maintain balance. If he could get past the learning curve, he'd have a blast.

A minute or so later, Amari hobbled past us in the other direction, carrying his ice bucket. He disappeared into the guest laundry room, which also held the vending and ice machines. We heard the *clunk-clunk-clunk* of ice falling into the bucket. He passed us again with a full bucket of ice on his way back to his room.

My sons returned after the resort closed late that evening, arriving just past ten o'clock, looking wiped out but happy. After they filled me in on the fun they'd had, I said, "Clean up and go right to bed. It'll be morning before you know it, and I'll need you two bright-eyed and bushy-tailed."

They murmured their agreement and headed down the hall.

Daphne and Jean-Paul returned shortly thereafter, bidding Rocky and me good night as they aimed for their room. "Bonne soirée!"

Laurie and Kyle had closed the place down, too. As they carried their gear inside at half past ten, I called, "How was the skiing?"

Kyle stopped to wipe his feet on the mat. "We're still getting our legs for the season. Had to take it slow and easy. We're slope pokes. Get it? *Slope pokes*?"

I groaned inwardly. "Another good one!"

Celeste and Emilio had put in a full day, too. They rolled through the doors on the Jensens' heels.

I greeted them with, "Welcome back. Did you have a good time?"

"Too good," Emilio said. "I'll need a full tube of muscle cream for my back and biceps."

"Don't worry, baby." Celeste gave her husband a flirtatious wink. "I'll rub it on for you."

No doubt I'd be replacing their menthol-scented sheets tomorrow.

Shortly thereafter, Sebastian Cochrane returned. He was damp with sweat, definitely in need of a hot shower and a change of clothes, yet that didn't stop him from flopping down in a chair in front of the fire. He yanked off his snow boots, releasing a stinky steam of foot odor. I fought the urge to pull the neck of my shirt up over my face. Molasses raised his head, sniffed the air, and released a whine. *Poor dog and his enhanced sense of smell.*

"What a day!" Sebastian lifted his stocking feet to place them on the ottoman.

Ugh. I made a mental note to use the fabric refresher spray on the chair and ottoman tomorrow. "I saw you racing Mr. Goodwin earlier."

Sebastian cocked his head. "You were at the resort?"

"No." I gestured to the monitors in the lobby. "I saw you on their webcams."

"You did? Then you saw it wasn't much of a contest. I'd bet him a beer. Should've bet him much more."

From what I'd seen, Goodwin had held his own against a man many years his junior, but no sense in arguing the point. Sebastian belched, adding the fetid aroma of half-digested beer to the body odors hanging in the air. Clearly, he'd visited the resort's taproom.

Rocky waved a hand in front of his face. "Smells like Goodwin paid up on that bet."

Sebastian chuckled, unfazed. He raised a finger, wagging it. "Which way to the hot tub?"

"Sorry," I said. "We don't have one."

"Yet." Rocky turned to me. "I found a ten-seater with loungers at each end for eighteen grand. It's a good deal. They're also offering zero-percent financing over four years. Should I pull the trigger?"

Before I could respond, Sebastian did it for me. "Hell yeah! Can you get it up and running by tomorrow night?"

Rocky said, "With some hard work, luck, and a 'yes' from Misty, maybe."

An extra eighteen thousand dollars wasn't in my budget, but paying it out over time would allow me to manage the expense. "Go ahead. Pull the trigger."

Sebastian stood and gathered up his things. "If there's no hot tub, guess I'll take a shower." He headed back to his room in his socks, leaving a trail of sweaty footprints behind.

When eleven o'clock rolled around, Rocky and I rose from our chairs. A glance at the monitors in the lobby told me the lenses of the outdoor security cameras were again coated with snow, but I didn't bother taking the duster out to clear them again. It was late, I was tired, and it clearly would be a futile endeavor. Rocky and I went to our rooms. I hadn't seen Goodwin return to the lodge, and figured he must've entered while I'd been checking on Yeti or moving the wet sheets into the dryer. But, as I learned the next morning, I was wrong. He'd never made it back inside the lodge that night.

CHAPTER 10

Misty

Temperatures had dipped down into the upper twenties overnight, and five more inches of snow fell on the mountain. To a resort town, the snow was a blessing that, ironically, made me want to curse. More snow meant more fun for the folks who'd come up to play in it. But, for me and my staff, it meant a lot more work. More risk, too. A guest could slip and fall, or the pipes could freeze. Storms sometimes made the electricity go out, too. Fingers crossed it would hold out.

Twice during the night, the *clunk-clunk-clunk* of the ice machine dispensing cubes down the hall woke me from my slumber. *Who's getting ice this time of night? Is it Amari Lott again?* Though I was glad he was icing his injury, I hoped the racket hadn't woken my guests. People sometimes became grumpy when their sleep was interrupted, and they tended to turn their ire on the innkeeper. I'd apologize for their inconsiderate fellow guest and offer a set of foam earplugs or an electric fan to create white noise that would drown out offending sounds.

I rose Tuesday morning and ran through my usual routine to get ready for the workday, leaving Yeti to her breakfast as I exited our room. The hallway was still dark, but I could see the glow of a computer monitor in the lobby and hear the sound of the printer as it spit out a piece of paper. *Someone is using the business center.* I heard the tap of paper against the desktop, as if the person were straightening a stack. As I tread quietly up the hall, Rayan headed down the opposite wing with a thin printout in his hand. He hadn't seemed to notice me, and I wasn't about to call out a greeting and risk disturbing my other guests. I continued to the lobby and glanced outside to see Rocky plowing the shared parking lot again.

When Patty brought over the food from her diner a short time later, my boys and Rocky had joined me in the lobby. Patty handed Rocky another pie and turned to me. "You'd better keep this man happy. I don't know what I'd do without him."

I didn't know what I'd do without Rocky, either. He'd been a godsend for my business, and he was a perfect personal companion, as well.

Snow continued to come down and, as my guests enjoyed their breakfast, I sent my sons out to blow the latest accumulation from the walkways. I gave them the long-handled duster, too, with instructions to wipe the snow from the security cameras.

Around 9:00, my boys came back into the lodge, laughing. J.J. held something in his hand. *A stone?*

"What's so funny?" I asked from my stool behind the desk.

J.J. said, "We were sledding outside and we found this rock. Doesn't it look like a nose?"

He handed it over the counter. The grayish-yellow rock was cold and hard, with two indentations that resembled nostrils. It did indeed look like a nose. In fact, it looked like one very particular nose. A pointed one with a flat round tip on the end the size of a dime—*Holy bleep!*

I dropped the frozen object like a hot potato and put my hands to my face, stifling my scream. Rocky looked up from a seat near the hearth, where he was lingering over his coffee. He stood, set down his mug, and rushed over, with Molasses slowly leveraging himself to his feet and ambling along behind him. Rocky leaned in over the counter and met my gaze. "You okay?"

When I couldn't speak, he looked at my boys. Mitch shrugged, but J.J. raised his hands in innocence. "All I did was hand her a rock! I swear!"

Mitch leaned over the counter and pointed. "It's down there. She dropped it."

I tried to say *It's not a rock!* But I only managed to stammer, "It's-it's-it's—"

Realizing something was very wrong, Rocky circled the counter, picked up the nose, and examined it closely. His eyes popped wide. He quickly tucked the nose into a drawer and slammed it shut. "Boys, where did you get that rock?"

Mitch hiked a thumb over his shoulder. "At the bottom of the sledding hill."

"Show me and your mother." Rocky turned to J.J. "You watch the desk, okay?"

J.J. looked confused, but agreed. "Sure."

Rocky didn't bother to don his coat, but I grabbed mine from the hook behind the desk and slid into it as we exited the lodge. Molasses, sensing excitement was afoot, trotted along with us. We hustled down the cleared walkway until we reached the end of the lodge. My sons had left a sled at the bottom of the slope, just past a long hump that hadn't been there before. It looked like a mogul, a bump in the snow. Mogul courses were popular with skiers who liked the challenge of navigating the humps. Mogul skiing was even an Olympic sport.

Mitch stopped and pointed to a spot a couple of feet before where the sled sat askew atop the snow. "There. That's where the rock was."

Rocky fell onto his knees in the snow and began to dig at the nearby lump. Molasses eyed his master, then began to dig, too. It seemed to be a natural instinct. His breed was often used in avalanche rescue.

It took only a few seconds before Rocky uncovered a face that had been hidden under the snow. *Goodwin's face.* His eyes stared upward, unseeing, fringed with icy lashes. A ragged hole of torn flesh appeared under them, where his nose had been before the metal runner on the sled had sliced off the tip. Though it was slightly gooey with blood, the fluid was too frozen to run. A faint dark blue line surrounded the hole in his face, the bruise curving inward where the wide part of his nose would have been when it had still been attached. The rest of the bump under the snow must be his body. The business mogul had become a snow mogul.

Though I'd expected something like this after my sons had brought Nigel Goodwin's nose inside, actually seeing the man's frozen corpse was nonetheless shocking. My head went woozy, twinkle lights surrounding my vision. I closed my eyes and bent forward, hands on my knees, to keep from collapsing.

After a few deep breaths, I opened my eyes to see that Mitch's mouth had fallen open. When he spoke, his voice was high and cracked, as if he were hitting puberty for a second time. "Is that who I think it is?"

Rocky cleared his throat, but his voice was tight when he spoke, too. "Afraid so."

Mitch whispered a string of surprised curses. I didn't bother to scold him. If I could speak right now, I'd probably be saying the same thing. If ever there was a *what the fudge* moment, this was it.

Rocky placed his fingers on Goodwin's cheek. "He's frozen solid. No point in trying to resuscitate him."

Finally, I found my voice. "Doesn't being cold slow the metabolism? I've heard of people being trapped in snow or cold water and surviving longer than they might otherwise."

Rocky gave me a pointed look. "His nose broke off, Misty. There's no coming back from this."

Rocky was right, of course. *What happened? How had Nigel Goodwin ended up dead and frozen outside my lodge?*

Rocky reached into his pocket, pulled out his cell phone, and called the authorities. The dispatcher said she'd send both police and an ambulance. While we waited for them to arrive, he enlisted Mitch to help him round up a tarp and sawhorses from the lodge's tool shed. Together, they formed a waist-high curtain of sorts that would prevent anyone who might wander up from getting a glimpse of Nigel's frigid, nose-less remains. When they finished, I noticed Rocky staring at the tool shed, an odd look on his face.

I was almost afraid to ask. "What is it?"

"Someone got into the shed last night. I can tell because the two bags of rock salt are gone."

"You mean they broke in? You keep the tool shed locked."

"I do," he said.

He eyed me and it was clear he was leaving something unsaid. Then it hit me. My boys. They had been in and out of the shed to get the snowblower and shovels, and to put them away later. They were the ones who'd forgotten to lock it back up yesterday.

"Is anything else missing?" Snowblowers were expensive. I hoped the thief hadn't gotten away with the equipment, or with any of Rocky's tools. He had quite a valuable set.

"No. Everything else is accounted for."

"Thank goodness. We've got enough to deal with right now." I shivered, but from nerves, not the cold. The thought that Nigel Goodwin had died out here was bad enough. I didn't want to think petty thieves had also been lurking about, stealing our property. But there were far more critical matters to concern ourselves with at the moment than some missing salt. "Should I get Aileen?"

Rocky considered a moment. "Not yet. She shouldn't see her husband like this. She'd never be able to get the image out of her head."

Neither will I. I feared the sight of Goodwin sans snout would haunt Mitchell, too, much like the monsters under his bed did when he was a small boy. I put an arm around his shoulders, and felt him trembling. I was tempted to tell him to go back inside, but the damage had already been done. Plus, I knew the authorities would want to speak to at least one of my sons about how they'd come to find Goodwin's pointed proboscis.

I looked around the area. Goodwin's skis and poles lay in a jumbled pile at the edge of the woods, not far from the road, as if they'd been tossed or dropped there. The bag that contained his ski boots lay even closer to the road, his jacket beside it. *Had he walked back from the ski resort last night and collapsed out here?* It seemed plausible. The guy was in good shape for his age, but everyone had their limits. He might have pushed himself too hard yesterday racing Sebastian. Sometimes people who seemed robust and healthy could suffer a sudden health issue. The fact that he'd discarded his jacket indicated he might have become overheated walking up the mountain carrying his heavy gear.

In what seemed like no time, help arrived. A quick response was one of the benefits of living in a small town: a police officer was never very far away. The Beech Mountain Police SUV turned into the parking lot, Officer Hardy at the wheel. Thankfully, he had kept the lights and siren off so as not to attract undue attention. The car eased into a spot near Rocky, Mitch, and me. Hardy climbed out and walked over. He glanced at Goodwin's face peering up out of the snow and grimaced. It was a ghastly sight. He closed his eyes and made the sign of the cross before turning to us. "What happened here?"

Mitch said, "My brother and I were sliding down the snow pile on sleds just a few minutes ago. After we went down the third time, J.J. saw something lying on the snow. We thought it was just a weird-shaped rock. He picked it up and we took it inside so we could show our mom." Mitch looked to me, inviting me to share my part of the story.

I gulped. "I realized the rock was actually a nose. Nigel Goodwin's."

"A nose?" Hardy's lip curled up. "That's a new one for me. Just when I thought I'd heard it all."

Mitch appeared pale, even against the background of white snow. He had been forced to face some very grown-up situations this morning. It broke my heart. Every mother wanted their children's lives to be easy and comfortable and carefree, without strife or trauma. In other words, every mother wished for the impossible. It took everything in me not to gather him in both my arms and hold him tight, but I knew he wouldn't appreciate me attempting to console him publicly. I turned to the officer. "May Mitch go back to his room?"

Hardy looked from me to my son. "Is there anything you haven't told me?"

Mitch shook his head.

"All right, then," the officer said. "You can go to your room. Just don't say anything to anyone inside. We need to figure things out before the rumors start to fly."

Looking relieved to be dismissed, Mitch strode off toward the door.

Once my son was gone, the officer glanced over at Goodwin's body again. "This'll be a case for the medics. Initially, at least. They should be here soon." Returning his attention to me, he said, "This may be a moot point now, but I went by Tyson Pell's place twice yesterday to arrest him for the property damage. There was no sign of the guy. I'll check again today. The other officers have been keeping an eye out for him, too. He's got a criminal record for poaching bear, so he was already on our radar."

With so much wilderness in the state, poaching was a real problem here. Wildlife authorities in Georgia and North Carolina had recently joined forces in an undercover operation to bust a bear-poaching ring. The effort was known as "Operation Something Bruin," *bruin* being an Old English word for *bear*. Ten men from North Carolina, Georgia, and Texas were arrested and charged. Unfortunately, the crime of poaching was only a misdemeanor in North Carolina, and fines were the only punishment. The criminals served no jail time, nor were their weapons seized or their right to own guns restricted. The slap on the wrist was a weak deterrent, and most offenders were never caught as their crimes took place in remote areas where there were few, if any, witnesses. To encourage reporting, the state had recently set up an award fund for those who reported poachers. Poachers who were convicted were assessed the amount of the award as part of their fine.

Hardy reached into his jacket pocket and pulled out a pair of gloves, sliding his hands into them. "By the way, Gus Bingenheimer called the department to find out whether he could file theft charges against Nigel Goodwin for refusing to return cameras he'd left at the resort site."

"What did you tell him?" I asked.

"That pursuing charges would be a double-edged sword. Gus clearly didn't intend to abandon the equipment, so Mr. Goodwin had a duty to return it. But I told Gus that raising a stink would surely push Goodwin to press trespassing charges. He said Goodwin had told him the same thing. Of course, a trespassing charge is small potatoes unless it disrupts the operation of a business. Since the resort hasn't even been built yet, a felony charge wouldn't apply. Gus said he'd give it some thought and get back in touch if he needed assistance."

I gestured to the lodge. "Gus's cameras are inside. Mr. Goodwin's assistant rounded them up yesterday afternoon."

"Good to know. Once we get things taken care of out here, I'll see about collecting them."

Rocky told the officer about the missing bags of rock salt. "They were in the shed yesterday. Someone must've snatched them last night."

Hardy's head bobbed and his eyes narrowed as he processed the information. "I'll note the theft in my report."

I gulped once more. "What about Nigel Goodwin's wife? She's inside, too. Should I get her?"

The officer's eyes narrowed slightly. "Has she been looking for her husband?"

"No. Not yet, anyway."

His eyes narrowed even more. "They're sharing a room, right?"

"Yes. The room, but not the bed."

"How do you know that?"

"They're the only two in the room, and someone's been sleeping on the foldout."

"Ah. I see." His head bobbed as he seemed to mentally file away the information.

I glanced back at the lodge. "Far as I know, Aileen has no idea what's happened."

"Let's keep it that way for now," he said. "I'll talk to her once the body and scene are processed."

My cell phone pinged in my pocket. I pulled it out to find a text from Patty. *What's going on over there? Tell me it's not another death.*

I turned to see her standing at the window of her diner, looking at the lodge from above the Help Wanted sign she'd posted in her window the day before. I texted her back. *Wish I could. I'll be in touch with details once things get sorted.*

She glanced down at the phone in her hand as my text arrived. A couple of seconds later, she looked back at me through the window, shaking her head in astonishment.

An ambulance arrived and parked close by, and in seconds the two-man medical team was bent down next to Goodwin, assessing his status. They immediately reached the same conclusion Rocky had—Goodwin was a goner. His soul had divested from his body.

With no patient to treat or transport, the EMTs summoned staff from the Watauga County Medical Examiner's Office to collect the body.

I looked from one EMT to the other. "What do you think happened? What killed him?"

"Hard to say," one of the medics replied with a shrug. "What do you know about this man? What he was doing prior to falling here?"

"Not much. He skied a good part of the day yesterday." I pointed to his gear and jacket lying not far away. "It looks like he might have walked back from the ski resort last night."

The EMT seemed to think out loud. "Other than the missing nose, which you've explained, there are no obvious signs of major trauma, just some minor bruising on his face that he could have suffered in his fall to the ground. My guess would be a heart attack or stroke."

"Or it could be hyponatremia," offered the other.

I wasn't familiar with the term. Evidently, Rocky wasn't either. "Hypo—?"

"Hyponatremia. That's what it's called when a person's sodium levels become too low and their electrolytes get out of balance. It happens sometimes to marathon runners. They sweat out a lot of salt."

The first EMT backpedaled a bit. "We're just spitballing here. We don't provide the official diagnosis. That'll be up the M.E.'s office."

My mind went back to Sebastian Cochrane, how he'd reeked of body odor the night before. My sons had, too. I knew from my own experience that skiing was a physically demanding activity and that, despite frigid outdoor temperatures, a person could sweat profusely. *How many times had I peeled off layers as the day went on?* In fact, because skiing and hiking produced an abundance of sweaty clothing, the lodge had an in-house laundry facility for guests to use. Between hours on the slopes and apparently walking back to the resort, Goodwin had undoubtedly worked up a sweat yesterday. Too bad there wasn't a shortcut between the resort and my lodge, like Amari had inquired about at the reception. Maybe Goodwin could have survived a shorter walk.

With nothing more to offer, and concerned that my long absence might raise questions among the guests, I begged off to go inside. Rocky could handle things out here. As I turned to head back into the lodge, I noticed that the layer of snow atop Sebastian Cochrane's car was markedly thinner than that on the other vehicles. *That's odd.* I supposed the SUVs on either side of it could have blocked the snowfall, but there had been little wind last night. The snow had fallen straight down rather than being blown at an angle.

I walked back into the lobby. Before I retook my seat at the desk, I grabbed the spare key to Rocky's room and retrieved his heavy coat and a knit beanie. I carried them outside and handed them over. He gave me a grateful nod. I also lured Molasses back into the lodge with a biscuit from the breakfast buffet. The dog didn't mind the cold weather, but he might get in the way of law enforcement and the medical examiner's staff. Better to keep him inside.

When I returned to the desk, J.J. whispered, "I saw a cop car and an ambulance drive into the parking lot. Mitch came inside but he went straight to our room without telling me anything. What's going on?"

Lest he freak out and alert the guests, I prepared him for the news I was about to deliver. "You are going to be very shocked by what I tell you. But for the sake of my guests, you need to stay calm and not react, okay?"

His eyes widened but he kept his voice barely above a whisper. "Okay."

I shared the news of our discovery.

When I finished, he looked green, as off-color as Goodwin's nose had been. He seemed to shrink, too, as his knees went soft. "Mitch and I were sledding over a . . . *dead person*?"

I grabbed his arm to steady him and nodded. He turned even greener, putting a hand over his mouth. I pointed down the hall. "Go join Mitch in your room." A handful of guests were still eating their breakfast. If J.J. was going to get sick, I didn't want it to be here.

He took off like a rocket. Daphne and Jean-Paul glanced over from the buffet line. Both were dressed in their usual bright, bold, form-fitting clothes, looking like fashionable clowns. After watching J.J. rush down the hall, they turned my way, expressions of mild concern on their faces. Thank goodness Nigel Goodwin had fallen on the side of the lodge and the emergency vehicles had parked at the end of the lot by the road. Rayan's long passenger van and the sledding hill would block the view from the lobby and the guest-room windows.

I forced a smile at them. *Nothing to see here, folks.* "You're not missing those famous French croissants, are you?"

"Not at all." Daphne chuckled and gestured to the warming trays. "I love coming to America. You people really know how to eat." Out of context, her words could be taken as an insult. But her amiable expression told me she was being sincere.

Once the Fourniers had taken seats, I went to tidy up the breakfast buffet as I normally did. I was curious to note that Amari was seated at a table with Rayan in the back corner of the great room. The two appeared engaged in an intense discussion. *Is Amari attempting to get insider information from Rayan? Or are the two talking about something else entirely?*

Aileen emerged from the hallway and made a bee-line for the box of assorted tea bags and the hot water dispenser. She still didn't seem to realize her husband was missing. *How can she be so oblivious?* Even if they were sleeping in separate beds, shouldn't she at least be aware of his presence, or lack thereof? Then again, I supposed it was possible she'd fallen asleep yesterday evening and assumed he'd come back to their room late last night, and that he'd risen and left the room before she awoke this morning. But she didn't even glance around the great room to look for him. *That's strange, isn't it?*

She fixed her tea, served herself a plate of food, and, as before, carried her breakfast back to her room. I felt guilty watching her go. But she'd have little appetite once she learned about her husband. It couldn't hurt to let her get a solid breakfast under her belt before she received the tragic news.

Sebastian swaggered up the hall, smelling much better than he had the night before, thank goodness. I greeted him with a "good morning," and stepped aside to give him access to the warming trays.

After Sebastian filled his plate, Kyle Jensen called out from a nearby table. "Hey, Sebastian! Join us." Laurie patted the empty seat to her left.

Their request surprised me. What would a middle-aged couple from South Dakota have in common with an entitled millennial? Sebastian seemed as surprised as I was. He emitted an elongated "Okaaaaay."

He carried his food and a mug of steaming coffee over to the table, set them down, and plopped down in the seat.

Laurie and Kyle glanced around, before Kyle leaned toward Sebastian and quietly asked, "Tell us about the issues in Alberta that you mentioned yesterday. What do you know?"

Sebastian snorted. "That resort has been a total fuster cluck. You know that area? Ever been up to Banff?"

The two shook their heads.

"It's amazing, I'll say that," Sebastian said. "Pristine wilderness. There's a big icefield with glaciers, and three turquoise blue lakes. Lake Louise, Moraine Lake, and Peyto Lake."

Though I'd never been to Banff either, I'd heard of Lake Louise and seen photos online. The color of the water was incredibly vivid.

"There's all kinds of wildlife, too," Sebastian added. "Grizzly bears. Mountain goats. Moose. The First Nations consider the mountains sacred."

Laurie tilted her head. "First nations?"

"That's what they call Indians up there . . . or Native Americans. Indigenous people?" Sebastian lifted one shoulder in a half-shrug. Internally, I added *insensitive to other cultures* to my increasing list of reasons not to like the guy. "I don't know what we're supposed to call them now, but you know what I mean. Anyway, the glaciers up there have shrunk due to climate change, and the area is considered vulnerable. Between the environmental impact, the wildlife habitat, and issues with sacred land, all kinds of folks joined together and filed a lawsuit in July to prevent the Alberta Adventure Resort from being built. It's gonna to be tied up in court for years. If Goodwin wins the lawsuits, which is a big *if*, it's going to cost a fortune in legal fees. Even without those problems, the Alberta resort isn't a good idea.

There's already three ski resorts up there: Mount Norquay, Lake Louise, and Sunshine Village."

Sunshine Village? My mind went back to the lift ticket I'd seen on Laurie's ski jacket, the one with a logo of snowcapped mountains superimposed over a sun. If she hadn't made it clear she'd never been to Banff, I might wonder if it had been from that particular resort. Some logos, including that of the Beech Mountain Ski Resort and the popular Marmot and REI brands of outdoor gear featured mountains with no background in their graphics. But it wasn't unusual to see mountains depicted against a backdrop that included the sun, moon, or sky. The Patagonia clothing brand logo featured a mountain range against a striped sky. The Aquafina water logo showed an orange sun peeking from behind mountain peaks.

Sebastian continued to apprise the Jensens—and me. "They offer a combined lift ticket for all three resorts. They call it Ski Big Three. The resorts are well established, and the area would be a tough market. I'd know. I've skied there lots of times. Goodwin should've done more due diligence before taking investor money and dragging them into a mess." He took a sip of his orange juice and added a big whammy. "I heard a rumor that one of the investors took his own life when he learned he'd probably lost everything."

Whoa. That information was unsettling. It was sad to think someone felt they couldn't bounce back from the financial hit if they lost their investment in the resort. The news was also surprising. Hadn't Goodwin said he made sure everyone who invested their money in his projects could afford to do so? Had something fallen through the cracks with that particular investor?

Kyle and Laurie appeared as horrified as I was by this piece of information, maybe even more so. Laurie returned her attention to Sebastian. "Is that why you asked Mr. Goodwin if he'd done his homework here? Because you knew about the problems with the Alberta project?"

"Yup." He scooped up a big spoonful of grits and shoveled them into his mouth. After swallowing, he gestured with his empty spoon. "Goodwin got lucky with his earlier projects. They were smaller, more manageable. He got too ambitious with the Alberta resort, got out over his skis."

An apt metaphor.

Worry puckered Laurie's forehead. "We'd really hoped that investing in the resort here would generate some wealth we could count on during retirement. We're both approaching fifty. Middle age snuck up on us much faster than we'd expected."

I could certainly relate to that sentiment. Seemed just yesterday I was a young newlywed, then *boom* the boys appeared and life since had been a busy blur.

Kyle picked up where Laurie had left off. "We're hoping to retire in ten or fifteen years, while we're still young enough to enjoy it. We're looking for secure investments. I know nothing is a sure thing, but the resort seemed like a good risk." He angled his head one way, then the other, considering. "Maybe Goodwin learned his lesson in Alberta. Maybe he won't make the same mistakes again here."

Sebastian shoveled another heaping spoonful of grits into his mouth, but this time he didn't bother to swallow before speaking around them. "Maybe. Maybe not. Either way, I'm not giving the guy a cent."

As Sebastian swallowed and swiped at his mouth with

a napkin, Kyle assessed him. "You've already decided without hearing the full pitch? You were never planning to invest?"

"Nope."

Kyle followed up with, "Then why did you bother to come here at all?"

Sebastian leaned back in his seat, raised his palms out to his sides, and smirked. "Free vacation, baby!"

CHAPTER 11

Yeti

The cat stood on her hind legs on the windowsill, stretching herself up as tall as she could, trying to see over the darn pile of snow that was in her way. Something was going on outside and she wanted to know what it was. She could hear vehicles and voices. She'd heard vehicles last night, too. Late. The first had a loud engine, and the driver had slammed the door. The other had driven slowly into the parking lot with its lights off. She'd heard the soft hum of the motor and the soft crunch of snow under its tires, followed by the softest of thumps as something fell to the ground on the other side of the snow pile. She'd gone to the window and used her claws to try to open the shutters to no avail. She hadn't been able to get a look then, and she couldn't get a look now with them open, either.

Could what was happening now have something to do with that late-night thump?

CHAPTER 12

Misty

Laurie heaved a deep breath and shook her head. "I can't believe we drove over fifteen-hundred miles for nothing."

Kyle's face was sour as he repeated Sebastian's words with far less enthusiasm. "Free vacation, baby."

Laurie addressed Sebastian again. "Are you going to tell the others? Warn them so that they don't lose their money, too?"

The young man shrugged. "I've raised the issue. It's up to them to look out for themselves and ask questions, like you have."

Daphne said something softly in French to her husband, and he eyed Sebastian and the Jensens suspiciously. My mind went back to the day before, when Daphne had bristled at Sebastian's comment that Goodwin had better have done his "homework." In light of her unconditional endorsement, as well as the fact that she'd referred to Goodwin by his first name, the thought crossed my mind that the Fourniers might be plants, cohorts of Goodwin who'd come along to help him sell the interests. Maybe they got a kickback or some other sort of payment for convincing others to invest. Then again, maybe they just wanted to see the development proceed as quickly and efficiently as possible. After all, the sooner the Retreat on Blue Ridge was completed and operational, the sooner they'd reap their returns. Then again, they might simply be cockeyed optimists, always seeing the good and hoping for the best.

Daphne and Jean-Paul stood and headed back to their room. Just after they'd gone, the doors opened behind me as Rocky came inside. I left the buffet and met him at the desk.

He spoke softly. "The assistant medical examiner has loaded Nigel's body into her vehicle. She'll come in to speak with Aileen before she takes him to the morgue."

I glanced back into the great room, where Goodwin's assistant was moving the podium and projector into place. Rayan had clearly been frustrated by the demands Goodwin had put on him, and I wondered how he'd react when he learned his boss wouldn't be continuing his pitch today—or ever—and that he no longer had a job. "What about Rayan? Who's going to tell him? And the others?" I wasn't sure whether it should be me or the authorities.

Rocky said, "Let the authorities handle it. This isn't their first rodeo."

I grimaced. "It's not mine, either." Guests of my lodge had perished twice before. "But I will gladly defer to the experts."

"It's weird," Rocky said. "Goodwin had taken off his jacket, and he wasn't wearing his ski pants, either. Just a base layer."

"He was in thermal underwear?"

"The sportier performance-style long johns and undershirt, but yeah. His pants were stuffed into his bag with his boots."

"He must've gotten overheated walking back from the

resort." I knew from personal experience that, despite frigid temperatures, outdoor exercise could raise a person's body temperature, making heavy, insulated clothing unbearable. I opted for a lightweight powder jacket any time I went skiing in outdoor temperatures above 35 degrees.

A few minutes later, Rocky and I were sitting side by side behind the desk when the assistant medical examiner came into the lobby, accompanied by Officer Hardy. She carried a small cooler in her hand, as if she were heading to a picnic. It was a quarter past nine by then and, fortunately, most of the guests had finished their breakfast and returned to their rooms to freshen up before today's pitch session. Only Amari Lott and the Salazars remained at the tables. Rayan was at the podium, setting up the equipment for Goodwin's presentation scheduled for later this morning. It was a wasted effort, but I couldn't tell him so. The four watched as the authorities approached my desk, and exchanged questioning glances.

The assistant M.E. stopped before me and Rocky and whispered, "Where's Goodwin's nose?"

Oh my gosh! It was still in the drawer. I'd forgotten all about it. Luckily for me, Rocky pulled the drawer open and pointed down into it. The assistant M.E. circled around the counter, donned a glove to pick it up, and discreetly secured it in a sealed plastic bag in her cooler. The morbid task complete, she asked, "Which room is his wife in?"

I told her the room number and directed her and Officer Hardy down the hall to my right. As they headed off, the Salazars rolled up the counter. Celeste lifted her chin to indicate the two retreating down the hall. "What's with the cop? Has something happened?"

I bit my lip. "There's been . . ." *What? An accident? A death?* I wasn't sure how to phrase things. I went with "an unfortunate incident. Someone will address your group shortly."

Her brows lifted, disappearing under her spiky bangs. She was obviously curious, but she didn't press me further. Emilio exhaled sharply. "Mountains are dangerous places."

I wondered if he was speaking from personal experience, or just making a general observation. But, like his wife, I didn't ask for clarification. I didn't need to. I'd heard stories of people falling off cliffs, being swept away in rushing water, becoming disoriented and lost without adequate food or water to sustain them, and what was supposed to be a day hike turning into a weeks-long search that often ended in recovery rather than rescue. Someone slid on ice and hit their head, suffering a concussion. A skier could go out of control and crash into a tree or a lift-support pole, suffer a severe brain injury or death. Vehicles, too, could slide and crash, injuring or killing passengers. Of course, bad things happened everywhere, not only in the mountains. No place on the planet was without risk.

A minute or so later, Officer Hardy returned without the assistant M.E. I supposed the woman was still in the room, questioning Aileen about her husband's medical history and filling her in on the next steps, what would be done with husband's body. The autopsy would pinpoint exactly what had happened to Nigel Goodwin.

The officer angled his head to indicate Rayan. "Is that Mr. Goodwin's employee?"

"Yes," I said. "His name is Rayan Gandapur."

He strode over to speak to the young man. Amari Lott had yet to move from the table where they'd eaten breakfast, and he watched the exchange with an eagle eye. From his vantage point, he might even be able to overhear their discussion.

The officer said something to Rayan, and Goodwin's assistant took an involuntary step back, as if attempting to distance himself from the disturbing information he'd just received. He reached out to grab the podium, gripping it tightly to steady himself. Hardy pulled a chair over and Rayan sank down onto the seat. Pulling a second chair over for himself, Hardy sat and huddled with Rayan, asking the younger man a few quick questions. Judging from his terse responses, Rayan wasn't able to offer much information.

The officer said something and gestured to me. My guess was he'd told Rayan that I'd mentioned the trail cams, how Rayan had removed them from the property and brought them back to the lodge the day before. Rayan cast a glance my way and rose from his chair. He walked down to his room, returning a short time later with the trail cams jumbled in his arms. The cameras clattered as he unceremoniously dumped them onto a table, making little effort to be careful with the equipment. Perhaps he was still upset that he'd had to trudge through deep snow yesterday afternoon to collect them, and was taking out his emotions on the devices. Or maybe he was angry at Gus for trespassing and putting the devices on the property in the first place, and didn't feel the need to show any more respect for the man's equipment than the man had shown for Nigel Goodwin's property rights. Either way, the pile of trail cams would be difficult for the police officer to handle.

"Hold on!" I called. A cardboard box from my latest cat food delivery remained behind the desk, serving as a lost-and-found depository. Guests constantly left mittens, gloves, scarves, knit caps, cell phones, or lip balm in the public areas of the lodge where the owner couldn't be readily identified. While cell phones were almost always claimed in short order, the other items were not. I opened an empty drawer behind the desk, then picked up the box and turned it over, dumping the contents into the drawer. I carried the empty box into the great room and addressed Officer Hardy. "How about I put the cameras in this box? It'll make them easier for you to carry."

The officer gave me a grateful nod. "That would be great. Thanks."

The pile included a variety of trail cams. Some were in camouflage cases, intended to blend in with their surroundings. Others were basic black, brown, green, or gray. Some had a single lens, while others had two or more; some aimed to the sides to provide wide-angle views. A couple of them even had small solar panels on top to provide electricity to the devices.

I picked up the trail cams one by one, placing them gently in the box. As I picked up the third camera, which had landed face down on the table, my eyes spotted a small number written in permanent marker on a round sticker: 13. A piece of clear shipping tape had been affixed over the numbered sticker, probably in an attempt to weatherproof it. I turned over the two cameras I'd already placed in the box. The numbers 7 and 9 appeared on their cases. I went through the pile, arranging the cameras in order by number. The lowest was 2 and the highest was 23. At least three numbers were missing—5, 11, and 18. More could be missing if the numbers went higher than 23, but I had no way of knowing how many cameras Gus had placed on the property. Besides, with Goodwin having been found dead outside this morning, we had a much bigger issue to deal with at the moment. Rayan had been seriously inconvenienced collecting the cameras yesterday, and Gus was lucky to be getting any of his equipment back. I pointed out the discrepancy to Officer Hardy and returned to the desk.

The rest of the guests began to return to the room. They glanced around, appearing surprised to see that the tables hadn't been rearranged since breakfast for today's pitch session. Many looked to Rayan, who bore the expression of a deer in the headlights. Fortunately, Hardy took the lead, stepped to the podium, and addressed them. "Take a seat, folks. I've got some information that I'll share once everyone is gathered."

Daphne and Jean-Paul strode up the hallway. Daphne stopped in her tracks when she spotted the police officer and threw out an arm to stop her husband, too. She turned to look at me. "Something is wrong. What is it?"

I swallowed hard. "Officer Hardy will fill you in."

They exchanged a concerned look before tentatively continuing on and perching on the edge of their seats.

The others convened in the room. Sebastian Cochrane was the last to arrive, coming down the hall at the last second just as he had the day before. When he spotted the officer, he hesitated for an instant. A look of alarm flitted across his face, but then he threw his hands in the air. "Uh-oh!" he called. "You caught me!" He barked a laugh as he dropped into a chair.

Hardy gave Sebastian a sour look. This was not the time for jokes. *Read the room, for goodness sake!*

Rayan turned to the officer. "Everyone is here now."

Officer Hardy nodded and faced the group. "Folks, I've got some bad news. Earlier this morning, Nigel Goodwin was found deceased."

The group issued a collective gasp. Kyle went stock-still in apparent shock, while Laurie's hand reflexively went to her throat, where her ever-present infinity scarf hung in a double loop. Daphne put her hands over her nose and mouth, her fingers muffling her cry of "Mon Dieu!" Jean-Paul shrunk against his seatback, his shoulders curving forward as if he were trying to disappear inside himself. Amari's eyes narrowed in question. He rested his elbows on the table where he sat and leaned forward, eagerly anticipating more information.

After Celeste and Emilio exchanged dark glances, Celeste turned back to look at the officer and asked, "What happened, exactly? Did he have an accident?"

"We don't know the cause of death yet," Hardy said. "The medical examiner's office will make that determination. The assistant medical examiner has some questions for all of you, so I'm asking everyone to stay put until she is finished speaking with Mrs. Goodwin."

Kyle glanced down the east wing toward the Goodwins' room. "He was found here? Inside the lodge?"

"No," the officer said. "He was found outside. Does anyone know why he might have been out there late last night or early this morning?"

While the others shook their heads or said words to indicate they had no information to offer, Rayan's eyes darted around, looking anywhere but at the officer in front of him. *Does he know something he's not telling the police?*

"I've got a question, too," Sebastian said. "Will we still get our lift tickets for the rest of the week?"

The group erupted in another collective gasp, though this was a gasp of outrage rather than surprise.

"For Pete's sake!" Kyle turned back and skewered Sebastian with his gaze. "Have some basic decency!"

Jean-Paul was only slightly more forgiving. He scowled at Sebastian. "You only think of yourself. Nigel is not even cold yet."

Jean-Paul was wrong about that last bit. Nigel Goodwin's body was indeed cold. Frozen solid, in fact. But I wasn't about to correct the guy. Rocky eyed me askance. He must've been thinking the same thing.

Many of the others shook their heads or scowled at Sebastian, too. For once seemingly cowed, he avoided their gazes, instead pulling out his cell phone and appearing to be checking emails or texts.

Rayan riffled through the materials on the podium and pulled out four stacks of lift tickets bound by rubber bands, one stack for each of the four remaining days in the week. Rather than pass the tickets out, he simply placed them on a nearby table for the guests to take for themselves. "Here are the lift tickets if you want them. They've already been paid for, so you might as well use them." Before stepping back, he finagled a single lift ticket from each stack for himself. He'd been too busy dealing with issues at the resort property to ski the day before, but now, with Goodwin dead, he'd be able to ski the rest of the week. This was one unexpected event that actually worked in his favor.

The group eyed each other. They'd just scolded Sebastian for being overly concerned about the lift tickets, but now that the issue had been raised, they appeared equally eager to get the perk they'd been promised. They rose slowly and made their way to the table, retrieving their tickets. Sebastian got in line, too, but not before discreetly rolling his eyes at their hypocrisy. After retrieving their tickets, they returned to their tables to await the assistant M.E.

A few minutes later, Rocky and I were still sitting

behind the desk, waiting, too, when the woman emerged from the Goodwins' room and came to the lobby. She walked over to the podium, but rather than stand behind it, she merely stood beside it in a less formal fashion. After identifying herself, she said, "It's my understanding that y'all spent yesterday afternoon and evening with Mr. Goodwin at the ski resort. I'm wondering if any of you noticed anything unusual going on with him, whether he mentioned feeling ill?"

Sebastian said, "He seemed fine to me. Hell, he put me to shame on the slopes. We raced down the mountain and nearly tied."

Nearly tied? That wasn't how Sebastian had put it last night. In fact, if I remembered correctly, he'd said it wasn't much of a contest. *Why the newfound love for the truth?* Maybe he'd had a bit of conscience since being such a disrespectful jerk earlier, and had realized he owed Nigel Goodwin at least a modicum of respect.

Jean-Paul said, "I rode a lift with Nigel. He pointed out that he was one of the oldest skiers on the mountain. But he was not complaining. He seemed proud."

I knew that feeling. I felt proud that I, too, was still able to ski, even if I could no longer ski for a full day and paid dearly for my fun in the form of a sore back and knees the next day.

Laurie's head tilted and, when she spoke, her voice was hesitant. "I'm not sure if this could have anything to do with his death, but when we were at the ski resort yesterday a teenager came out of the equipment rental place carrying his skis flat across his shoulders. Someone called to him, and he turned around and whacked Nigel Goodwin right in the face with his skis. Thank goodness Mr. Goodwin had his goggles on to protect his eyes. It was a pretty hard smack and the kid seemed embarrassed, but Mr. Goodwin was nice about it. He didn't make the kid feel any worse than he already did."

That could explain the bruising around Goodwin's nose. New skiers were often not familiar with the proper way to carry skis, and didn't realize they turned into a human-centered propeller when they carried their skis sideways. I'd seen more than one person take a hit to the head or body when someone transported their skis in a careless manner. For that very reason, I gave the equipment rental area a wide berth when I went to the resort.

Celeste said, "I saw him pull to the side on the runs a few times, but he was taking photos with his phone. It didn't look like he'd stopped to rest or because he was in trouble or anything like that."

The assistant M.E. asked, "What about alcohol or drug use? Anyone aware of Mr. Goodwin drinking excessively yesterday or using recreational drugs?"

Officer Hardy raised his palms and added, "We're not looking to make any arrests for drug use. We're just trying to figure out what happened."

Everyone shook their heads and murmured in the negative. Sebastian didn't mention that he'd had a beer with Goodwin the evening before, after beating the older man in their race. But I supposed his silence didn't necessarily mean anything. Goodwin might have had only one or two beers, an amount Sebastian wouldn't consider excessive.

The assistant M.E. passed out her business cards. "If there's anything you'd like to tell me privately, or something you think of later, please get in touch. We'd like to resolve this investigation as soon as possible. Mrs. Goodwin has a plane ticket to London Saturday evening. It's a red-eye flight. She'll have to leave here Saturday afternoon to drive down to Charlotte to make sure she doesn't miss her plane. She'd like to have her husband cremated before she leaves so that she can take his remains back with her."

Though Aileen seemed to be moving awfully fast with her plans, I supposed the situation wasn't necessarily suspect. It seemed clear she hadn't wanted to leave London in the first place, and she'd be even more eager to get back to the comfort of home in light of her husband's death.

Having done what they could for the time being, the assistant M.E. thanked everyone and departed. Officer Hardy went with her.

With the authorities gone now, the guests looked to Rayan for guidance.

Amari asked, "What now? Does this mean the plans for the resort will be canceled?"

Rayan appeared unsure, shrugging and shaking his head. "I . . . I don't know what will happen. I suppose Nigel's solicitors back in London will sort things out."

Sebastian was back to his old, offensive self. "But we can stay in our rooms here until Friday, right? That was the deal." He looked from Rayan to the desk where I sat and raised his brows in question.

My gut clenched. If the guests left early, would I be able to fill the rooms at the last minute like this? With the snow continuing to fall, maybe. But until I released the rooms, anyone trying to make a reservation on my website would get a message that we were currently fully booked and no rooms were available. When Goodwin reserved the large room block, one of the terms was that the reservations would be nonrefundable. I couldn't run the risk that my entire lodge would sit empty for days if he canceled. To that end, I'd already charged all five nights to his corporate credit card. But did our agreement still apply now that he was dead? Would I be a horrible person if I held a dead man to a promise he'd made while he was still alive?

Fortunately, Rayan took the burden off my shoulders. "Mr. Goodwin's number-one priority was making sure his guests had a good time at his resorts. I am sure he would want the same for you. The rooms have already been paid for, same as the lift tickets. Enjoy the rest of the week here."

That's a relief.

As the guests left the great room, Rayan gathered up the materials he'd brought for today's session and returned them to the file box. He came to the desk and held out four lift tickets, one for each remaining weekday. "These were left over. Could your boys use them?"

"Thanks, Rayan, but they have season passes." So did Pebble. I knew that the only reason there were lift tickets remaining was because Nigel Goodwin had bought tickets for himself, too. But, again, no sense letting them go to waste. I suggested Rayan offer them to someone in line at the resort, and recalled how I'd had to scrimp and save when the boys were younger to afford their lift tickets. "Maybe give them to a family with kids. You'll make their day."

"Good idea."

He set off to his room with the box and lift tickets. I noticed he didn't check in on Aileen. *Someone should, right?* I supposed that someone would be me.

After informing Rocky of my intentions and asking him to watch the desk for a moment, I walked down the hall and stood before the door to Aileen's room, my hand raised to knock. Hesitating, I considered what I should say. *What words would console someone who'd suffered such a sad and shocking loss?* I didn't know. Realistically, there were none. After all, grief was a process and couldn't be healed with mere words. It would take time. Despite the disagreement I'd overheard between Aileen and Nigel Sunday evening, she seemed to love the man. After all, she wouldn't have been upset by his lack of attention if she hadn't wanted to spend more quality time with him, and she'd only want to spend more time with him if she truly cared about him, right?

I rapped softly. "Mrs. Goodwin? It's Misty. No need to come to the door if you'd rather not. I'm so sorry for what's happened. If there's anything at all I can do, bring you a cup of tea or something to eat, please don't hesitate to call the desk."

A disembodied voice came from inside the room. "Thank you. A cup of tea would be wonderful."

"I'll be right back."

Grateful I could help her in this small way, I hurried to the great room, fixed her a hot mug of tea, and carried it back to her room. I rapped softly again and she opened the door just far enough for me to hand the mug through. She looked down at the mug, so I didn't get a good look at her face. It was just as well. I already had her husband's horrid, frozen face branded on my brain. I didn't need her grief-stricken one, as well.

After she took the mug, she said, "You can skip the cleaning today. I'd like to be alone."

"Of course."

She quietly closed her door. I returned to the check-in counter, took my seat on the stool next to Rocky, and texted Patty. *Come over when you can.* A death at my lodge was better discussed in person.

A mere minute later, Patty strode through the door in

her snow boots, her heavy coat hanging open over her apron and clothing because she hadn't taken the time to zip it. She rushed up to the desk. "Who was it?" she whispered, looking from me to Rocky and back again. "What happened?"

"Nigel Goodwin." I'd been thrilled when he'd booked his group here, and had told her all about him and his plans for the resort then, so no explanation was needed now.

Rocky added, "Misty's sons found evidence that there was a body outside. Goodwin was covered in snow at the bottom of the sledding hill beside the lodge."

I was glad Rocky hadn't specifically mentioned the detached nose. It was too macabre.

Patty's mouth fell open nonetheless. "How'd he end up there?"

"We're not sure. His ski equipment was out there, too, so it looks like he walked back from the resort after it closed last night. The EMTs speculated that he suffered a heart attack or stroke, or"—hard as I tried, I couldn't remember the name they'd given for the electrolyte issue—"some kind of mineral imbalance. The medical examiner's office will do an autopsy to find out."

Patty reached across the counter and took my hands in hers, giving them a supportive squeeze. "I'm so sorry, Misty. You've been through so much with the death of the yoga instructor and the woman from the ladies' motorcycle club. But at least this death doesn't look like a murder, right?"

CHAPTER 13

Misty

Patty gave my hands another squeeze before releasing them. "I'd better collect the breakfast trays and get back. The lunch rush will be starting soon and I'm short-staffed."

As Emilio had surmised, getting reliable help on the mountain was a constant challenge due to the small local population and the long, sometimes treacherous drive for those who lived in larger towns nearby. Patty's diner ran lean. "I'll help you," I offered.

Rocky slid off his stool beside me. "So will I."

As the three of us stacked the warming trays and gathered up the bussing bins and errant silverware, glasses, and mugs, the guests emerged from their rooms in their ski gear and skulked out of the lodge. Many of them clearly felt uncomfortable enjoying themselves on Nigel Goodwin's dime when the man lay dead in the morgue, but wasting the man's money would be even worse, wouldn't it?

Soon after Patty left the lodge to return to the diner, Rocky's phone came to life with an incoming call. He took it and stepped to the window, staring out at the snow as he talked with the person on the other end. "I understand. No sense taking chances."

He ended the call and turned to me. At least I knew that anything he might say couldn't be any worse than what had already happened here today.

"The hot tub delivery is going to be delayed. The truck driver doesn't dare venture up the mountain in all of this snow."

"No problem. The hot tub can wait." The spa was the least of my worries, though a relaxing soak in a hot tub sounded darn good at the moment.

Now that things had settled down in the lodge, we re-grouped. We'd lost most of the morning. Rocky needed to go plow some residential driveways, and my sons and I had better get started on the housekeeping rounds. I went down to their room to check on them. Fortunately, both of them had recovered from their initial shock and looked far calmer and collected. While Yeti lounged on the couch between them, they played Butterfly Brawl on their laptops, trash talking other players through their headsets. Though it might seem insensitive that they were playing a video game not long after a man had been found dead here, I knew their games served the same purpose as the novels I read—mental escape. If ever they'd needed a distraction from reality, it was today.

J.J. looked up from his laptop and gestured to his screen. "This is the highest level I've ever reached."

"Same," Mitch replied, looking proud.

With everything that had happened that morning, I was glad my boys had experienced something posi-tive in their day, even if it was only a good score on a video game. I felt guilty tearing them away from the much-needed distraction, but cleaning the rooms could be a good distraction, too, and there was no way I could complete all the work myself. "Time to get to work, boys."

They told the other players that they had to go, signed out of their games, and removed their headsets. Leaving Yeti behind to enjoy yet another cat nap, we went together to the housekeeping closet, retrieved our carts, and rolled off in opposite directions.

As I was cleaning Daphne and Jean-Paul's room a while later, I spotted a piece of paper folded in quarters in their trash can. I supplied recycle bins for the rooms as well, so I figured they must have simply dropped the paper in the wrong bin inadvertently. As I picked it up, it unfolded enough for me to see an image of an ice-cream cone. *What's that about?*

Curious, I unfolded the paper. It contained a photograph at the top of an ice-cream shop that was available for rent in the nearby town of Boone. Below the image were details about the space, including square footage, seating, and freezer capacity. Stapled to the top corner of the paper was a business card from a local commercial realtor. *Had the Fourniers gone to see this property? Is that why they'd turned left out of the parking lot yesterday after the pitch session rather than right like everyone else?*

I wondered why they would have taken a look at an ice-cream shop. I also realized I had no idea what the couple did for a living. It hadn't come up in conversation. I only knew that, whatever they did, they must earn a very good living to have been able to afford an interest in each of Goodwin's resorts.

I placed the paper in the recycling bin on my cart, and dumped the rest of the trash into the trash bag. Now, for the bed.

I turned to straighten the sheets and sighed. Daphne wore copious amounts of makeup, and I'd spotted traces of it on her pillowcase yesterday. I'd exchanged it for a fresh one. There was even more makeup on her pillowcase today, including smudges of bright red lipstick that looked like a virtual bloodbath. *Sigh.* I doubted the stains would come out, but I'd try. I was beginning to see why hotels supplied makeup remover towelettes. Providing the cloths was probably cheaper than having to constantly replace stained pillowcases.

I changed the pillowcase, made the bed, vacuumed, and disinfected the bathroom. When I saw Daphne's tube of red lipstick on the bathroom counter among her myriad cosmetics, I had to fight the urge to accidentally-on-purpose knock it into the trash can. When I finished in their room, I took the stained pillowcase to the laundry room. I generously spritzed the makeup spots with stain remover, scrubbed them hard with a laundry brush, and rinsed the case under the faucet in the utility sink. *Out, damned spot! Out, I say!* The stains were lighter, but still visible. I repeated the process to no avail. Brynn favored natural, non-toxic products, and many of them worked as well as or better than the harsh chemicals, but so far they weren't cutting it in this case. I feared nothing would. I made a paste out of the laundry detergent she'd ordered for the lodge to see if that could wipe out the stains. I applied the paste to the stains and scrubbed again.

My ringtone sounded in my pocket, and I tossed the pillowcase into the sink to check the screen. Rocky had placed a Facetime call. I tapped the icon to accept it, and his face appeared on the screen, the shadowy, snowy woods behind him. "Where are you?"

"At Goodwin's property." Steam formed in the frigid

air as he spoke. "I was passing by on my way to plow a driveway when something caught my attention. I thought you should see this." He turned the phone away from himself and aimed it at the resort's sign—or what was left of it, anyway. The wood was riddled with so many bullet holes it had splintered in places. The words had been obliterated, only a few letters still legible. A *B*, a *T*, an *N*, and an *S*.

The shock was like a punch to the gut. *It had to be Pell, didn't it?* Turning over a table and breaking the model was one thing. Heck, even Jesus had turned over tables when he'd gotten angry. But firing a gun on another person's property was another thing entirely. "It looks like Pell used an entire arsenal on that sign!"

"You're not exaggerating." Rocky aimed his phone down at the ground, where there were dozens of holes in the snow, presumably from where the shotgun shells and bullet casings fell and were now buried under fresh snowflakes. "He's left a lot of evidence behind."

With Tyson Pell living so close to the resort property, I worried that he might see Rocky at the scene of his crime, come over, and fill my handyman/boyfriend with lead, too. "Are you safe? Is Pell at his house?"

On my screen, Rocky's face reappeared, though he looked off into the distance. "There's no lights on at his place. No sign of his truck. It's either gone or parked in his garage. Haven't seen or heard his dogs, either." He turned back to face the screen. "I've called the police. An officer is on the way." He looked away again as the sound of a motor came through the phone. "In fact, here he is now. I'll let you go. We'll talk when I get back to the lodge."

We ended the call and I turned back to the pillowcase, taking out my fears and frustrations on the fabric. After scrubbing the stains with the brush again, I tossed the case in the washing machine to soak. It was likely a futile effort.

As I exited the laundry room, Mitch summoned me from down the hall. "Hey, Mom!"

I turned to see him standing outside the open door to Sebastian Cochrane's room. He waved me forward, and I walked down the hall. "What's up?"

He pulled me into the room, where J.J. was dusting the shutters. "A bath towel is missing. We weren't sure what to do."

To ensure my guests had plenty of bath towels, hand towels, and washcloths, I normally left four complete sets in each room when I cleaned, along with a fresh bath mat, replenishing the stock as needed. Brynn and I had trained my boys to do the same. But Mitch was right. Only three full-size towels remained in Sebastian's bathroom. Two clean, dry ones sat folded on the shelf and a damp one hung from the rack. I stepped back out of the bath and walked farther into the room, glancing around. The missing towel wasn't draped over a chair or the arm of the sofa. It wasn't lying on the floor either, or tangled up in the bedsheets. The bath towel had gone AWOL.

The situation was frustrating, but not unusual. People sometimes took a towel with them to wipe down their ski boots and equipment before packing them up. I only wished they'd ask before using a good towel. My housekeeping closet held a substantial supply of bath towels with stains or holes that had been relegated to cleaning cloths. I would gladly offer them one of those towels to use instead.

"Leave two fresh bath towels," I instructed Mitch. "If another towel goes missing tomorrow, I'll ask Sebastian about them."

As I turned to leave, I noticed a bag on the floor. Given the shape, my first thought was that Sebastian had forgotten to take his ski boots with him today. But when I took a quick peek in the bag, I realized it contained a pair of hockey skates, not ski boots. Sebastian Cochrane wasn't just a Carolina Hurricanes hockey fan, he was a hockey player himself. I wondered why he'd brought the skates along on this trip. Did he plan to join in a hockey game somewhere in the area? Or maybe just skate for fun?

J.J. interrupted my thoughts by picking up a one-dollar bill Sebastian had left on the night table. "The big tipper strikes again."

I shook my head. The tiny tip wouldn't even cover the cost of the missing towel.

Leaving my sons to finish their rounds, I headed back up the hall toward the lobby. There, I found a large cardboard box on the reception desk. It was addressed to Rayan. It must be the security cameras Goodwin had told him to order yesterday, the ones to be shipped via overnight express. The mail carrier had braved the weather to ensure an on-time delivery. He must've slipped inside while I was talking towels with my boys. I wondered whether Rayan would go ahead and install the cameras, or send them back. Could the resort even move ahead without Goodwin? I had my doubts. I'd gotten the impression that he and Adventure Capital were essentially one and the same, that without him there was no business.

After taking the box to Rayan's room and leaving it on his table, I moved down the hall to the Jensens' room. While all of their towels were accounted for, their box of tissues was empty. They'd run through it quickly. Not uncommon, especially this time of year when people were constantly going in and out of heated spaces and the cold outdoors, and the temperature and humidity changes could trigger a runny nose. They might have put tissues in their pockets to take with them when they skied. Some women also used tissues and cold cream or liquid makeup remover to clean off their makeup. *Too bad Daphne doesn't.*

I didn't see an abundance of tissues in the trash can when I went to empty it, but they could have been buried under the fast-food bags and napkins stuffed into the bin. Looked like the Jensens had cleaned their car of the trash they'd accumulated on their long drive from South Dakota. I replaced the box of tissues in the bathroom and left a second one atop the dresser for good measure.

An hour later, my sons found me wiping a mirror in a guest room.

Mitch said, "We've finished our rounds. Anything else you need us to do before we leave?"

"No, thanks. You boys have fun." To my surprise, Mitch and J.J. stepped over and grabbed me in a group hug. They must've realized I was upset by Goodwin's death. While it had been a momentary shock for the two of them, I'd be dealing with the aftermath for days, at least. Maybe longer. I gave them each a peck on the cheek. "Thanks, you two. I needed that."

Their hugs delivered, they took off to snowboard.

When I finished my rounds, I returned to the desk to await Rocky. I was eager to find out whether the search for Tyson Pell had been escalated since he'd used the sign for target practice. *Where has that man gone?*

I didn't know where Pell was, but Gus Bingenheimer ventured into my lodge late that afternoon. "Hey, Misty."

He offered me his usual gap-toothed smile. "I'm hoping tempers have cooled and that I can collect the rest of my cameras."

He hasn't heard. Part of me was shocked. News traveled fast in small mountain towns, especially among those who were active on the local Facebook groups. Not that the rumor mill was always accurate, by any means. But another part of me realized that this guy spent a lot of time wandering around the woods by himself. Maybe it wasn't so surprising he'd be out of touch. Before I'd share the news about Goodwin, I wanted clarification. "The *rest* of your cameras? So, you removed some of the cameras from the property yourself? Despite Nigel Goodwin telling you not to step foot on his property?" Okay, maybe I was still sore that someone had stolen the rock salt from the lodge's tool shed, even though we had no intention of ever using it, and I was taking it out on Gus. *People need to show respect for each other's property.*

The burly man's eyes went wide and he froze, a sasquatch caught in headlights.

Before he could attempt to deny it, I said, "I noticed the cameras were numbered, and some of them were missing. Five. Eleven. Eighteen. Maybe more if the numbers went higher than twenty-three."

"All right." He raised his hands in surrender and the sleeves of his coat pulled back an inch or two, revealing scratches along the inside of his wrists. "I suppose I might as well come clean. When I left here yesterday, I went right to the property to remove my cameras."

I supposed that fact could explain the scratches on his wrists. He'd probably rubbed them up against the rough bark of the trees as he'd pulled the cameras down.

He exhaled a sharp breath. "I was only able to round

up three of them before Goodwin's partner showed up and I had to sneak off. But can you blame me?" He raised his hands palms up to the sides this time, the scratches visible again. "The camera equipment is valuable and Goodwin was being stubborn about it. All I've ever tried to do is protect the wildlife. He could've worked with me, been more reasonable. I'm hoping he'll be more receptive today now that he's had time to calm down."

Oh, he's calmed down all right. He's calmed all the way down. "Gus," I said, taking a deep breath to steel myself for delivering the tragic news, "Mr. Goodwin was found dead this morning."

It took a beat for him to register what I'd said, but when he did his eyes went round again and he took a big step back, as if playing an inverse game of Mother, May I? "What?! What do you mean he's dead?"

How else could I put this? "He's no longer living."

The man's chest heaved twice before he got his breathing under control. He took a tentative baby step back in my direction and lowered his voice. "What happened to him?"

"We don't know yet. The medical examiner is doing an autopsy."

The man looked down at the floor and slowly shook his head. When he looked back up, he said, "Does this mean I can get my cameras then? From his business partner?"

Rayan was Mr. Goodwin's assistant, not his partner, but I didn't bother correcting Gus. "Officer Hardy has your cameras. Rayan turned them over."

His eyes flashed. "I don't see why he had to involve the police."

I cocked my head, confused. "Officer Hardy told

us you'd called the department wanting to know your rights. You'd already involved the police." He had no grounds to complain.

Realizing my logic was inarguable, he said, "I guess you're right. It's just now that the police have custody of them, it's going to be a hassle getting them back. They'll probably treat them as evidence or whatever."

"I can't speak for the police, but with Goodwin gone I don't foresee a problem. His wife and his assistant aren't likely to pursue trespassing charges. They've got much more important things to deal with right now."

Gus cast a glance out the front windows. "Guess I'll head over to the police department now and see about getting my cameras." He turned back to me. "Thanks for the information."

"Sure." Though Gus was a grown man, the mother in me couldn't help but gesture at his wrists and add, "You should put some ointment on those scratches before they get infected."

He looked down at his wrists, then back up at me. "I will. Thanks." With that, he left the lodge.

While Pell was still AWOL an hour later, someone else turned up at the lodge, someone I was happy to see. Phoebe. Over her shoulder, she carried what was intended to be an overnight bag, but which she'd stuffed with at least a week's worth of clothing. The bag was so full, the zipper wouldn't shut. The sight of Rocky's vivacious daughter was a bright spot in my otherwise dark day. Like my boys, Phoebe would be joining us here at the lodge for the next few weeks while she was on break from Appalachian State. She entered quietly, her face tentative. Rocky must've already filled her in on what had happened at the lodge this morning.

"Hey, Pebble." I circled around the desk and gave her

a hug, having to work around the bag. I backed up, still holding her by the upper arms. "It's great to see you."

"You, too." She blushed slightly and offered a small smile before she winced. "Sorry about your guest."

"Me, too," I released her and took a step back. "His wife is in her room, but the other guests have all gone to the ski resort."

"J.J. and Mitch, too?"

"Yep. It's just us girls for now. Why don't I pour us some Cheerwine and you can tell me about your final exams?"

"That sounds nice." She hefted her bag higher on her shoulder, having to lean to the side to balance herself. "I'll just go stash this in my dad's room first."

"I'll meet you back here in a bit." As she headed off to her room, I aimed for mine. Yeti lay napping on my bed, but the smudges on the interior of the window told me she'd spent quite a bit of time with her nose at the glass today, probably watching the goings-on in the parking lot and beside the lodge. Not that she could see much from here with the snow pile in the way. I ruffled her ears and grabbed two cans of Cheerwine from my minifridge. Despite its name, the cherry-flavored soft drink contained no alcohol. I'd noticed at Thanksgiving that it seemed to be Pebble's favorite, and it was made right here in North Carolina.

I returned to the great room. Pebble had pulled two chairs up by the fireplace and positioned a single ottoman between them. She sat in one of the chairs, her snow boots kicked off, her feet atop the ottoman. I poured the drinks into two coffee mugs and handed one to her.

"Thanks," she said. "I love Cheerwine."

"I noticed. You drank at least ten gallons of it at Thanksgiving."

She issued a soft snort of amusement and eyed me over her mug. "You bought it just for me?"

"Of course." From what Rocky had told me, his ex-wife had been a terrible mother, though she'd evidently had an awful childhood herself. Rocky had done his best with his girls, but surely they'd missed having a female role model, bonding over girly things, having a mother who knew all of their likes and dislikes, who spoiled and indulged them. I was glad my small gesture meant something to Pebble. She deserved to feel special. I kicked off my boots, too, and put my feet up next to hers. "Now, tell me about your finals. How'd they go? Were they difficult?"

"I kicked butt. Earned all As. Well, one A minus, but that still counts, right?"

"That's wonderful, Pebble" I remembered my college days, waiting days for grades to be posted on the bulletin board outside the classrooms. Students were lucky that their tests could be processed and grades posted online almost immediately after they were completed now. I raised my mug in toast and held up the other hand for a high five. "Congratulations."

She slapped my hand and clinked her mug against mine, and we sipped our drinks.

By then, it was nearing dinnertime. My boys and the rest of my guests would likely grab something to eat at the resort or one of the restaurants around town. I had doubted that Aileen would have much appetite, but to my surprise she called the front desk. I set down my mug and scurried to the desk in my socks to take her call.

"I phoned in an order at the diner," she said. "Would you mind picking it up for me?"

"Of course. I'll bring it to your room as soon as it's

ready." I hung up the phone and turned to Pebble. "Would you like something to eat from the diner?"

"The answer to that question will never be no." She came to the counter and looked over the menu I kept there. I called in orders for ourselves, and one for Rocky, as well.

The hostess said, "Give us twenty minutes to get it ready."

Pebble and I retook our seats in front of the fire to wait. Molasses rolled over on the rug to warm his other side, as if he were a hot dog on a rotisserie. Pebble reached down and scratched his belly.

"What do you plan to do with your free time over the holidays?" I asked.

"Snowboard as much as possible," she said. "But I want to make some money, too." She looked up at me. "Any chance you need any more help around here?'

"My boys are more than enough help around the lodge, but there's a Help Wanted sign in the diner window." I hiked a thumb over my shoulder in the general direction of the restaurant.

"Oh, yeah?" Pebble sat up and looked out the front windows across the parking lot. "It would be nice to be able to walk to work and not have to buy gas. Plus, my commute would only take fifteen seconds."

I was sure Patty would hire the girl in a heartbeat. Patty was the one who'd initially sung Rocky's praises to me, convinced me to hire him to perform repair work on my lodge. She'd used his handyman services around her diner for years. With Pebble being a chip off the old block—or the old rock, in this case—she'd surely be a hard worker, too.

I went to the desk and rounded up some cash from

my purse, enough to cover our meals and Aileen's. I returned to the great room and held it out to Pebble. "Why don't you pick up our orders and ask about the job at the same time?"

"All right." She took the money, tucked it into her pocket, slid her feet into her boots, and stood. "Wish me luck!"

She'd just exited the lodge when Rocky pulled up out front. He came inside and asked, "Where's my daughter off to?"

"Picking up our dinner," I said, "and applying for a job at the diner."

He put a hand to his heart, as if it were broken. "You mean she doesn't want to plow driveways with me during her school break?"

"That girl adores you, but she needs a job where she can socialize with people her own age."

"It's probably just as well. She'd want to listen to all that horrible pop music in my truck." He grimaced in distaste. "You know I love my classic rock."

Did I ever. He sang along to his playlist whenever he worked outside. "She aced her finals, by the way."

Rocky raised a victorious fist. "Yes!"

While he went to his room to clean up, I rounded up plates, silverware, and napkins, and set a table in the great room for the three of us.

Pebble returned shortly with four bags of food and a new job. "Patty hired me!"

"When do you start?" I asked.

She groaned. "Six a.m. tomorrow. I never get up that early. I'm a night person! I always pick classes that start at ten or later."

"Look on the bright side," I replied. "Your shift will

be over in time for you to hit the slopes by early afternoon."

She set the bags on the table. I read the names written
on them and chose the one for Aileen. To my surprise,
the bag was quite heavy. I opened the top and peeked
inside. She'd ordered a big meal—an entrée with sides,
cornbread, a salad, and a slab of Patty's apple-cranberry
crunch pie for dessert. It struck me as strange that she'd
have such an appetite on the day she'd received such up-
setting news. Then again, Patty's diner offerings were
delicious and hearty, the ultimate comfort foods. Some
people had no appetite when they were upset. Others
used food for consolation. It appeared Aileen was the latter type.

I carried the food down the hall and knocked on her
door. "I've got your dinner, Aileen."

As before, the door opened slightly and she reached
a hand out to take the bag, avoiding eye contact with me.
"Thanks," she rasped. "What do I owe you?"

"Nothing," I said. "It's on the house." No way would
I nickel-and-dime the woman under the circumstances,
though it was considerate of her to offer.

I walked back to the lobby to find Rocky unpacking
our food bags and Pebble filling him in on her new job.
"I'll start as a hostess, but Patty said she'll train me to
work as a server, too."

Rocky reached out and chucked her chin. "I'm proud
of you, Pebble. 'Our labor preserves us from three great
evils—weariness, vice, and want.'"

She rolled her eyes. "Which annoying philosopher
came up with that?"

"Voltaire," Rocky said. "You'd know that if you took
a philosophy class like I keep suggesting."

His daughter shrugged. "Why do I need a class when I've got you quoting ancient Greeks to me nonstop?"

"Voltaire wasn't Greek," Rocky said. "He was French. And he lived and wrote during the Enlightenment."

"The Enlightenment?" Pebble rolled her eyes again, adding a groan for good measure. "That's back when you were born, right?"

Ignoring her jibe, he beamed at his daughter. "Rumor has it you aced your finals."

She leaned back in her chair and raised her palms. "Was there ever any doubt?"

"Wish I could say the same about my boys." Both had been honor-roll students in high school but found college a little more challenging. J.J. had finally realized he couldn't squeak by with just an hour or two of studying each night, and had begun to apply himself more. Mitch was struggling to stay on top of things, despite being in a study group. Of course, the study group itself might very well be the problem. I suspected a certain cute blonde was proving to be a distraction. I hoped Mitch would learn how to better juggle things next semester.

As we ate, Rocky got us up to date on what had transpired since our earlier Facetime call.

"The officer collected bullet casings and shotgun shells. They're going to check them for fingerprints. Since Tyson Pell has a record, his prints will already be in their system."

"I hope they get a match." Even if Tyson Pell had been the one to shoot up the sign, it was possible he'd worn gloves while loading his guns so that the shells and casings wouldn't bear his prints. But in light of the impulsive behavior he'd displayed at my lodge when he'd broken the model, I doubted the guy would have the patience and forethought to ensure he didn't leave fingerprints. He might not even care if he was caught. After all, he'd received a mere fine for his poaching offense. I wasn't sure what the North Carolina penal code set forth as the punishment for property damage, but it wasn't likely much worse, especially when the property value was relatively low.

I thought aloud now. "Rayan didn't mention the sign being shot up when he went to collect Gus's trail cams or install the No Trespassing signs yesterday. The sign must've been shot up afterward, last night, or earlier today. That's too bad. If the trail cams had still been at the property, maybe one of them would've caught the shooter in action." Photographic evidence would have been a slam dunk for law enforcement.

The fact that the sign had been shot up late yesterday or earlier today also meant that Tyson Pell had been skulking around the mountain, managing to hide from law enforcement. The thought gave me the creeps. The guy was dangerous and unhinged. I hoped he'd stay far away from my lodge.

I remembered then that Goodwin had told Paulette and her entourage that they could come back here on Friday to discuss their remaining concerns. Pell might be planning to return to the lodge then, along with the others. I decided to nip things in the bud. I pulled out my phone, used my thumbs to type "Frost Property Management Beech Mountain" into my browser, and tapped the highlighted number to dial it. The phone rang four times before transferring me to voice mail.

Paulette's recorded voice came over the line, sounding much more cheerful than it had when she'd been at my lodge yesterday. "Hello! You've reached Paulette Frost, president of Frost Property Management. I'm handling a property matter at the moment, but your call is very important to me. Please leave a message and I'll get back to you as soon as possible. Have a wonderful day!"

I waited for the beep and left a message. "Hello, Paulette. It's Misty Murphy from the Mountaintop Lodge. I just wanted to let you know that there's been an unfortunate incident. Mr. Goodwin has passed away unexpectedly. Please inform the others in your group and let them know there won't be a meeting at my lodge on Friday after all. Thank you."

Paulette would probably call me back for details. Not that I had many. But I supposed I could put her in touch with Rayan so he could give her contact information for Goodwin's attorneys—or solicitors, as they called them in England. I certainly wouldn't put her calls through to Aileen. The poor woman had been through enough.

CHAPTER 14

Misty

My guests were far more solemn when they returned from the slopes Tuesday evening than they had been the night before. Most went straight to their rooms, including Sebastian. I was glad he didn't choose to fill the great room with his range of rank body odors again.

My sons and Pebble watched a movie in their room before calling it a night at ten o'clock. All of them had to get up early for work tomorrow. *Welcome to adulthood.*

I checked the local weather forecast on my phone before turning off my light. Temperatures were expected to plummet overnight, with high winds and heavy snowfall. Near-blizzard conditions would continue into the morning. My guests and I were likely to be snowbound tomorrow. Sighing, I returned my phone to my night table, turned off the light, and settled in.

Even with Yeti's warm, comforting body curled up against me, I slept fitfully. A *tap-tap-tap* sounded in my dreams, like the finger of Nigel Goodwin's ghost tapping on my window. I woke to realize the sound was real. Tossing back the covers, I went to the window and opened the interior shutters to discover the brisk wind rattling a sled that had been haphazardly leaned against the outside wall. Lest the noise bother my guests across the hall, too, I felt around my floor for my snow boots, slid my feet into them, and ambled out of my room. I'd only be outside for a matter of seconds, so I hadn't bothered with my coat. *Big mistake.* I exited the lodge through the exterior door at the end of the hall, still in my nightgown and still half-asleep. A gust of frigid wind blew straight up my gown, raising it to my waist. *Yikes!* My eyes popped wide and every orifice in my body puckered. If a blast of arctic air on bare skin wasn't enough to instantly render someone fully awake, I didn't know what was.

I pulled the sled away from the wall and lay it flat on the snow. The noise dealt with, I hurried back inside before my nether regions suffered frostbite. I climbed back into my warm bed and pulled Yeti up next to me. She stretched out a paw, yawned, and began to purr, the sound and sensation soothing me.

Wednesday morning came much too quickly. After getting a fire going in the great room, I waited at the door of my lodge for the breakfast buffet to be delivered. Today, Pebble had been assigned the task of bringing the food over. I saw her in the dimly lit parking lot, fighting the wind as she attempted to keep the stainless-steel cart on course. The wind caught it and took it full circle as she desperately hung onto the handle, sliding on the pavement. She looked like an unwitting rider on a carnival spinning-teacup ride. If she couldn't get the cart under control, it might crash into one of my guest's vehicles.

I threw on my thick coat, attached my crampons to

my snow boots for traction, and rushed outside, meeting her halfway across the parking lot. I grabbed the front of the cart, helping to hold it steady. Sleet pelted our faces like icy buckshot, and we had to blink it out of our eyes as we made our way to the door. No doubt today's weather would further delay the hot tub delivery.

As we drew close to the lodge, a gust of wind blasted us, causing both us and the cart to veer toward Sebastian's Challenger. I threw my body between the cart and his car. I'd rather suffer a bruise than have to pay for damage to Sebastian's vehicle. Luckily for me, my thick coat cushioned the cart's blow. A second gust from the opposite direction blew us toward the Jensens' Outback and, even with the spiky cleats on my boots, I scrambled to stay on my feet.

Bam! I barked my shin on the Outback's trailer hitch. The impact felt like someone had taken a sledgehammer to my leg. I cried out in agony, borrowing a curse substitute from Rocky. "Mountain climber!"

When we'd finally managed to wrangle the cart inside, Pebble swiped snow and sleet from her face and exhaled in relief. "What a way to start a new job!"

"You're definitely earning your pay today." I was too. My shin throbbed.

My boys emerged from their room a few seconds too late to join in the rescue, but they helped Pebble unload the cart as I started the coffee. Rocky and Molasses came up the hall, too. After greeting us, Rocky attempted to take Molasses outside for a potty break. The dog wasn't having it. He took two steps outside and attempted to turn around and reenter the lodge. When Rocky didn't allow him back inside, he raised his rear leg and relieved himself on the wooden black bear statue that stood beside the doors. Normally, I'd be none too happy about the dog soiling my bear and the entrance but, in these conditions, I couldn't blame him. Rocky let the dog back inside, where Molasses shook the snow off his fur, his tags and collar jangling. Rocky grabbed a snow shovel to relocate the offending yellow snow from the bear's base to the woods.

Once the breakfast buffet was set up, Pebble glanced out the windows, where the wind continued to roar and snow filled the air, blocking the view of the woods behind the lodge. "There's no way the lifts will be operating today." She released a soft sigh. "My first day of vacation and I won't get to snowboard."

J.J. stepped up next to her. "Yeah. This storm blows. But think how epic the powder will be once it's over."

I gestured to the restaurant cart. "Go get your coat and help Pebble get that back to the diner."

J.J.'s eyes brightened at the opportunity to play her hero. He hurried back to his room and returned in full winter gear. The two of them headed out the door with the cart. Rather than looking terrified by the wind as she had earlier, Pebble threw back her head and laughed as she and J.J. slipped and slid their way across the parking lot. Thank goodness no diners had yet ventured out in this mess. The two would've had a hard time avoiding cars.

When Rocky came back inside, the two of us grabbed cups of coffee and filled our plates. Mitch did the same, and the three of us took seats near the fire. J.J. joined us when he returned from the diner.

We were just starting our meal when a Watauga County Sheriff's Department SUV eased up in front of the lodge. Although the vehicle was four-wheel drive, conditions outside were so bad that chains had been installed on all four tires.

Deputy Yona Highcloud slid out of the SUV. I'd met her back in September at the same time I'd met Officer Hardy, after the death of the yoga instructor. Deputy Highcloud was a petite woman in her late fifties, a member of the Cherokee tribe, with long black hair intermixed with snowy-white strands. Her hair was gathered into a braid that hung down the back of her thick coat. For extra warmth, she wore a knit beanie under her standard sheriff's campaign hat today.

Her arrival caught me off guard, and sent a cold shiver through my body, much as the blast of cold air up my nightgown had done last night. *This can't be good.* On the upside, her unanticipated visit took my mind off my smashed shin.

I scurried to the door and opened it for her. "Good morning, Deputy Highcloud."

She came inside and stamped her feet to clear her boots of snow. "Someone must have angered Oonawieh Unggi." When she saw my puzzled expression, she clarified. "Cherokee wind spirit."

"Ah." Turning from the weather to the reason for her visit, I bit my lip. "Given that you're out in a blizzard, I take it this isn't a social call."

"Not in the least."

I exhaled a long breath. "Can I get you a cup of coffee before you ruin my day?"

She chuckled mirthlessly. "I'd love one. Thanks."

She came farther into the lodge. Rayan was the only guest who'd already come out for breakfast. I supposed it wasn't a surprise. He probably had yet to fully adjust to Eastern Time from Greenwich Mean Time. And a recently deceased boss might give anyone a sleepless night. He'd likely have to search for a new job when he returned to London.

He'd just taken a bite when he glanced up from his plate. His eyes flashed in alarm when he spotted the uniformed deputy sheriff, but he made no effort to address her. He seemed to have trouble swallowing his food. He probably realized the deputy's visit pertained to his dead boss. *Could his throat be clogged with emotion? Or was it something else?* Given the season, my mind went to Scrooge's reaction in *A Christmas Carol*, when he saw the ghost of Jacob Marley and chalked up the apparition to his meal coming back on him. *"You may be an undigested bit of beef, a blot of mustard, a crumb of cheese, a fragment of underdone potato. There's more of gravy than of grave about you, whatever you are!"*

Rocky stood to shake her hand. "'Mornin', Deputy."

She pulled off her gloves, shoved them into the pockets of her coat, and took his hand. "Rocky."

I introduced her to my sons, then poured her a mug of coffee. As she took it from me, she angled her head to indicate the west wing. "Let's take this down to your room."

I turned to my boys. "I'll be tied up for a bit."

"No worries," Mitch said. "We can take care of things out here."

Deputy Highcloud followed me down the hall to my room. We stepped inside and I held out a hand, inviting her to take a seat at the table. I closed the door quietly behind her. Once she'd sat, I joined her. Yeti sauntered over, swishing her tail. The deputy reached down to allow my cat to sniff her hand. "Remember me, girl?"

After giving the woman's hand a sniff, Yeti rubbed against it. The deputy scratched the cat's ears for a few seconds before returning her attention to me. "I need to see your exterior security camera footage from Monday night."

Uh-oh. "I'm afraid there might not be much to see."

"Why's that?"

I winced. "Because I didn't clean the lenses before I went to bed." I explained how snow had repeatedly accumulated on the cameras throughout the day, and how I'd twice used the long-handled duster to clear them. "It seemed like a futile exercise."

"Show me the footage anyway," she said. "Start the feed from the last time you cleaned the camera."

"Of course. We can use the computer at the front desk or I can pull it up on my personal laptop here."

"Laptop's fine."

I rounded up my laptop, plugged it in, and booted it up. After logging in, I pulled up the website where my security camera files were stored. I selected the feed for the exterior camera on the western side of the building and scrolled through the grayish blur on the feed until the video showed the blur becoming lighter and lighter. Finally, it cleared entirely and an image broke through—me, looking up at the lens, the duster in my hand. I tapped the handle against my other hand to shake the snow from it, then trudged off to clean snow from the guest room windows and the remaining exterior cameras. Bit by bit, snow accumulated on the lens again, until the feed was totally blocked out again twenty minutes later. The feed became dark gray and remained that way as we forwarded through the night. As the sun rose, the blur lightened slightly to a pale gray. The next thing we saw was the duster moving back and forth across the lens again, then J.J.'s face as he looked up at the camera, the cleaning tool in his hand.

The feed went on to show J.J. tossing the duster aside, grabbing a sled, and climbing the steps of the ladder to the top of the snow pile. Mitch grabbed another sled and joined him. They slid down the hill several times, until J.J. bent over and picked something up from the snow at the bottom. *Goodwin's nose.* He held it out to show it to Mitch. The two returned the sleds to the side of the lodge and walked out of camera range as they headed inside.

We took a quick look at the feeds from the other exterior cameras. They, too, were blocked by snow for most of the day and all of the night. The deputy released a long, frustrated breath.

"I'm so sorry," I said. "I should have made sure to clean the lenses again before I went to bed."

"The snow would have just blocked them again," she said. "It wouldn't have mattered."

I was afraid to ask, but I had to know. "Why *does* the video matter?"

Highcloud pinned me with a pointed look. "Aileen Goodwin wants to take her husband's remains with her when she flies back to London this weekend, so the medical examiner expedited his autopsy. They got the results last night and sent them over to my office."

A queasy feeling overtook me. The M.E.'s office would only have involved the sheriff's department if the death was suspicious. "What did the report say?"

"The assistant M.E. noted some slight bruising around and under Mr. Goodwin's nose. One of your guests told her they'd seen him get hit in the face with skis."

"That's right," I said. "Laurie Jensen mentioned it."

"The bruises could have been caused by his goggles and the skis themselves. There was no evidence of major trauma, no toxicity. He had some alcohol in his system, but well below the level to be intoxicated."

"But that's good news, isn't it?" After all, if he'd

been murdered, they'd have found a stab wound, a bullet wound, some sign of blunt force trauma, or, at the very least, some proof he'd been poisoned. *Right?*

"Turns out he died of a heart attack."

"A heart attack," I repeated, relieved. I'd upset myself for nothing. "Natural causes, then?"

"Not exactly."

"What do you mean?"

"Do you recall how cold it was overnight Monday?"

I thought back. "It snowed, so it must have been below freezing. I don't think it was much under thirty-two degrees though."

"You're right. It was thirty degrees overnight here in Beech Mountain Monday." She explained that it was routine practice for the medical examiner to check the deceased's core temperature immediately when they arrived on a scene. "The victim's body temperature helps the M.E. determine how long the person has been dead. Over time, the body's core temperature will adjust and eventually reach equilibrium with the surrounding ambient temperature."

"Makes sense." Science had never been my forte, but this principle was easy enough to understand and relatable. After all, items taken out of the oven or refrigerator would eventually become room temperature if left out long enough—not that I should be comparing a human being to a tray of blueberry muffins or a package of frozen peas.

"Of course, the fact that Nigel Goodwin was buried in snow has to be taken into consideration." Highcloud explained that the assistant M.E. also used an infrared thermometer to verify the temperature of the snow. "The snowpack was twenty-five degrees. In light of this fact, Mr. Goodwin's body temperature should have measured somewhere between a low of twenty-five degrees and a high of ninety-eight point six, the normal human body temperature."

I nodded to let her know I was following.

She cocked her head. "Guess what Nigel Goodwin's body temperature was when the assistant medical examiner arrived and recorded it?"

My mind flashed an image of the man, his lifeless eyes fringed with snowy lashes. I gulped, forcing down the horror that clogged my throat. "Lower than twenty-five?"

She tapped her nose to indicate I was correct. "It was nineteen."

My mind spun like the catering cart in the parking lot earlier. "How could that be?" The number didn't jibe with the facts—or at least the facts as we currently knew them.

"That's what I'm here to find out," said the deputy. "Someone, somehow, for some reason decided to turn Nigel Goodwin into a human popsicle."

That explains why Goodwin wasn't wearing his ski jacket and pants when they found him buried in the snow outside my lodge. My mind went woozy, and I feared I'd fall out of my chair. I bent over and put my head between my legs. Yeti took my position as an invitation to play with my hair and batted it about with her paws.

The deputy put a reassuring hand on my back. "Take a slow, deep breath, Misty. I'm sorry, but it looks like I'm going to need your help on this."

After a few seconds passed, I freed Yeti's claws from my tangled hair and was able to sit back up without feeling like I'd keel over. "I don't understand. I thought they'd determined Goodwin died of a heart attack."

"He did. The assistant M.E. believes he suffered the heart attack while . . ." Highcloud seemed to be trying to come up with words that wouldn't make me woozy again. She went with "during the process." She gave me a pointed look. "I've made you privy to this information only because I need your help. You've witnessed the interactions Mr. Goodwin has had with people here at the lodge, and you're likely to offer the most objective assessment." She pulled a notepad and pen from her pocket, prepared to take notes old-school style. "Do you know anyone who had a beef with Nigel Goodwin?"

The most obvious people were the locals. After all, they'd come to my lodge ready to do battle with the developer. "Tyson Pell is the first person who comes to mind. He lives across the road from the resort property. He came to the lodge Monday afternoon with a group of local business owners and residents to confront Goodwin. They weren't happy about the proposed development. Pell might have also shot up the sign at the resort property. Rocky called the local police about that yesterday. There's a guy named Gus, too. He's a wildlife photographer and rehabilitator. He left cameras on the resort property to document the animal activity there. He doesn't want the resort to be built, either. He's afraid it will negatively impact wildlife."

She nodded. "I'm familiar with those two. The Beech Mountain Police have filled me in. I've been told that Goodwin's assistant collected the cameras from the property and turned them over to the police yesterday."

"That's right," I said, "though I think Gus has the cameras now."

A V formed between her brows. "What makes you think that?"

"Gus came to the lodge late yesterday afternoon

asking for them. He didn't know that they'd been turned over to the police, or that Goodwin had died. I broke the news to him on both counts. He seemed a little irritated that Rayan had turned the cameras over to Officer Hardy. He thought it was going to involve a lot of red tape to get them released from the police department. I reminded him that he had called the department earlier asking about his rights to collect them after Goodwin told him to stay off the resort property. It's my understanding that he went straight to the police station to get the cameras after he left the lodge."

"That's not *my* understanding," she said, looking thoughtful, "but Officer Hardy can clear things up when he arrives. For now, tell me more about this group of local protestors."

"A woman named Paulette Frost was the group's ringleader," I said, "or maybe *spokesperson* is a better word. She runs a property management company. She's afraid the resort's hotel would compete with the rentals she manages. I called her yesterday evening and left her a voice mail to let her know that Goodwin had passed away, so there was no reason for her group to come back on Friday when they had planned to meet with him again."

"Did she ask a lot of questions when she called you back?"

"She didn't call me back," I said. "Not yet anyway." *That was surprising, wasn't it? Shouldn't she be curious?* I certainly would have wanted more details if I'd been in her position.

Highcloud seemed to have the same thought. Her brows quirked in question. "Anyone else?"

"None of the others in the group stood out to me."

"What about your guests?" she asked. "The potential investors?"

The only one of my guests who'd seemed directly at odds with Goodwin was Cochrane. "I overheard Sebastian Cochrane telling other investors he'd only come here for the free ski vacation."

She mused aloud. "He'd taken a spot from a legitimate investor." Her eyes narrowed slightly, her crow's feet crinkling. "Do you know if Goodwin was aware that Cochrane had no intention of investing in the resort?"

"He might have sensed it. Sebastian heckled him during the first pitch session. He said Goodwin had better have done his homework this time because a resort Goodwin had planned to build in Canada hadn't worked out." It wouldn't be a huge surprise if the two men had later had words over the issue. *Could the bruising around Goodwin's nose have been caused by Sebastian punching him while Goodwin was wearing his goggles?* I barely had time to consider the thought before the deputy moved on.

"What about Mr. Goodwin's assistant? Rayan Gandapur?"

"Rayan clearly wasn't happy with the way things were going." I told her how he'd confronted Goodwin about his dissatisfaction with his work. "He said, 'This job is nothing like you said it would be.' Rayan expected to see the world and enjoy the places they traveled to, but there were always unanticipated problems coming up that Goodwin made his assistant deal with."

"Like tramping through deep snow to remove wildlife cameras from the resort property?"

"Exactly."

"Anyone else?" she asked.

"This might be nothing," I added, "but Aileen and Nigel Goodwin didn't share a bed." I told her how the convertible sofa bed had been used, and mentioned the CPAP machine I'd seen. "Maybe they only sleep in separate beds because one of them snores. But they don't seem to share a real connection. Aileen took their rental car yesterday even after Nigel told her he'd need it to take the investors to see the resort property. He wasn't happy about it at all."

"Did she undermine him on purpose?"

"I don't know." I told her about the argument I'd overheard. "I felt bad for Aileen. It seemed like she wanted her husband's attention, but he wasn't giving it to her."

The deputy's head bobbed slowly as she processed this information and jotted down some notes. She reached into the pocket of her coat, pulled out a cell phone, and placed it on the table. She typed in a code and tapped the icon to bring up the text messages. "This is Nigel Goodwin's phone. Take a look."

I leaned in to better see the screen. There was a series of five text messages from Nigel Goodwin to his wife Monday night between 8:30 and 9:42, asking her to come to the ski resort to pick him up. She'd never responded. Highcloud showed me his recent calls list, which indicated he'd placed two outgoing calls to her that night, as well. The short length of the calls—twenty-one and eighteen seconds—indicated he'd probably left her a voice mail each time. A conversation would have taken longer.

The deputy asked, "When did Aileen return to the lodge?"

I thought back. "I don't recall the exact time, but it was early evening. She had a take-out bag from an Italian restaurant in Banner Elk. Rocky and I sat down to have dinner ourselves right after she returned."

"Did she leave the lodge later that evening?"

"Not to my knowledge, but I can't say for certain. I was back and forth to my room a few times and took care of some things around the lodge. The footage from my interior security cameras would tell you whether she left."

Deputy Highcloud showed me another set of texts, these sent from Goodwin to Rayan between 8:30 and 9:30 Monday evening, the verbiage evidencing his increasing frustration with his assistant.

The first read: *I need a ride back to the lodge from the ski resort. Let me know when you can come.*

The second was more insistent: *Rayan, come get me at the ski resort. NOW.*

By the third, Goodwin's patience was gone: *I've left you three voice mails! Where the bloody hell are you?*

I looked from the screen to the deputy. "Rayan ignored the messages? Just like Aileen did?"

"It certainly looks that way."

I wondered what excuses they might offer for failing to respond to Nigel's pleas, whether they'd tell the truth when questioned.

Highcloud tapped her pen against her pad. "Let's look at this another way. Do you know anyone who would have the ability to freeze something the size of Nigel Goodwin?"

Yikes! The question made me shudder. But then I myself froze as an image flashed in my mind. The printout of the ice-cream shop that was for rent down the mountain in Boone. "I have something to show you! I'll be right back."

The deputy made a motion as if she was locking her lips and pointed at me, silently directing me to remain mum about the information she'd shared. I gave her a nod to let her know I understood. I left my room and strode to the housekeeping closet, closing the door behind me in case a guest happened by. I bent over the large recycling bin where I accumulated the items from the individual bins in the guest rooms. I rummaged through it until I found the printout. Lest Daphne and Jean-Paul come to breakfast now and see me with the paper, I tucked it into the back pocket of my jeans, out of sight.

I returned to my room, removed the printout from my pocket, and handed it to Deputy Highcloud. "I found that in the Fourniers' trash can yesterday. I picked it out and placed it with the recyclables."

She ran her eyes down the page. "Why would they be looking at an ice-cream shop to rent?"

I raised my palms. "I have no idea." No idea unrelated to murder, at least.

It crossed my mind that properties up for sale or rent often had keys kept in a lockbox on-site for easy access. Maybe the Fourniers had watched the realtor open the box and made note of the code. Or maybe the ice-cream shop had a keyless entry with a numeric pad and they'd obtained the entry code. I had no idea how they might have accessed the ice-cream shop late Monday night, but I did know one thing. A commercial ice-cream freezer would be big enough to hold a human body. *Gulp.*

I recalled how Daphne had become defensive when Sebastian had questioned Goodwin's record with the adventure resorts. "Daphne claimed that she and her husband had invested in all of Goodwin's resorts and been happy with their returns." *But with the Alberta resort being tied up in court, that couldn't be true, could it?* "She even initiated a wire transfer right then and there to invest in the resort here."

The deputy's expression told me she found the situation questionable, too.

I recalled the first time I'd met Tyson Pell, when he'd stopped at the resort property while Rocky and I were checking things out. "Tyson Pell has a large deep freezer in his garage. The wide chest kind." I held my hands out as far as I could to each side to illustrate its size. "There's a huge gun cabinet in the garage, too."

She jotted some notes, and tapped on Goodwin's phone again, bringing up his photos. "I need to know who's who. Tell me who these people are."

The first image she showed me was a closeup of Goodwin on a ski lift, snow-covered ridges in the distance behind him, the ever-present smile on his face, to which his nose was still happily attached. *What a thought.* Most of the images on Goodwin's phone were selfies. As Highcloud scrolled through Goodwin's recent photos and videos, I named the people in the images. There was Goodwin at the top of the mountain flanked by Celeste and Emilio Salazar, smiles all around. One of him and Amari Lott at the base of the mountain, Amari looking stiff and unsure on his skis. Goodwin taking a break to warm up at one of the ski resort's fire pits with Kyle and Laurie Jensen. Various photos of him with the other potential investors. A pic of Goodwin and Sebastian Cochrane raising mugs of beer in the resort's taproom. The final photo was of Goodwin by himself, the mountain behind him, the resort's lights bright against the dark night sky. The data above the photo said the picture had been snapped at 9:26 p.m. Monday night. Goodwin had probably snapped it just before boarding the lift for his final run of the day.

The deputy went to turn off the screen when something caught my eye. I pushed her hand aside and cried, "Wait!"

CHAPTER 15

Misty

Highcloud's brows lifted as I used my fingers to enlarge the image. There, on Goodwin's ski goggles, was the faint reflection of a platinum-haired woman in a dark gray blazer, a fuzzy white circle on her lapel.

I pointed to the image. Though the reflection was blurry and indistinct, I had no doubt the woman was Paulette Frost. "That's the woman who owns the property management company. Paulette Frost. I'm sure of it. She's wearing the same blazer she had on when she came to my lodge." I pointed to the white circle. "That's her snowflake pin." *What had she been doing at the resort? Confronting Goodwin again?* She wasn't in ski gear, so she certainly hadn't been skiing.

"If she returns your call," Highcloud said firmly, "don't tell her anything. Give her my number and tell her to call me."

"Of course."

The deputy jotted a note on her pad, turned off the phone, and tucked it back into her pocket. "Play me the footage from your interior security cameras. If I can't see what was going on outside the lodge, I'd at least like to see what was happening inside."

I pulled up the interior camera feeds. The video currently showed Rocky and my boys eating breakfast in real time, and Rayan surreptitiously keeping a close eye on the hallway where the deputy and I had gone. At least, he assumed he was being surreptitious. He had no idea we were watching him on the monitor. He only poked at his food now, apparently having lost his appetite. Maybe his gut was too full of guilt to hold the serving of grits on his plate.

The deputy directed me to start the feed Monday morning, as the pitch session wrapped up and the locals arrived to voice their protests. The screen showed a fish-eye view of the investors leaving the great room, then returning to the lobby minutes later in their ski gear to collect their lift tickets from Goodwin. They crossed paths with Paulette Frost as she barged into my lodge, leading her army of anxious residents and business owners. The security camera had no audio, so I paraphrased the confrontation I'd overheard between the group and Goodwin, informing the deputy of the concerns they'd expressed. After a few minutes, most of the group departed, leaving only Tyson Pell and Gus behind. When Pell flicked the tiny human figure into the fireplace, the deputy issued a *hmm*. When he flipped over the table, breaking the model, she issued a longer *hmmmm*.

Her eyes narrowed as she watched Gus continue to plead with Goodwin, even after Pell's temper tantrum. "Gus doesn't know when to quit, does he?"

"He's persistent, that's for sure. He's devoted his life to helping animals."

Gus's body language spoke volumes as Goodwin advised him on screen that his cameras would not be returned. He went stiff, his face contorted in anger, his hands fisted. Then he turned and stormed out of the lodge.

Highcloud reached out and stopped the feed. "He's a big, strong guy. He could have carried Goodwin's body with no problem."

"I just can't see it." I recalled what he'd said the first time I'd met him: *"I believe we should live and let live."* "He rescues wildlife and he's against hunting. He might've gotten angry at Goodwin, but I don't think it's in his nature to be violent."

"Violence is in everyone's nature," Highcloud said. "Under the right circumstances."

I supposed she was right. I'd fight to the death to protect my sons.

The deputy restarted the video, which now showed the interaction between Goodwin and his assistant. Rayan looked only slightly less angry than Gus, and stormed out of the lodge with just marginally less rage.

We fast-forwarded through the afternoon, which showed me and my boys going in and out of rooms with our housekeeping carts, until my sons finished and left to snowboard at the ski resort. Highcloud made a backward rotating motion with her hand. "Go back. I want to see when Aileen left the lodge."

I looked up at the ceiling in thought. *When had she gone?* I recalled knocking on the door to the Goodwins' room Monday morning, not long after Nigel had begun his pitch session. I had listened in for about a quarter hour before starting my housekeeping rounds. The Goodwins' room was the first one I'd cleaned. Aileen had headed off when I arrived.

I took the video back to 10:15. On the screen, I started

off down the hall with my cart, shrinking and becoming less distinct as the distance between me and the security camera increased. I raised a hand to knock on the Goodwins' door, and my mouth flapped as I called out. Aileen emerged. My housekeeping cart blocked the exit door at the end of the hall as I disappeared into the room. She slunk up the hall, stopping at the corner to peek into the great room where her husband was making his presentation. She waited until he turned his back, then bent low behind his audience and scurried, hunched over, out of the lodge.

Whoa. There was no doubt in my mind now. She hadn't forgotten that he'd planned to use the SUV to transport the investors to the resort site. She'd clearly been trying to abscond in the vehicle without him noticing and stopping her. I turned to Deputy Highcloud. "It looks like she was trying to sabotage her husband by taking off in their rental car." *But why would she undermine him?* After all, she stood to lose, too, if the investors didn't put their money into the resort project. From what I'd overheard her say during their argument in the hallway—that she'd given up a job she loved for him—I surmised she wasn't currently employed. Presumably, she relied on her husband's income. But maybe the other resorts were earning enough that they could live on the profits. The Goodwins might have amassed sufficient wealth by now that they could live out the rest of their lives in comfort regardless of whether any more resorts were built.

Highcloud directed me to find the footage of Aileen's return. We watched her come into the lodge early that evening with her take-out order and go straight to her room. Rayan returned not long after his boss's wife and

went to his room, as well. Then, Amari Lott limped his
way in.

The deputy pointed at the screen. "Did he get injured?"

"I'm not sure why he was limping," I said. "I noticed
it at the time. He had a ski lesson that afternoon, and
from what I saw on the resort's webcam he was a beginner. I figured he'd gotten a blister or maybe put too
much pressure on his knee trying to execute turns." He
certainly wouldn't be the first person to do that—or the
last.

On the screen, Amari went into his room, coming out
a short time later with his ice bucket. Hobbling down the
hall, he filled the bucket with ice from the machine in
the guest laundry and returned to his room.

We sped up the feed through the lulls and slowed
it to actual speed at critical moments. The remaining
guests trickled in throughout the evening. Just after ten
o'clock, my boys returned, followed not long afterward
by Daphne and Jean-Paul, Kyle and Laurie, Celeste and
Emilio, and finally Sebastian. Sebastian pulled off his
boots and put his feet up on the ottoman. The stench
of his foot odor was obvious from the expressions on
Rocky's face and mine. A few minutes later, Sebastian got up and went to his room. Shortly thereafter, I
dimmed the interior lights in the lobby, and Rocky and
I turned in, too.

We sped up the feed again. To my surprise, Sebastian came out of his room not long after I'd retired. He
exited the lodge. Seconds later, beams from headlights
flashed across the front windows. Maybe even more than
one set. He must've left in his car. But had someone else
been outside, too? In a second vehicle?

Highcloud paused the feed. "Do you know where Sebastian went?"

"I have no idea. This is the first I've become aware that he left the lodge Monday night."

We continued to watch the feed. Around midnight, Amari came out of his room in his pajamas and slippers. As earlier, he had his ice bucket in his hand, and lumbered to the laundry room to refill it. At least now I knew for sure who was responsible for the late-night noise that had woken me.

Highcloud squinted at the screen. "Looks like he suffered way more than a blister. Maybe he took a hit to the knee—or a kick."

Though she hadn't come right out and said so, the implication was clear. Amari's knee could have been injured in a struggle with Nigel Goodwin.

The deputy turned from the screen to me. "I take it he sat out on skiing yesterday?"

"No, he didn't sit out. He went to the resort along with the rest of them."

Her brows inched up. "Was he still limping yesterday morning?"

I thought back, but couldn't recall. "I didn't notice."

"No problem." She turned back to the screen. "The camera will tell us."

Amari returned to his room. A few minutes later, Aileen emerged from hers. She, too, was in her nightclothes, though she'd covered them with a thick robe and had donned a knit cap. Rather than slippers, she wore her snow boots. She headed to the front door and went outside, disappearing into the parking lot. She was gone for a quarter of an hour. We saw no headlights come on during the time she was outside. *Does that mean she'd stuck around? What had she been doing outside?* She walked back into the lodge, her hands shoved into the pockets of her robe.

Sebastian returned a little after 2:00 in the morning, the flash of his headlights foretelling his arrival before he walked through the lodge's front door. The fact that he'd driven his car during the night explained why there'd been less snow accumulation on it Tuesday morning relative to the other vehicles. Some of the snow had likely blown off while the car was in motion, and the heat from the engine likely melted much of it, too. He also would have used the wipers and defroster to clear the windshield so he could see while he drove. *But where had he been? And with whom?*

The lodge was completely still for a couple of hours until 4:08 a.m., when Amari came out of his room a third time with his ice bucket in hand. Though he still favored the one leg, his limp was less pronounced than earlier. In my peripheral vision, I noticed the deputy tilt her head ever so slightly. Her head tilted more as he emerged from the guest laundry with yet another full bucket of ice.

"He used a lot of ice," Highcloud observed. "Does he have a cooler in his room?"

"I don't know. He put out the Do Not Disturb placard and declined housekeeping service, so I haven't been into his room since he checked in. I don't recall him bringing a cooler into the lodge when he first arrived, but he wouldn't allow us to help with his things. He said they were *sensitive*."

"Sensitive how?"

"He didn't explain and I thought it would be rude to ask."

After Amari returned to his room, the lodge was quiet again until Rayan came down the dimly lit hall to use the computer in the lobby. He spent only a short time at the device, retrieved his printout, and headed back to his room at the same time I walked up the opposite hall.

I gestured to the screen. "Do you think Rayan's printout could be a clue to Goodwin's murder?" Rayan had seemingly risen early to use the business center while everyone else was still in bed. *Did he have something to hide?*

The epaulets on Highcloud's uniform bunched as she shrugged. "I'll ask him about it."

A few minutes later in the footage, my boys joined me and we started breakfast preparations. Rocky came in from plowing the snow, and Patty brought over the food for the buffet and the pie for Rocky. Some of the guests wandered into the great room for breakfast, including Rayan and Amari, who now moved without any perceptible limp. The two took seats at the table in the back corner. The boys brought Goodwin's nose inside, and the video showed my reaction when I realized what it was. Rocky snatched the nose up off the floor where I'd dropped it and secured it in the drawer.

J.J. watched the desk for a few minutes before Mitch came back inside, walked right past his brother without saying a word, and headed to their room. About half an hour passed before I came back inside, informed J.J. what was going on, and took over at the desk as he rushed down the hall to join Mitch in their room.

The Fourniers arrived in the great room and filled their plates. Aileen got her tea and breakfast without inquiring about her husband or looking around for him. Sebastian arrived, and took a seat with the Jensens. Not long after, the police officer and assistant medical examiner came inside and headed down the hall to speak with Aileen. Highcloud closely watched the reactions of the guests as, minutes later, the officer and assistant M.E. informed them that Goodwin had been found dead.

When we wrapped up the footage, I closed my laptop and Deputy Highcloud phoned Officer Hardy, requesting he come to the lodge to help her interview the guests. When she ended the call, she stood and glanced over at Yeti, who now lay on the windowsill staring out at the snowfall. The enormous flakes were falling straighter now rather than coming in from the sides. "Looks like the wind might have calmed a bit."

I reminded the deputy that the windows in my lodge could be opened from the inside. My inn was only one story, so there was little risk of someone being severely injured if they fell out a window. The windows also gave guests a means of escape in the event of a fire. The lodge had no central air-conditioning. With summer temperatures reaching only into the low seventies, A/C wasn't necessary here. Windows helped keep things fresh and facilitated airflow. "It's possible someone went out their window to avoid being picked up on the interior security cameras."

"Did you notice footsteps outside anyone's window or around the lodge yesterday morning before Goodwin was found?"

"No." Unlike earlier, where my failure to keep the camera lenses free of snow meant critical video evidence hadn't been collected, in this case my insistence that my sons clear the sidewalks of snow bright and early meant that any footprints along the front of the lodge would have been eradicated by the snowblower. "We can ask my boys if they noticed anything. If someone came out a window on the back of the lodge, there would have been footprints, but I walked around with the duster brushing snow off the cameras and windows yesterday, so they might have gotten mixed in with mine. I didn't notice any footprints along the back of the lodge, but I hadn't been looking."

The deputy gave Yeti a final scratch behind the ears and we left my room. We emerged from the hall to see that several of the guests had come for breakfast by then, and either sat at tables with their food in front of them, or stood at the buffet, filling their plates.

Rocky stood and came over from the table where he'd been drinking coffee. Though the deputy didn't look happy about it, she didn't tell him to buzz off. She seemed to trust him, like she trusted me.

Rocky ran his eyes over my face, assessing, before meeting the deputy's gaze. "Someone killed Goodwin," he surmised softly. "That's why you're here."

The deputy cast a glance my way. "You weren't supposed to say anything."

"I didn't!"

"Body language," she said. "It can speak volumes."

"Don't blame Misty," he said. "I'm a good guesser."

We continued on to the front desk. Molasses sat on his haunches between J.J. and Mitch, enjoying their attention. Highcloud quietly asked my sons if they'd noticed any footprints on the front walkway before they'd cleared it yesterday morning.

"We did," J.J. said, responding for the two. "But they didn't go all the way to the side of the lodge. They only went partway, to where the cars were parked. But there were a bunch of footprints around the bottom of the sledding hill when we first got out there."

The deputy, Rocky, and I exchanged glances. Those footprints probably belonged to the person or persons who'd dumped Goodwin there.

"Where did they lead?" she asked.

J.J. said, "To an empty space in the parking lot."

"Could you tell how many sets there were?"

"No," my son said. "They were all jumbled up, like there were a lot of people, or maybe one person who'd walked around a lot."

The deputy looked to Mitch, who concurred with his brother. After she thanked them, I dismissed my boys. "I'll take over at the desk. You two are free until it's time to start housekeeping rounds."

They headed down the hall to their room.

Officer Hardy's Beech Mountain Police Department SUV pulled up behind the deputy's vehicle outside, the windshield wipers on high speed, throwing off the heavy snow. Rocky held the front door open for the officer as he leaped from his vehicle, slammed the door behind him, and hurried inside, bringing a blast of cold air and a flurry of snow in with him.

Hardy approached the deputy, giving me a nod in greeting as he stepped up to the desk.

"Got a question for you," she said. "That man you told me about, the wildlife guy. Did he pick up his trail cams from the police department?"

"Not yet," Hardy said. "Far as I know, nobody's heard any more from him since his initial call."

Highcloud glanced my way and lifted her chin, silently directing me to fill Officer Hardy in. I told him about Gus's visit to the lodge late yesterday afternoon, how Gus had admitted to removing several cameras before Rayan arrived at the property. "The fact that he'd removed a few of the cameras explained why the numbers weren't all sequential. He gave me the impression that he was heading your way when he left here. I suggested he put some ointment on his scratches and off he went."

"Scratches?" Highcloud and Hardy asked in unison.

"On his wrists." I raised my own hands and turned them over, the inside of my wrists pointed upward to demonstrate. "I figured he got the scratches from the tree bark when he was removing the cameras."

They exchanged a look and Hardy mused aloud. "Could be defense wounds."

"Defense wounds?" It took a second for the meaning to sink in, that Gus might have been scratched defending himself when Goodwin fought back. *Ughhh.* I closed my eyes and sent up a silent prayer. *Please don't let the killer be Gus! The animals need him!*

Highcloud said, "We need to see those scratch marks, find out how he got them."

Hardy said out loud what I was thinking. "He might have decided not to come pick up the cameras from the police department once he realized the scratches were noticeable and would raise questions. Maybe he plans to wait until they heal to come by the station and retrieve his cameras."

Though Hardy's theory made perfect sense, I really hoped he was wrong. Gus might have become angry at Goodwin, but he had good reason to be upset.

Turning to another suspect, Hardy said, "We got a match on the fingerprints found on the shell casings at the resort property."

"Tyson Pell?" the deputy asked, her lack of inflection making the question sound more like a statement than a true inquiry.

"Tyson Pell," Hardy repeated.

"Those prints give us grounds for a search warrant." Highcloud straightened, as if the news had taken some weight off her shoulders. "We can see about searching his place once we're done with the folks here. Let's talk to Aileen Goodwin first."

Hardy angled his head to indicate the east wing. "This way."

As the two walked off, I wondered what they would learn, and whether they'd soon be taking one of my guests away in handcuffs.

CHAPTER 16

Misty

After Officer Hardy and Deputy Highcloud spoke with Aileen Goodwin, they instructed the guests eating breakfast in the great room to stay put, then made their way up and down the hall, knocking on doors, rounding up all of my guests once again. They assembled in the great room—all but Aileen, of course. Many looked rumpled and ungroomed, as if they'd been roused from their beds and had thrown on the first thing they could find. Sebastian was still in his pajamas. If not for Daphne's flaming red hair, I would not have recognized her. She was surprisingly plain without her makeup, especially her lipstick. The group spoke softly among themselves, trying to figure out if anyone knew what was going on. Finally, the entire group was assembled.

Wasting no time, Deputy Highcloud got down to brass tacks. She ran her eyes over the crowd. "We have reason to believe that Nigel Goodwin's death was the result of foul play."

Just like the day before, the group erupted in gasps and murmurs upon hearing the disturbing news. Laurie reflexively put her hands to her infinity scarf once again, grasping it tightly, creating a virtual noose around her own neck. As she began to shake with emotion, Kyle draped an arm over her shoulders. Daphne reached over to take Jean-Paul's hand in hers, holding it tight for reassurance. Sebastian leaned his head back, stared up at the ceiling, and muttered a curse. Amari pulled his phone from his pocket and worked his thumbs over the screen, apparently searching to see what information might have already been made public. Rayan stared at the floor, avoiding eye contact with the others. Was he feeling guilty? And, if so, was it because he'd killed his boss or merely because he'd argued with the man, harbored some anger toward him over how things had played out on Monday?

The always-bold Celeste demanded details. "What makes you think he was intentionally killed?"

Kyle looked from Celeste to the officers and added a question of his own. "Wouldn't it have been obvious from the start if he'd been murdered?"

Daphne said, "Not if he were poisoned." When all heads snapped in her direction, she realized her blunder and blushed darker than her usual rouge. "I did not kill Nigel! I just read a lot of crime novels."

The deputy shut down the speculation. "We are not ready yet to disclose the manner of death."

Sebastian crossed his arms over his chest and snorted. "That means you think one of us killed him, doesn't it?"

Highcloud didn't back down. "We haven't ruled anyone out at this point, including all of you in this room."

Most of the guests appeared taken aback, their eyes going wide as they glanced suspiciously at one another.

"That's it." Sebastian threw up his hands. "I'm going home. The vibe here has gotten way too dark." His chair scraped against the wood floor as he stood.

The deputy made a downward motion with her hand, directing the insolent young man to sit back down. With a begrudging scowl, he slowly lowered himself until he was perched on the edge of the chair, his refusal to fully seat himself another act of rebellion. The deputy kept her eyes locked on him, though her words addressed everyone in the room. "Nobody is leaving the lodge until we've completed our interviews. I'd like all of you to return to your rooms. Officer Hardy and I will come speak to you one by one."

Sebastian glowered at her from his seat. "I know my rights! You can't make me stay. Unless you're putting me under arrest, I have the right to leave."

"That's a common misconception," Officer Hardy said. "Law enforcement has the legal right to detain a person without arrest for a reasonable time for questioning and investigation."

Sebastian's frown faltered. "Well . . . I don't have to say anything to you."

Hardy shrugged. "You're correct there. You have the option to remain silent if you choose, or to get an attorney."

Emilio rolled forward a few inches and stared Sebastian down. "What's your problem? You got something to hide?"

Sebastian jerked his head back as if Emilio had thrown a punch. "No! I didn't do anything!"

"Then stop being a jerk and cooperate. You owe it to the rest of us. You owe it to Nigel Goodwin, too. You basically stole from him, coming here with no intention of investing. You screwed us over, too. A serious investor could have had your space." With that, Emilio rolled himself back into place beside his wife.

Highcloud arched a brow at Sebastian. Cowed by

Emilio's rebuke, he exhaled sharply but stopped arguing. Highcloud dismissed the group, and they shuffled off to their rooms.

The snow continued to come down outside while the officers interviewed the guests. Rocky took a seat by the fire with his dog and a book, and I spent the morning at the desk, fielding questions from guests who'd completed their interrogations and wanted answers they assumed I might have. I rebuffed their inquiries, feigning ignorance, trying hard to sound nonchalant.

Celeste didn't buy my casual act. She narrowed her eyes at me. "There's more, and you know it, don't you?"

I wasn't sure how to respond, and I was afraid to look like a liar, so I simply said, "I'm sure Deputy Highcloud and Officer Hardy will get to the bottom of things. When they do, the information will be made public."

Celeste issued a *harrumph*, turned, and rolled away. Emilio rolled after her.

As I watched them go, I wondered if they could have had something to do with Goodwin's death, and if their visit to my desk had been an attempt to pump me for information. *Had Emilio's reproof of Sebastian been an attempt to gain favor with law enforcement and throw suspicion off himself, or off both himself and his wife? Did the two have reason to want Goodwin dead? If so, what might that reason be?*

Other than their tidiness habits, or lack thereof, I knew only a few details about my guests, things I'd overheard at the meet and greet or gleaned from their behavior or belongings. I decided to do a little digging online, see what else I might learn about them, starting with the most obvious suspects. Aileen and her husband seemed to be at odds, and she'd ventured outside last night for some unknown reason. Even so, I didn't think the spindly woman had the strength to lift her husband's corpse on her own, even if fueled by the fear of detection. For that reason, I mentally set her aside and focused on Sebastian.

The young man's social media accounts were replete with references to the Carolina Hurricanes hockey games, players, and scores. They also contained images of him playing goalie for an amateur hockey team in Raleigh called the Rusty Blades. One photo showed him taking a puck to the chest. Another showed him defending the goal, enormous pads protecting his legs, his knees buckled inward as he hovered just above the ice.

Ice! Oh my gosh! My heart tossed blood about in a frenzy. *Could Sebastian Cochrane have frozen Nigel Goodwin's body on a skating rink before dumping him outside my lodge?*

I pondered the possibility. Beech Mountain Resort had recently eliminated its ice-skating rink to install additional fire pits. The nearest rink was an outdoor recreational one at the Sugar Mountain Resort, a mere five miles—and a twenty-minute winding drive—away. Appalachian Ski Mountain in the nearby town of Blowing Rock also had an outdoor rink. That facility was a twelve-mile, fifty-minute drive from the lodge. Sebastian had been gone long enough Monday night to drive to and from either place with Goodwin's body. *But just how cold is the ice in a rink? And how long would Goodwin have to lie on the ice for his body temperature to be brought down to 19 degrees Fahrenheit?*

A quick internet search told me that the best ice temperature for playing hockey was around 16 degrees Fahrenheit, the low temp making the ice hard and fast. A slightly higher temperature was preferred by figure skaters, for softer landings.

It dawned on me that Lake Coffey, a small lake only a short drive from my lodge, had frozen over. Sebastian could have driven to Lake Coffey in mere minutes and had more time to put Goodwin—literally—on ice. Maybe he'd used the missing towel to prevent Goodwin's frozen corpse from dripping water in his car, or laid the dead man on it to drag him from the car to the bottom of the sledding hill. It was possible, wasn't it?

My search had brought up related sites on ice temperature, and a link referencing "salt" caught my eye. I clicked on the link and read the article. The piece discussed the complex interplay between ice and salt, noting that salt reduces the freezing and melting point of water to below the usual 32 degrees. While salt was often used to break up and melt ice on pavement, the salt actually made the temperature of the ice drop to as low as –21 Celsius, or around –5 Fahrenheit. According to the article, the temperature dropped because as the ice melted, energy, in the form of heat, needed to be drawn from the environment to break the hydrogen bond that held the water molecules together. The salt also caused freezing-point depression, meaning it lowered the freezing point of water, making it take longer to refreeze. There was even a formula for freezing-point depression that included a K, an F, a b, and an i. The K and F represented something called the "cryoscopic constant," the b stood for "molality"—*whatever that is*—and the i stood for the van 't Hoff factor—another term unknown to me. The formula was far above my pay grade, but I could vaguely understand the concept. As more ice melted in salty water, more heat would be absorbed, and the temperature of the icy salt water would fall further. The article explained that this interesting interaction between salt and ice was how ice cream could be made without a freezer. The ingredients need only be placed in a bag suspended in a bucket of salted ice, and the contents would freeze quickly due to the extremely low temperature of the salted ice.

I sat back on my stool to process this information. The reference to ice cream in the article naturally made me think of Daphne and Jean-Paul, and their suspicious visit to the ice-cream shop in Boone. But it also made me think of the bags of rock salt that had gone missing from the tool shed, and of Amari Lott and his multiple visits to the lodge's ice machine. Goodwin's body was too big to fit inside the ice machine's storage bin, but if Amari had filled his bathtub with ice and rock salt, he might have been able to soak Goodwin's body in the frigid water and freeze it.

I recalled that one of the suitcases Amari brought to the lodge had appeared to be especially heavy. He'd had a hard time pulling it. Could it have been filled with fifty-pound bags of rock salt? Maybe he hadn't taken the rock salt from our tool shed, but had brought his own supply. The stuff was stocked in hardware stores all over the region this time of year, and was even stacked in front of some of the local grocery stores for sale. The thought that such an everyday item could be used for such a nefarious purpose turned my own blood to ice in my veins.

The sun suddenly broke through the clouds outside, filling the outdoors with brilliant light, as if the universe was telling me I was on the right track. Over the next minute or two, the snow dwindled to a smattering of flakes falling here and there. The storm was finally over. *Thank goodness*. The only thing creepier than knowing a murderer might be staying at my lodge would be being trapped by the snow and unable to escape if the killer sought a second victim.

The sunshine brought my mind back to something Sebastian had said, that Banff had three ski resorts, including one called Sunshine Village. I typed the name of the resort into my computer browser to run a search. Once I had the resort's website pulled up on my screen, I leaned in for a better look at the logo. *Hmm.* The emblem contained snowcapped mountains and a sun, like the one I'd seen on the crinkled, torn lift ticket on Laurie's jacket. But was it the same image? I couldn't be certain. It wasn't especially unique, and I hadn't considered the lift ticket or logo to be significant at the time. *Too bad I didn't pay more attention.* But Rocky had worked at the ski resort here at Beech Mountain when he was young. I figured he might know of other resorts with *sun* in their name, or with logos that featured a sun.

I softly cleared my throat, hoping not to attract attention from the guests lingering over late coffee in the great room. When Rocky looked up from his book, I waved him over to the desk and whispered, "Do you know any ski resorts with the word *sun* in their name or with a sun in their logo?"

Rocky looked up in thought. "Just off the top of my head, there's Sun Valley Idaho, Sun Mountain in Washington State, and Sunlight Mountain. I think that last one is somewhere in Colorado." He angled his head. "Why?"

"Sebastian mentioned that there's a ski resort called Sunshine Village in Banff. I saw an old lift ticket on Laurie's ski jacket that had mountains with a sun in the background on it, and I'm trying to determine if it could be from that resort. She said she's never been to Banff."

Well, she hadn't said it, exactly, but she had shaken her head when Sebastian had asked Kyle and her if they'd ever been there.

A cloud crossed Rocky's face. "You think she might have lied about it? Why?"

I shrugged. "No reason that I know of. I don't know what to think. I'm feeling suspicious of everyone right now. If there's a killer in my lodge, I want to know who it is right away."

"Me, too." He glanced out the window. The sun reflected off the deep snow in the parking lot, and the effect was blinding. "I suppose I'd better get out there and plow the lot again. Folks will get cabin fever if they can't leave the lodge soon."

His words now had me thinking of the haunted hotel in *The Shining*, the guests' ghosts who haunted it and the caretaker who'd gone off the deep end. *Yeesh*. Not exactly a Christmas classic.

As Rocky went to his room to secure his dog and grab his coat, I looked up the ski resorts he'd mentioned. The logo for Sun Valley included a sun with a face. *That's definitely not the logo I saw on Laurie's lift ticket.* The logo for Sun Mountain Lodge in Washington State didn't include a sun at all, just three triangles representing peaks. Sunlight Mountain's logo was just the opposite. It contained no mountains, just a semicircle of yellow sun with pointed rays over an orange arch edged in blue. I found another place called Sunday River in Maine, and its logo had a mountain superimposed over a sun, but the logo was red, clearly not the one I'd seen. *Had Laurie lied about having visited Banff?*

Rocky walked out into the arctic tundra the mountain had become, climbed into his truck, and began to plow the parking lot again. Meanwhile, I searched *Laurie*

Jensen along with the word *Banff*, but nothing came up. Ditto for her name and *Alberta*. When I ran a search for *Laurie Jensen and Rapid City*, several links popped up, including one for an obituary. It was for a Joshua Wagner of Missoula, Montana. He'd died nine months earlier, in late March, at the age of only thirty-eight, killed in an unspecified accident. He was described as an avid outdoorsman who loved the mountains. My thoughts went back to what Emilio had said: *Mountains are dangerous places.* Had Joshua Wagner been killed while climbing or hiking? Taken a fall? Survivors were named and included his wife, three daughters, and his sister Laurie Jensen and brother-in-law Dr. Kyle Jensen of Rapid City, South Dakota. I thought of my sons, the deep bond they shared, and my heart went out to Laurie. Losing a sibling would be devastating, especially one who should have had so many years ahead of him.

The other links detailed various charity boards on which Laurie served, including the Friends of the Library and one that provided school supplies and clothing to underprivileged local children. By all accounts, she seemed like a nice, normal person—generous and selfless even—but I knew from experience that people weren't always who they appeared to be.

My mind circled back to the unidentified lift ticket. *Could it have been from the resort in Banff?* If so, I supposed it was possible that Laurie had lent her ski jacket to someone who'd gone to Sunshine Village. Not everyone owned the proper gear, and it was expensive to outfit yourself. People sometimes borrowed pants, jackets, goggles, or helmets from family or friends. I realized, too, that the lift ticket could have been from a resort in another country, or maybe the logo I'd seen was from another resort with a name that had nothing to do with the sun. In fact, with a little more digging, I discovered that Hunter Mountain ski resort in upstate New York had a logo with a sun and mountains, despite not having the word *sun* in its name.

Hunter. The word took me back to Tyson Pell, his hunting dogs, and the rack of hunting rifles in his truck. I recalled the ball cap he'd been wearing the first time I'd met him, the one with the trophy hunter emblem on it, a deer with an impressive rack of antlers. *Does he only hunt for trophies, or does he also hunt for meat?* The large deep freezer in his garage said he probably ate what he killed, at least the deer anyway. I only wondered if Nigel Goodwin might have shared the frigid space with frozen venison.

Law enforcement had yet to determine how Goodwin got from the ski resort to the sledding area outside my lodge. Maybe Goodwin had been walking back to the lodge and Pell had spotted him. He might have offered Goodwin a ride or, more likely, threatened Goodwin at gunpoint to get into his truck. Having a gun pointed at you, especially at point-blank range, would certainly be enough to cause a heart attack. Could Pell have then put Goodwin in his deep freezer before dumping him outside my lodge? Maybe he'd put Goodwin's body in the freezer while debating how to dispose of him. Pell was clearly an impulsive guy. He might have seized the opportunity to put an end to both Goodwin and the resort, acting without a premeditated plan. Maybe he'd subsequently decided that, rather than dump Goodwin's body someplace it would never be found, he'd ditch it here at my lodge as a warning to others who might attempt to develop the mountain. Or maybe he'd panicked and attempted to make Goodwin's death look like an accident caused by the heart attack or cold temperatures. It seemed to be a viable theory but, at this point, it was only a theory.

The thought of deep freezers brought my mind back to Paulette Frost. She managed a lot of properties in the area. *Are any of them hunting cabins? Do any of them contain a deep freezer?* It seemed ironic that Goodwin had been found buried in snow after Paulette had made her comment that *an avalanche buries everyone.* I couldn't help but think her presence at the ski resort shortly before closing time had been no coincidence. Unlike Pell, who hadn't been seen on the mountain since he'd left my lodge, Paulette had been at the ski resort. Her reflection in Goodwin's goggles proved it. She still hadn't returned my phone call, which seemed suspicious. *Had she offered Goodwin a ride back to the lodge when neither his wife nor his assistant responded to his texts and voice mails, and then taken advantage of the situation to eliminate her competition? Had she done or said something to terrify or upset him so much he suffered a heart attack? Had she been the last person to see him alive?*

CHAPTER 17

Misty

I logged onto the Frost Property Management website and clicked on the menu option titled Vacation Rentals. A dropdown menu popped up, requesting I input the number of people in my party and the dates of my trip so it could search available rentals for a suitable match. The menu also provided a list of amenities that could be checked to narrow down the search. The number of beds, bedrooms, and bathrooms. Slope-side ski-in/ski-out location. Views. Fireplace and outdoor fire pit. Pets allowed. And, of course, there was an option to narrow the listings to those that came with a hot tub.

Unfortunately, yet not surprisingly, a deep freezer was not listed among the searchable amenities. A little inconvenience wasn't going to stop me, though. I put in a variety of dates and search options to view as many listings as possible. The property owners had devised clever names for their properties in the hopes of catching the attention of renters. Hostel La Vista. Sky High House. Black Bear Bungalow. They'd put puns in their descriptions, too. *This property will really 'peak' your interest!* And *Ski bum it on the summit!* The lighthearted, cheesy verbiage almost had me missing Kyle Jensen's dad jokes. They might be corny, but at least they were upbeat. Kyle hadn't made a joke since Goodwin was found dead. Murder was no laughing matter.

I clicked through the photos on each rental option, ignoring the décor and gorgeous mountain views, looking only for a deep freezer. Even a little corner of one would do, just enough to let me know that the property had a deep freezer on site. *Nope. Nope. Nope. Yep!*

A three-story rental called the Treetopper featured a garage on the first floor, a nice amenity for those who didn't want to have to scrape snow from their vehicle's windshield every time they left their rental. Underneath the rudimentary, open staircase that led from the garage up to the first floor were two bright orange plastic sleds, visible through the stair treads. They rested atop a white deep freezer. *Could Paulette have stowed Goodwin's body in that freezer?*

If the property had been rented by vacationers Monday night, it was unlikely, though not impossible. She'd have to have a lot of nerve to sneak a corpse into the garage while renters were upstairs. Then again, the photo also showed that the garage had a service door on the side. She could have dragged Goodwin through the side door without raising the garage door with its accompanying ruckus. The renters might not have even been on site at the time if they'd stayed at the ski resort until it closed and then gone for drinks or food somewhere afterward.

There were a lot of ifs remaining, and they were best resolved by law enforcement. There was a fine line between being helpful and getting in the way, and I didn't want to cross that line. Though I was dying to dig deeper into this theory, I had to satisfy myself with printing out the photos and details in the listing for Deputy High-cloud and Officer Hardy to review.

Now that Mother Nature was done punishing us, one of the town's snowplows rolled slowly by on the parkway, clearing the road as well as my mind. Deputy Highcloud and Officer Hardy would gather the available evidence and do their best to nail the culprit. While I'd keep a keen eye out for clues that might arise, I should stop driving myself crazy with speculation.

Rocky was still in his pickup out in the parking lot. He drove his truck to the exit and drove slowly sideways across it, pushing the pile created by the town's snow-plow onto the area beside my lodge. The pile was so high now it would be months before it could fully melt.

As the deputy finished with each of my guests, many of them left the lodge, presumably to head over to the slopes. Celeste and Emilio. Laurie and Kyle Jensen. Daphne and Jean-Paul. The latter surprised me a little. I'd thought they might have been the ones to put Good-win on ice. Though I'd been trying to keep my mind open to other possibilities, the Fourniers were at the top of my suspects list thanks to the flyer I'd found in their room about the ice-cream shop for rent.

When Sebastian passed the desk in his ski gear, I called out to him. "Have you decided to stay, after all?"

"Yeah," he said. "Figured I might as well finish out the week. It's already paid for."

I wondered if law enforcement had also requested he remain in the area in case they had follow-up questions. "By the way, I noticed a towel was missing from your room yesterday."

He rolled his eyes. "Why is everyone on my case today? First the cops and now you."

On his case? A man had been murdered! *Sheesh.* I

fought a frown. "It's not a big deal," I said. "I just wondered if I'd overlooked it somewhere. A wet towel can mildew if it's not washed right away."

"Look," he snapped. "I took a bath towel with me to the ski resort to wipe down my skis and boots before I put them back in their bags. Gear can't be put away wet or it'll rust."

"I understand. I'd be happy to wash the towel for you. Is it in your car?"

He gave the eye roll an encore performance. "I threw it out at the resort. I didn't realize you'd be giving me the third degree over a two-dollar towel." He reached into his pocket, pulled out his wallet, and retrieved a five-dollar bill. He slapped it down on the counter in front of me. "There. We're even. You can even keep the change."

With that, he paraded out of the lodge. *Jerk.* He'd all but called me cheap. And I'd paid way more than two bucks apiece for the lodge's towels. They were extra-thick premium quality. *Could his rage be feigned, an attempt to throw me off-kilter? To get me to back off?*

I tucked the bill into my pocket. I'd use it to treat myself to a chai tea latte at the local coffee shop or maybe some candy from Fred's General Mercantile. I deserved to enjoy myself after putting up with these sometimes rude and potentially murderous guests.

I heard voices down the hall. Seconds later, the deputy, Officer Hardy, and Amari Lott came out of the hallway and turned into the great room, taking seats around a table at the far back corner. *Had he refused to allow law enforcement into his room?* If that wasn't enough to raise suspicions, I didn't know what was.

I pretended to be working online when, in reality, I was straining so hard to hear their conversation it was a wonder I didn't suffer an aneurysm. Only a few phrases that Amari spoke were discernible. *Security breach. Smoke and mirrors. Got out at the right time.* I tried to write a narrative in my head in which all of those phrases made sense together, but I couldn't.

When the officers dismissed him, Lott walked past my desk. He didn't acknowledge me with so much as a glance. He appeared to be both troubled and lost in thought. *Had his interview with Deputy Highcloud and Officer Hardy gone poorly? Was he afraid he'd inadvertently tipped them off with something he'd said? Had he, in fact, frozen Nigel Goodwin with rock salt and ice in the bathtub in his room? If so, why?*

I turned back to my computer and searched for Amari Lott online. I found only long-ago references to awards won at high school science fairs and first-place wins with the school's robotics team. He had no social media accounts. The guy seemed to value his privacy.

The officers continued their interrogations. As guests completed their interviews and left the lodge, I directed my sons to their rooms to perform housekeeping duties.

Pebble finished her first shift at the diner and returned to the lodge.

"How was your first day on the new job?" I hoped things had gotten better after the rocky start she'd had bringing the breakfast over.

"It was epic!" She stopped and pumped her hands over her head in a raise-the-roof motion. She reached into her pocket and pulled out a wad of bills. "I made over sixty dollars in tips, and that was even with it being a slow day 'cause of the snow." She came around the desk and grabbed me in a hug. "Thank you so much!"

I'd had little to do with her landing the job, but I wasn't about to turn down a hug from the girl. It felt nice to be appreciated, especially for something so minor. I patted her back. "I'm glad it went well."

She released me and inquired about my sons. "When does their shift end? I was hoping we could hit the slopes together this afternoon."

The nature of housekeeping work meant that it wasn't amenable to a specific time schedule, and was finished when it was finished. My boys had worked hard that morning, though, and I figured I could clean any rooms they hadn't finished on their wing. "Let's see how far they've gotten." I motioned for Pebble to follow me.

We found my sons cleaning Celeste and Emilio's room. A pair of ski goggles sat on their night table. I hoped they were a spare pair. As bright as the reflection was off the fresh snow now, it wouldn't be a good day to be without eye protection. At least they'd remembered to apply sunscreen. A tube of 50 SPF lotion stood upright on the dresser. Skiers could get badly sunburned in these conditions without proper precautions.

"Pick up the pace, boys," Pebble teased. "The slopes aren't going to shred themselves."

J.J. said, "I'm planning to work on my nose grab today."

"What?!" I cried. *Hadn't my boys grabbed enough noses recently?*

"Chill, Mom," J.J. said. "It's just a snowboard move." Though he was playing it cool, it was likely for Pebble's benefit.

Mitch shuddered, still as openly freaked out as I was. "Why don't you work on your melon instead?"

I knew squat about snowboarding tricks. They might as well be speaking another language. "When you're done with this room, you're free to go. I'll finish your rounds for you."

J.J., who'd just chastised me for my ignorance, now gave me a grateful smile. "Really? Thanks, Mom!"

A ping sounded as a text arrived on Mitch's phone. He pulled it from his pocket and took a look at the screen. I glanced over. The text read *I'm sooooo bored. You're lucky you're somewhere fun.*

"Who's that from?" I asked.

His face went red and he slid the phone back into his pocket. "No one."

Yeah, right. I ventured a guess. "The cute blonde from your study group?"

J.J. barked a laugh and Pebble tilted her head, brows raised. "You got a boo?"

Mitch ignored the two of them and instead turned on me. "Have you been stalking me on social media?"

Of course I had! The twerp rarely returned my emails or voice mails, claiming nobody talked on the phone anymore and that he didn't check his emails regularly. He'd left me no choice but to peruse his social media posts to see what he was up to down there in Chapel Hill. He had some nerve making accusations. "You can hardly call it stalking. You put your posts out there for all the world to see. And I wouldn't have to check your posts if you'd call me once in a while."

He couldn't argue with that, and he didn't try. He just rolled his eyes and groaned.

I rolled my eyes and groaned right back. Had he not yet realized that I was a cool mom? *Sheesh.* Knowing I'd be pushing my luck to ask for more details, I let the subject drop. As I left the room, I glanced back at the ski goggles. While we'd all assumed the bruises on Goodwin's face had been caused by his ski goggles when he'd either been hit in the face or fallen, my mind produced the image again. The bruises had curved *inward* around the tip of his nose, hadn't they? But ski goggles angled *away* from the nose. Something else must have caused the bruises. *But what?*

My nerves crackled with the thought that I might be on to something. An image of the Goodwins' room popped up in my mind, including Aileen's CPAP machine. The mask on the device curved inward around the nose, but it extended farther down to cover the mouth, as well. It couldn't have been her mask then. Something else had caused the bruising.

I thought back to what I knew about Goodwin's day. He'd made his pitch presentation here at the lodge. He'd then gone to the ski resort, where he'd been hit in the face by an inexperienced skier who'd been carrying his skis horizontally across his shoulders rather than vertically in his arms. But even if Goodwin been hit in the face with the curved tips of the skis, they couldn't have made bruises in the correct shape on either side of his nose, could they? It didn't seem so. The angles would be all wrong. He'd had a beer with Sebastian in the taproom. Could that be where he'd obtained the bruise? Maybe someone had bumped him hard as he'd held the frosty mug of beer to his face. The glass would curve inward and could explain the bruise. But, even if it explained the bruise, it wasn't clear the bruise had anything to do with his death. After all, I had a huge, throbbing bruise on my shin from my run-in with the Jensen's trailer hitch in the parking lot that morning. Like Emilio said, mountains are dangerous places and people got bumped, bruised, and broken up here all the time.

Half an hour later, my boys had finished cleaning the Salazars' room, and all three kids had changed into their snowboarding clothes and packed up their gear. "Have fun!" I called as they headed out of the lodge. "I'll be looking for you on the webcam."

"Creeper!" Mitch called back over his shoulder.

If he'd been trying to get a rise out of me, he'd succeeded. I scurried around my desk, followed them out the door, and grabbed a handful of snow. After quickly forming it into a snowball, I hurled it at Mitch's back. *Thump!*

"Hey!" He turned around, surprise on his face.

"That's payback for calling me a creeper!" I backed inside and closed the door. Standing at the glass, I put my thumbs in my ears and wiggled my fingers. He bent down, grabbed some snow, and formed a loose snowball of his own. He gently tossed it my way. It hit the glass right in front of my face with a soft *clunk*, shattering. They laughed on their side of the glass, and I did the same on mine. I'd needed a moment of levity, and I could always count on my sons to provide it.

CHAPTER 18

Misty

I finished cleaning the unoccupied rooms on the west wing and returned to my perch behind the registration desk. Finally, the officers wrapped things up and came to the counter. I was dying to know what they'd been told, but I realized they had to be careful with what they shared with me.

Fortunately, Deputy Highcloud was fairly generous with her information. "I'm going to share more than I normally would because, with everyone leaving your lodge in two days, this investigation is under a severe time crunch. I need eyes and ears on these folks here, and that means you."

I felt both flattered and pressured. I wanted to help in any way I could, but my sleuthing skills were limited. I was only an armchair detective. I might not even recognize a clue when I saw it, or I might mistake something for proof of guilt when it wasn't. But I supposed I could report what I saw and heard, and let the professionals assess the information. After all, I'd done it before.

"Everyone's stories check out so far," she said. "There were no obvious inconsistencies. Of course, there's things we plan to follow up on. Aileen said she fell asleep early Monday evening and had turned her cell phone to silent mode so she wouldn't be disturbed. She woke up in the middle of the night, saw the texts, and noticed Nigel hadn't returned, but she said it's not unusual for him to stay out late entertaining investors. She figured he'd changed his plans after he'd tried to contact her, and that he'd return to the lodge later. She'd been using Nigel's phone charger in their room, but he'd taken it with him when he left for the resort. Her phone battery was low, so she went outside to get the charger they'd left in the rental vehicle."

I pointed out the obvious. "But that should've taken only a minute or two."

"You're right. She said she plugged the charger into a USB port in the SUV, and placed a short call to a friend back home who's an early riser. She made the call from her car so that she wouldn't risk waking up Rayan in the next room, or being overheard. She called her friend for emotional support. Her cell phone history supports her story. She claims her husband was a workaholic and that she's been lonely and miserable for years. The only way she could get his attention was by acting out."

"Like taking the SUV when she knew he needed it?"

"Exactly. And by refusing to return his calls and texts."

I wasn't entirely sure I bought Aileen's explanation but, as Deputy Highcloud had noted, there were no obvious holes in it.

Highcloud continued to enlighten me. "The CPAP machine is Aileen's. It has a full-face mask because she's a mouth breather. She was born with a deviated septum."

"So, it wasn't the cause of the bruises on Nigel Goodwin's face."

"No," the deputy said, confirming my earlier conclusion. "Sebastian claims that after he went to his room Monday night, he got a text from some guy he'd met at the resort's taproom who's a fan of the San Jose Sharks hockey team. The guy invited him down to a rental in Sugar Mountain to watch the Hurricanes and Sharks play. The guy and his friends were still up here in Beech when he texted. They swung by the lodge so Sebastian could follow them to their place."

"That jibes with the two sets of headlights we saw in the security camera footage."

Highcloud nodded. "The game was in San Jose, so it was played on Pacific Time. It didn't start until ten thirty Eastern and was already underway when they came by here. At any rate, Sebastian says the Sharks were beating the Hurricanes, and the other guys started 'acting like douchebags.'" She made air quotes with her fingers. "He got annoyed with them, left the party, and came back to the lodge."

"Did Sebastian show you the text? Have you contacted the Sharks fan so you can verify that Sebastian watched the game with him?"

"I couldn't. Sebastian said he deleted the text from his phone after he left the party. He doesn't know the guy's number."

"That's awfully convenient."

"I thought the same thing."

Hardy said, "I'm planning to check the Banner Elk webcam, see if his car passed by late Monday night."

I told them about the information I'd found online, about the ice temperatures. "I saw hockey skates in Sebastian's room when I was cleaning before. It crossed my mind that Sebastian could've frozen Goodwin's body on an ice rink."

"There's a rink at Sugar," Hardy said, using the abbreviated term often used by locals to refer to the Sugar Mountain Resort.

"And Appalachian Ski Mountain," I added.

Highcloud turned to Hardy. "Check them out, would you?"

"No problem."

The assignment made, she turned back to me. "Daphne and Jean-Paul own a sorbet company in France called Sorbet du Calais. They've invested in Goodwin's resorts in return for exclusive retail space. They said having their sorbet shops in his resorts has been extremely lucrative."

That explained why Daphne had downplayed the problems with the Alberta resort. "What about the shop in Boone?"

"They said they've been looking to expand into the American market, and decided to take a look at the space in Boone on a whim when they spotted a For Rent sign from the street."

The explanation seemed a bit flimsy to me. *Successful businesspeople are generally more methodical, aren't they?* Then again, I supposed some people might have considered my purchase of the lodge a whim. Prior to launching the Mountaintop Lodge, I hadn't held a fulltime job in years, and I'd never worked in a hotel. But what I'd lacked in experience, I'd made up for in determination. To paraphrase Mark Twain, the only things a person needs to succeed are ignorance and confidence.

Highcloud moved on to the next potential suspect. "Rayan admitted that he intentionally ignored Goodwin's texts and calls Monday night because he was angry. Goodwin made him feel used and exploited. He says he feels terrible about not responding, after what happened to his boss Monday night."

It was only right that Rayan feel terrible. If he wasn't the one who'd killed Goodwin, he might have inadvertently created an opportunity for someone else to put an end to the man. Either way, he bore some blame. "Did you ask him what he'd printed from the lodge computer?"

"We did. It was the receipt for the security cameras Goodwin told him to order. He showed us the document. He'd printed it out to give to the company's accounting department when they got back to London."

In other words, the document had nothing to do with Goodwin's murder.

Highcloud moved on. "Neither the Salazars nor the Jensens said anything that pinged my radar."

I raised a finger to interject. "This could be nothing, but when I was cleaning the Jensens' room on Monday, I saw an old lift ticket on Laurie's ski jacket. Probably from last season by the looks of it. All I remember is that it had a logo with mountains and a sun behind them." I told her how the Jensens had called Sebastian over at breakfast Tuesday to pick his brain about the problems with the Alberta resort. "I overheard Sebastian mention that one of the resorts in Banff is called Sunshine. The Jensens shook their heads when Sebastian asked them if they'd ever been to Banff, but I think it's possible the lift ticket could have been from the Sunshine resort. I looked up the logo, but I can't say for sure. If it's not the same logo, it's very similar." I told her how I'd searched the other resorts' logos, too, looking for one that would jog my memory, that would be a perfect match. "None of the others looked right."

Highcloud's eyes narrowed. "But you're not completely certain about the logo you saw."

"No."

"And the Jensens were questioning Sebastian about the Albert resort *after* Goodwin was already dead, when the resort here would surely be put on hold for the time being and problems with the Canadian resort had become moot."

In other words, if they knew Goodwin was dead, they wouldn't have bothered gathering more information about his business operations. I sighed. "You're right. That doesn't make sense. I must've been mistaken."

"Not necessarily," Highcloud said, backpedaling. "I'm just pointing out some other facts that need to be taken into consideration so that we've both got a fuller picture. The logo you saw may very well have been from the Banff resort, but there's also a concept called 'confirmation bias.' It's something we in law enforcement have to be very careful to avoid. It happens when a person forms a belief, and inadvertently interprets later data and facts in a way that supports that belief. Investigators have to be careful to keep an open mind. The Jensens told us that the first they'd heard about the problems with the Banff resort was here, when Sebastian raised the matter. I figured anyone who lost money in Alberta would have a potential motive for killing Goodwin. Rayan provided me with a list of investors. The Jensens' names weren't on it. They hadn't invested in it, hadn't lost any money. I'm not aware of any motive they'd have to kill Goodwin. Of course, the Fourniers were on that list. I'm not ruling them out yet."

"What about Amari Lott? Has he been ruled out?"

Highcloud and Hardy exchanged looks of exasperation. "He wouldn't let us in his room, and we don't have any basis for a search warrant."

"Too bad I can't give you access." Before opening my lodge, I'd made sure to school myself in the legalities of innkeeping. As the owner of the lodge, I had the legal right to ignore a Do Not Disturb sign put out by a guest in order to complete cleaning or maintenance, but I would hate to wrongfully violate Amari's privacy without a valid reason. Ironically, while the owner of a hotel had a right to enter a guest room at any time, the innkeeper could not legally allow law enforcement to go into a guest's room without the guest's consent or a search warrant. The Fourth Amendment protected the guest from illegal search and seizure, and the room was considered their protected space during their stay. The restriction expired at the end of the guest's tenancy, however, meaning if Amari stayed past checkout time on Friday, I could let the deputy and officer into his room.

"Amari is a computer programmer," Highcloud said. "He claims he brought work with him and that he's under strict orders from his client to keep the details of the project secure."

I recalled how Amari had declined the Wi-Fi password when he'd arrived, stating that he wouldn't need it. *Could a programmer work without internet access?* I supposed it was possible. The work could be stored on his computer or an external hard drive. "Do you believe him?" I asked.

Highcloud and Hardy exchanged glances and shrugs before she said, "It's an odd situation, that's for sure, but he said he'd check with his client to see if he could break with protocols and give us some basic information. He seemed forthcoming in response to the personal questions we asked him. He purportedly made his fortune in bitcoin and other cryptocurrencies. He says he realized from the git-go that they were nothing more than high-tech smoke and mirrors, but he figured if someone was going to make big money off other people's foolishness, it might as well be him. He got in, made a fast profit, and got out before the market tanked."

"What about the ice?" I asked.

Hardy said, "He claims he twisted his knee during his ski lesson yesterday, and that he'd used the ice he got from the machine to ice his knee."

I racked my brain, searching for holes in his story. "Wouldn't he need a plastic bag for the ice?"

"You'd think so," Highcloud said. "But the guy's a smart cookie, resourceful. He used the shower cap you provided in his room to hold the ice, and he sat on the side of the tub while he was icing his knee in case of drips. He claims he popped a couple of ibuprofen early Tuesday morning, and that his knee felt much better. He decided to go ahead and take a chance on the slopes. He didn't want to hang around the lodge after Nigel Goodwin had been found dead here."

Amari had filled the holes in his story, though I still wondered what he might be hiding in his room. *Was he being truthful when he claimed his work was subject to security protocols?* It seemed like a convenient—and questionable—excuse. And there was still the possibility that he'd snuck out of his window during the night to bury Nigel Goodwin in the snow, wasn't there? I posed the question to the officers.

Highcloud says, "He claims he has an airtight alibi. One your sons can corroborate."

"My sons?" My heart rate increased twofold in an

instant. I didn't want my boys dragged into this mess any more than they already were. "What do you mean?"

Hardy elaborated. "Lott told us that he was in too much pain to sleep well Monday night, and that he got online to play a video game. He claims he played against your sons until the wee hours of the night."

I shook my head. "That can't be right. My sons knew I needed them at their best the next morning. I told them so. They went straight to bed after going to their room."

The officer issued a soft snort and cocked his head. "You sure about that?"

I heaved a sigh. "I suppose not." It wouldn't be the first time my sons had disobeyed me. It probably wouldn't be the last, either.

Hardy said, "Lott even gave us J.J.'s screen name. JX2."

I remembered J.J. offering that bit of information when Amari checked in. "Did he give you Mitch's screen name, too?"

"No," Highcloud said. "He said he couldn't recall it, that it wasn't anything memorable. Do you know it?"

"No." I felt a little ashamed to be so out of touch with my sons' online lives, but Jack and I had given them strict instructions when they were younger to never reveal their real names or where they lived or went to school, anything that could enable some creep to track them down. My ex had kept an eye and ear on their online gaming back then but, as they'd grown older, we'd relaxed our oversight. I mentioned the Wi-Fi issue. "How could Amari play an online game without connecting to the internet?"

Hardy said, "Maybe he played from a phone app. Or he could have a mobile hotspot."

If only I could get into Amari's room and find out.

"We need to speak to your sons," Highcloud said. "See whether they confirm Amari's story."

I gave the deputy both of their cell phone numbers, and she tried each in succession to no avail. Neither of my sons answered their phones. She left both of them a short voice mail, asking them to call her back.

I cringed. "Sorry, deputy. They keep their phones on silent most of the time. Even if they have them on vibrate, they're not likely to notice it while they're snowboarding." Their padded ski pants and jackets would absorb the vibration and, even if they felt a jiggle while riding a lift, they might mistake it for the movement of the chair. But while I couldn't put the officers in immediate contact with my sons, I could share my thoughts about hunters and deep freezers.

Naturally, the two professional investigators had already considered the possibility. Hardy said, "The thought crossed our minds, too. A deep freezer would be big enough to hold a body, and it could chill a corpse in no time."

Of course, Tyson Pell wasn't the only one with access to such an appliance. I held out the vacation rental details and photos I'd printed out earlier. "Paulette Frost might also have access to a deep freezer."

The two put their heads together as they paged through the document. When they finished, Highcloud looked up at me. "You've got a knack for investigation. If you ever decide you're tired of running this lodge, let me know. I'd put you on my team."

I felt myself beam at her compliment. Like my cat, I had a natural curiosity. Some might even call me nosy. *Nosy.* Ugh. I groaned inwardly. *Will I ever think of noses the same again?*

Hardy folded the printout in two, and tucked it into

the large inside pocket of his coat. "I'll visit with Paulette Frost after I track Gus down and confirm Sebastian's story about going down to Sugar Mountain."

As we wrapped up our convo, I posed a final question to them. "I'm curious. What does Sebastian do for a living?"

Highcloud issued a soft snort. "He calls himself a professional investor, and he's bought a few small parcels of undeveloped land here and there, but from what we gleaned, he's mostly living off inheritance. His ancestors were tobacco barons. They owned tobacco farms all over North Carolina and Virginia."

Hardy elaborated. "He also mooches, looks for a free ride whenever he can get one. He seemed proud of all these things he's done on someone else's dime. He said it's amazing what people will give for free to wealthy individuals when they think they'll get something bigger in return."

"Like a free ski trip," I said sourly.

"Exactly." Deputy Highcloud tapped her knuckles on my desk. "Keep your eyes and ears open. If anyone does something suspicious or says anything contrary to what I've shared with you, call me immediately."

"I will."

The two bade me goodbye and headed toward the doors. Deputy Highcloud exclaimed when she saw the sun shining outside and the parking lot that Rocky had plowed. "Will you look at that! Things have really cleared up."

Had they? While the sun illuminated the sky with a brilliant light, it produced a reflection off the pristine white snow that was nearly blinding. I felt mentally blinded, too, more confused than ever. *What is it we aren't seeing?*

CHAPTER 19

Yeti

The cat was glad the sun was back. Misty had opened the shutters to let the rays shine in, and Yeti basked in the wide, warm swath of sunlight that angled across the bed. Misty had come to the room for lunch but, rather than eating quickly and leaving as usual, she'd lingered this time, sitting on the bed and running her hand across Yeti's side. As much as Yeti enjoyed Misty's attention, she sensed that Misty wasn't doing it only for her. Misty was doing it for herself, as well. The repetitive motion seemed to calm them both.

Still, the cat wondered what had rattled Misty in the first place. Yes, the world revolved around Yeti, but Misty was the most important object in her orbit. It was critical that Misty be okay. To that end, Yeti did the only thing she could. She turned her head, extended her tongue, and gave Misty one of the kitty kisses she reserved only for very specific circumstances.

Misty responded by bending over and giving Yeti a soft kiss of her own atop the cat's head. Yeti felt her purr

ignite on its own accord, her rumble much more pleasant than that of the pesky snowplow that had rolled by
earlier. She closed her eyes in feline bliss.

CHAPTER 20

Misty

After taking a longer-than-usual lunch break to mentally regroup, I ventured back out to resume my housekeeping duties. A stack of mail sat atop the registration desk, along with a small box. Rocky must have brought the mail in for me when he finished plowing. *Such a thoughtful man.*

I walked over and riffled through it. On top was a postcard from Brynn, sent from Bethlehem, Pennsylvania, in recognition of the upcoming Christmas season. She'd written a snarky message. *No sign of virgins or wise men here, but I won some gold at the casino.*

I decided to open the box next. I hadn't been expecting a delivery, so I was curious what was inside. I rustled up a small knife from a drawer behind the desk and sliced through the tape securing the box. The abundance of tissue paper inside told me to be careful with the contents. Gingerly, I removed the paper to find a beautiful three-dimensional glass Christmas ornament—a Moravian star, according to the paper insert—also sent by Brynn from Bethlehem. It was absolutely beautiful, just the heartwarming touch I needed today to remind me that not everyone was a sick killer.

My first thought was to hang the ornament front and center on the lodge's Christmas tree, but I quickly thought better of it. Lots of families stayed at the lodge, and children would surely want to touch the sparkling glass. The star wouldn't last long if kiddos could get their hands on it. Instead, I decided to hang it over the desk. To that end, I rounded up a stepstool and a hook. In no time, the gorgeous ornament sparkled brightly over my head. I snapped a photo and texted it to Brynn along with the kissy face emoji. *Thanks so much! The star is gorgeous!*

I sorted through the remainder of the mail. There were the usual circulars from local grocers. The monthly water bill. A promotional calendar for the upcoming year from a local auto repair shop—the bottom of each page included coupons for oil changes, tire rotations, and tune-ups. On the bottom of the stack was a catalog from the dental supply company my ex-husband worked for. Although they sent me regular emails featuring their products and encouraging me to visit their website, their marketing strategy included old-fashioned print materials, too.

Maybe I should consider sending out some type of marketing mailers for the lodge. Everyone's inbox was jam-packed these days, and it was easy to overlook or bypass promotions received via email. Meanwhile, snail mail had dwindled to a mere trickle and the items that arrived via USPS garnered more attention. It was definitely something for me to think about. I'd run the idea by Patty, see what she thought of it. Maybe I'd also splurge and order promotional toothbrushes printed with the name of the lodge. Enough people forgot to bring their toothbrushes from home when they traveled, and often asked for one at the desk. After they returned home, the toothbrush could serve as a reminder of the good service they'd received at the Mountaintop Lodge. Maybe it would encourage repeat business. I'd have to see how much more it would cost to have the toothbrushes personalized with the name of the inn. If the additional expense was nominal, I'd do it. But that was a question for later. Right now, I needed to finish cleaning the guest rooms. I set the catalog aside to peruse later.

Daphne and Jean-Paul cut their ski day short and returned to the lodge in the middle of the afternoon. I'd just finished a room and was returning the glass cleaner to my cart when they passed by me in the hall. "Back so soon?" I said, trying to keep my voice light. In reality, a nervous tickle ran up my spine. My boys and Pebble were at the ski resort, Rocky was off plowing driveways around town, and other than Aileen who was holed up in her room, I was the only person here. If the Fourniers had murdered Goodwin, might they also decide to end my life for turning over the paper I'd found in their trash can to law enforcement?

Daphne's bright red lips turned down, making her look like a sad clown. "It did not feel right to ski today. It was hard enough yesterday when we knew Nigel was gone, but now, knowing someone killed him on purpose . . ."

"It feels disrespectful," Jean-Paul said, completing his wife's thought.

The two continued on to their room. A few minutes later, I was vacuuming a doorway when I saw them walk down the hall to Aileen's room and knock on the door. A moment later, the door opened, and the two disappeared inside. *Had they gone to Aileen's room to express their condolences? Or was there more to their visit?*

I shut off the vacuum, left it in the hall with my housekeeping cart, and grabbed the shorter-handled duster to use as a prop in my one-act play. I scurried down the hall and let myself into Rayan's room, closing the door as quietly as possible behind me. I'd cleaned the room earlier, but with Rayan's room adjoining the Goodwins', it was the perfect place to eavesdrop on the conversation between the Fourniers and Aileen Goodwin.

As I walked into the room, I spotted a one-page invoice for the security cameras sitting atop his table. He must have left it there after showing it to law enforcement. I wondered why he had bothered to print out the receipt. He'd ordered the devices online, and surely had received the receipt via email. Couldn't he have simply forwarded the emailed receipt to the accounting department back in London? It seemed the more logical way to handle things. After all, he had a lot of marketing materials and equipment to transport. A physical printout could get lost in the shuffle. And hadn't I heard him tap the printout against the desktop as if to straighten the pages? I was fairly certain I had. That meant he had printed more than this single page, right? Of course, the additional pages might have been blank or have contained irrelevant information, promotional offers or the like. He might have felt there was no point in showing any additional pages to law enforcement.

I tiptoed to the door that connected the rooms, and put my ear to the frame. The first thing I heard was Daphne and Jean-Paul expressing their condolences.

"He was such a good man," Daphne said.

"Yes," agreed Jean-Paul. "He provided opportunities for so many. He did not deserve what happened to him."

Aileen said nothing, or at least nothing I could hear. In light of what Deputy Highcloud had told me earlier—that Aileen had resented her husband focusing so much on his work to the neglect of his wife—the accolades Daphne and Jean-Paul were bestowing on her deceased husband were not likely sitting well.

"Of course, Jean-Paul and I helped Nigel bring in the money," Daphne said. "We made sure the other investors believed they were making a good choice to put their money in your husband's resorts."

Aileen's voice was dull and lifeless. "I know you've invested in his projects and attended many of his pitch sessions, but that's all I know. He made it clear from the start that he didn't want me actively involved in his business. I had to beg him to let me tag along on his trips. I'd never have seen Nigel otherwise."

My heart went out to her. Until today, I thought she'd been distant and drab and cold, but my opinion had changed after hearing what she'd told Deputy Highcloud and Officer Hardy, and what I was hearing now. Nigel Goodwin was a mover and a shaker, and Ailene had faded into the background of her husband's life. He'd focused almost exclusively on his resort projects, which received the attention she so desperately needed. The only saving grace was that she'd grown accustomed to being alone and on her own, so his death wouldn't leave much of a void. That didn't mean she wasn't grieving, though, as much for what could have been as for the husband she'd lost.

"I'm sorry, Aileen," Daphne said. "I'm sure he loved you."

Aileen was silent once again.

After a long pause, Jean-Paul said, "With Nigel gone, the resort here is not likely to move forward. We would like to get our funds returned. Daphne sent the wire on Monday to the company account at the bank in London. Surely, the funds are still sitting in the account."

Aileen said, "I can't help with that. I wouldn't know where to start. Even if the resort isn't built, there will be costs for listing and selling the property here, and the loan Nigel took out to buy the property will have to be paid off. Sebastian Cochrane has approached me, too. He offered to buy the resort property to help make things easy on me. I told him the same thing."

Daphne tried another tack. "Your name is on the corporate paperwork, Aileen. I've seen it. You are listed as an officer. Surely you have some authority."

"Nigel only put my name on the documents as a formality," Aileen said, "a safeguard in case something happened to him."

Daphne pushed. "That is precisely the situation we are in."

"You'll need to contact Nigel's solicitors," Aileen said. "Rayan will know who they are."

Daphne's voice contained barely controlled rage now. "We wired over two hundred thousand pounds to your husband, as a favor. You are telling us we will get nothing for it? That it is all lost?"

"That's not what I'm saying at all!" Aileen cried. "I'm saying that I don't control any of this. You need to contact Nigel's solicitors!"

Jean-Paul piled on. "This is a terrible way to treat friends."

"You aren't *my* friends!" Aileen cried. "You might have been Nigel's, but I hardly know you."

While I didn't blame Daphne and Jean-Paul for feeling duped, now was neither the time nor the place to be discussing this matter, and their relentless pursuit of their money seemed ill-timed and heartless. At least they seemed to realize they were getting nowhere and left Aileen's room, but not before slamming her door. Once she was alone again, Aileen burst into sobs I could easily hear even after I backed away from the door.

I waited until I heard another door slam down the hall and walked over to peek through the peephole. The hallway was empty. I exited Rayan's room as quickly as possible, swishing my decoy duster about just in case one of the Fourniers happened to come out of their room at that moment, but I got lucky. The hallway remained quiet.

I rounded up my cart and continued down the hall. As I approached Amari's room, my gaze landed on the Do Not Disturb sign he'd put out. I had no legal right to enter his room merely to snoop. Though I could go into his room to clean without legal repercussions, I feared that doing so could create other repercussions, ones that would be far worse for me. If Amari returned and saw that I'd entered his room to clean despite his explicit request that I stay out, he might write a scathing online review of the lodge. I'd changed the name of the lodge when I'd bought it, in part because the reviews for the Ridgeview Inn had been largely subpar. I was making a fresh start, and I wanted to give the lodge a fresh start, too. As a relatively new entity, the Mountaintop Lodge had amassed only a few reviews so far, all of them four and five stars. A single one-star review could seriously hurt my rating and turn potential guests off. I couldn't afford to lose any business, especially after ordering the expensive hot tub.

Bad reviews weren't the only thing I feared. With Amari working in tech, he could be one of those gadget collectors. He might have installed motion sensors and cameras in his room, so that he could verify whether the space had been breached and his privacy violated. I didn't want video of me flitting about with my prop duster posted on YouTube under the title "Mountaintop Lodge Owner Caught Spying on Guest." I'd heard there were gadgets that could detect signals from hidden cameras and other such devices and alert a person to their presence. The problem was, even if I had one of those devices, I'd have to take it into the room in order to search for the hidden cameras. By the time I'd found any such cameras, they would have already recorded me sneaking about. *Argh!*

My gaze traveled down from the Do Not Disturb sign hanging from the doorknob to the thin, bright telltale line of natural light shining under his door. *He must've left his shutters open when he left the lodge to go skiing.*

My heart pounded in excitement. Maybe it was wrong of me, but I decided to seize this opportunity to gather what evidence I legally and ethically could. After all, anyone who left their shutters open should expect that passersby might glance through the window, right? At least that's what I told myself to assuage my guilt.

I went to the housekeeping closet and sorted through the bin of cleaning rags until I found one with a small hole in it. I positioned the hole over my cell phone camera lens, and wrapped the rest of the rag loosely around my phone to obscure it. After donning my heavy coat and gloves, I went out front with my improvised intelligence-gathering device and the long-handled duster. I worked my way down the walkway to Amari's room, cleaning the windows along the way.

At his window, once I'd cleaned the snowflakes from it with the long-handled duster, I could see through the glass that he'd left the interior shutters open halfway. Unfortunately, with the sun reflecting off his window, I couldn't see farther into the room. I'd anticipated this problem though, hence, my makeshift spy cam. I sneaked my thumb up inside the cleaning rag to push the button on my phone to start the video recorder. I put the rag to the window with the phone inside, the camera lens against the glass, and slowly moved the rag up and down and round and round until I feared that keeping at the task any longer would look suspicious should any camera inside the room be capturing my image. I continued on down the row, cleaning the remaining windows.

Back inside the lodge a few minutes later, I sat at the desk, staring down at my phone screen. I'd donned a pair of reading glasses and enlarged the image to better see the details. My eyes could barely make out two large flat-screen computer monitors angled in a wide V formation atop the table in the room. A desktop-style central processing unit stood between them, with a small rectangular black box sitting in front of it. *Is that a mobile hotspot?*

CHAPTER 21

Misty

Rocky returned to the lodge late Wednesday afternoon with the supplies to install the water line from the back of the lodge to the hot tub. He handed me the receipt for the materials, and I set it on the desk, placing my empty coffee mug atop it to serve as a paper weight. I'd scan a copy into my computer and enter the expense in my bookkeeping system later. Right now, Rocky needed my assistance.

I grabbed a snow shovel and helped to clear the area he would be working in. It was the least I could do. The delivery of the hot tub was on indefinite hold until the road conditions improved, but we wanted to be ready when it arrived so that we could enjoy it as soon as possible.

Pebble and my sons returned around seven o'clock, having worked up a big appetite on the slopes. I showed the photo of the black box to my sons. Mitch didn't waste a second before saying, "It's a portable hotspot."

J.J. cocked his head. "The lodge has Wi-Fi. Why would a customer need a hotspot?"

Mitch said, "They could be worried that their computer might get hacked if they connect to a public Wi-Fi. Or maybe they're doing something they don't want anyone else to know about."

J.J. wagged his brows. "Bow chicka bow wow."

Pebble chastised my son for me. "Gross!"

Maybe Amari was telling the truth, after all, that he needed to keep his work secure. Or maybe Mitch was right and the guy was watching dirty movies in his room. *Ew.* I'd be sure to use plenty of disinfectant after he checked out.

I made a huge pot of spaghetti on the electric hot plate in my room, topped it with a jar of store-bought pomodoro sauce, and paired it with a simple bagged salad. The kids, Rocky, and I ate our dinner together at a table in front of the fire in the great room.

Pebble fished a long noodle from her plate, stuck one end in her mouth, and bent over, letting the other end hang in front of Molasses. When the dog started eating the noodle from the other end, she released it from her teeth.

Rocky frowned, but a grin tugged at his lips at the same time. "What have I told you time and time again, young lady?"

Pebble rolled her eyes. "I know, I know. No *Lady and the Tramp* at the table."

We were finishing up our meal when my phone came alive with an incoming call from Deputy Highcloud. I looked down at the screen, then over at Rocky. "I hope she's got some good news." I tapped the icon to accept the call and put the phone to my ear. "Hello, deputy."

"We're searching Tyson Pell's place," she said. "There's been a development."

Though she could simply tell me what was going

on, I wanted to see for myself and hoped she wouldn't stop me. "I'll be right there." We ended the call and I addressed Rocky now. "I'm going to Pell's cabin. The police are searching it now."

J.J. wanted details. "What's going on?"

"I don't know," I said as I rose from the table. "I'll fill you all in when I get back."

As much as I wanted Rocky to come with me for moral support, I wasn't about to leave our kids at the lodge without one of us there with them for safety. We still didn't know whether one or more of the guests at the lodge could be a killer, and I wasn't about to take any chances.

Rocky walked me out to my car. The night was cold and clear, the crescent moon was big, and the stars were bright in the dark sky above us, seeming almost close enough to reach out and touch. Rocky opened the door for me. "I hope Deputy Highcloud's phone call means the case is resolved."

"Me, too." I'd love to put this murder behind us quickly so that my guests could enjoy what little time they had left here, and Rocky and I could get on with our lives. My stomach was raw. My anxiety had felt like rats gnawing on the inside of it all day.

I climbed into my car and headed out of the parking lot, turning right to drive down the backside of the mountain. Minutes later, I passed the shot-up sign for the Retreat on Blue Ridge and approached Pell's driveway. I turned into it and made my way up the slope, stopping behind a crime scene van. The woods and cabin were dark, but bright portable lights had been set up around the open garage. A line of yellow cordon tape had been stretched across the drive. The deputy stood just inside it. A couple of crime scene technicians in paper

caps, coveralls, gloves, and booties worked in the garage.
One knelt on the floor, examining the cement, probably
looking for blood or other sources of DNA. The other
was dusting the top of the freezer with a small brush and
dark powder, looking for fingerprints.

As I walked up, Highcloud said, "Stay behind the
tape. We don't want Pell's defense attorney claiming the
crime scene was contaminated."

"Crime scene?" I repeated. "You're sure Pell did it,
then? He killed Goodwin here?"

"It's looking more and more that way." She gestured
into the garage. "Something went on in that freezer."

I moved over to a spot behind the tape where I could
get a good view into the garage. The gun safe stood open.
My goodness! The man seemed to own every gun on
the market. Pointed upward in the bottom were at least a
dozen assorted long guns, including long-barreled rifles
and double-barreled shotguns, each with different fea-
tures. I knew squat about rifles, but I'd heard of muzzle-
loaders and single-shot, bolt-action, and pump-action
rifles. Given how many were in his locker, it was a safe
bet it held one of each variety. On the lower shelf above
were smaller hard-sided plastic handgun cases and nylon
zippered cases with the names and logos of the manufacturer printed on them. Glock. Colt. A red phoenix with
a white *R* on its belly. *Ruger, maybe?* Smith & Wes-
son, the letters and ampersand on its logo as tangled as
the Christmas lights still sitting at the registration desk
at my lodge. Box after box of ammunition was stacked
on the upper shelf, enough bullets to shoot up the sign
of every resort in North America. Knowing these guns
were in the hands of someone with such poor impulse
control was truly terrifying.

My focus shifted to the freezer. The dents and dings

and rusty nicks on the exterior said it was an older model. The tech who'd been brushing the top had opened it to work on the interior rim. I stood on tiptoe to get a glimpse into it. Frozen meat packed in clear bags filled the bottom half of the space. The top half was empty. A thick layer of frost had built up on the sides. The steel lining showed through in places where the frost had been slashed away. The tech moved aside, revealing several large dents on the inside of the freezer's lid at one end. *Oh my gosh! Had Goodwin been trapped inside and tried to kick and claw his way out? Is that how he suffered the heart attack?*

Though I'd suspected all along that Goodwin might have been put in a freezer, seeing this evidence for myself made it real. *Too* real. My stomach dropped and my head went light. Maybe coming here had been a mistake. The deputy reached over the cordon tape to grab my arm and prevent me from collapsing. "Deep breaths, Misty," she said, just as she'd done last time. "Deep breaths."

After a few slow inhales and exhales, my head cleared and I could stand on my own again.

Highcloud released my arm. "The techs found a short brown hair in the freezer. It could be Goodwin's, it could be Pell's, or it could belong to someone else entirely. It could even be from an animal. They've collected another hair sample from Pell's bed pillow to compare DNA and, of course, they have access to Goodwin's DNA at the morgue. I'm not going to consider this case solved until we hear back from the forensics lab. If it's Goodwin's hair, we'll know Pell is our guy. Then, of course, we'd need to find Pell. He's doing a damn good job of hiding."

"The hell I am!"

The deputy and I turned to see Tyson Pell storming up his driveway on foot, his face purple and tight with rage, a gun in a holster at his waist. Highcloud shoved me in the direction of her SUV. "Get behind my car!" As I scurried for safety, she yanked her pepper spray from her belt and threw up her left hand in a halt motion. "Stop right there, Mr. Pell! Put your hands in the air!"

The crime scene techs turned, eyes going wide when Pell ignored the deputy's orders and continued coming at her. Highcloud had no choice. She pressed the button on the canister and released a stream of noxious spray at the man storming toward her. The air filled with the acrid scent of chemicals and the sound of Tyson Pell releasing his own stream—of expletives. Through the windows of the SUV, I saw him whip his head back and forth and slap at his face, desperately trying to wipe the spray from his eyes and nose.

Highcloud was eight inches shorter and eighty pounds lighter than Pell, but that didn't prevent her from seizing this opportunity to subdue him before he could go for his gun. She hurled herself at the man, tackling him to the ground. They rolled off the driveway and into the snow, like a couple of tomcats fighting in an alley. The techs sprinted out of the garage and ran over to help the deputy, but by the time they got there she was sitting on Pell's back, riding him like a bronco. She reached down and yanked one arm up behind him. When he fell to the side, she put a foot out to brace herself and grabbed his other arm. He sank to the snowy ground and she straddled him. The techs held his arms while she affixed handcuffs to his wrists and removed his gun from the holster. Despite her orders to the contrary, Pell continued to thrash and kick out, sending up snow and making an inadvertent and angry snow angel. Lest he injure them, the deputy and techs stood and backed away.

The deputy squeezed the button on her shoulder-mounted radio and called for backup. As she brushed frozen flakes from her uniform, Pell buried his face in the snow in an apparent attempt to relieve the sting of the pepper spray, still cursing and hollering as loud as his chemical-filled lungs would allow. Thankfully, the snowpack muffled his protestations. In minutes, two officers from the Beech Mountain Police Department arrived and helped the deputy shackle Pell's legs. They hauled him to his feet and dragged him to Highcloud's SUV. I backed up to give them room to work. After wrangling the man into the back seat, they slammed the door.

My mouth gaped, releasing puffs of steam as I panted in disbelief at what I'd just witnessed. *That man is nuts!*

Highcloud said, "I'll let you know once the evidence is processed. In the meantime, I need you to move your car." She gestured to my Crosstrek, which sat behind her vehicle.

"Oh. Yeah. Sure." I shook my head, trying to clear it, but it only made my thoughts float around inside like glitter in a snow globe. Pell glared at me between wet, weepy blinks as I walked past the deputy's SUV to return to my car.

I carefully backed down the driveway and onto the main road. In minutes, I was back at the lodge, telling Rocky and the kids what I'd witnessed.

"Holy sh—" J.J. caught himself before he cursed and incurred my wrath.

Mitch couldn't stop shaking his head. "That man is messed up." He whipped out his phone and began texting, probably messaging the cute blonde from school.

Pebble simply said, "People be crazy."

Rocky enveloped me in his arms, and I fought the urge to burst into tears. All I'd wanted when I moved up here was to enjoy the peace and beauty of the mountains. Maybe now that Tyson Pell had been arrested, I could get back to that.

I heard the sound of a door opening down the hall and saw Aileen emerge. As she made her way toward us, she held up her phone and said, "I just heard from the deputy. They've made an arrest."

Noise came from the front door now, as Emilio and Celeste came in. Our faces, as well as the fact that Aileen had finally emerged from her room, must have said it all. The two immediately clued in that something big had occurred.

"What is it?" Emilio came up so fast he nearly rolled over my foot. His gaze darted between me and Aileen. "What's happened?"

Aileen said, "They arrested a local man."

Celeste pulled to a stop by her husband. "They did? Was it the one who flipped the model over or the guy with the wildlife cameras?"

None of the guests had remained at the lodge when the local group—including Tyson Pell—had confronted Goodwin. The Salazars must have obtained the information from Rayan. *But when?* I hadn't seen the three interact much at the lodge. I supposed they must have spoken at the ski resort.

"The first one," Aileen said. "The guy who broke the model." Now that the news had sunk in, tears began to stream down her face. She swiped at them just as Pell had swiped at his eyes after being blasted with the pepper spray.

The Salazars exchanged a glance before Celeste

turned back to Aileen. "I'm glad they got him. I hope he spends the rest of his life in jail."

"Me, too," Aileen said softly. "He didn't need to kill Nigel. If he didn't want the resort to be built, he could've tried other ways to stop it."

"Exactly. Like the people in Alberta did." Celeste reached over and gave Aileen's clenched hand a soft, supportive pat. With that, the Salazars bade us good night, turned, and headed to their room.

Aileen sniffled. I hurried to the desk and came back with a box of tissue. She snatched one from the box and held it to her face.

Though the tissue was helpful, I wanted to offer the distraught woman comfort, too. I didn't know her well enough to hug her, though. I offered what else I could. "Can I get you a cup of tea?"

"Please," she squeaked.

While I prepared her tea, Rocky put an arm around her shoulders and gently guided her over to a table to sit down.

When I placed the steaming mug of tea in front of her, she thanked me, though she didn't look up. Rather, she stared into the wafting steam. Maybe she was thinking how life was like the steam. There one second and then *poof!* gone.

Rocky and I took seats on either side of her, sensing she needed companionship if not conversation. When J.J., Mitch, and Pebble looked to me, I quirked my head, indicating they could leave the room. They were clearly uncomfortable, too young to be facing such raw grief and tragedy. Better they maintain what innocence they still had.

After a minute or so, Aileen picked up her mug and took a small sip. She cradled it in her hands, seemingly comforted by its warmth. She continued to sip her tea and dab at her eyes for the next few minutes. Several of the guests returned, including the Jensens. The couple came in chatting, but when Laurie spotted Aileen, she slowed her pace. Her expression was hesitant. "Has there been a development?"

Aileen nodded and swallowed hard. Her voice was raspy when they spoke. "They arrested a local hunter."

Kyle stopped next to his wife at the edge of the great room and gestured to where the model had sat on the table only two days earlier, but what felt like eons ago. "The guy who turned the table over?" So, he, too, knew about Tyson Pell. Rayan seemed to have filled in the entire group.

Aileen nodded.

Laurie exhaled a loud breath and put her hand to her scarf again, clutching it. "It's a relief to know he's behind bars!"

Kyle put a reassuring hand on his wife's back. "I knew Nigel's killer couldn't be any of the investors. Everyone seems so normal. It was impossible to fathom."

Aileen stood, leaving her mug on the table. "I'm going back to my room now. I've got calls to make."

I stood, too. "Let me know if you need anything."

As Aileen headed off, the Jensens watched until she'd gone into her room, then rushed me, eager for information.

"What happened?" Laurie asked.

I wasn't sure how much I was permitted to share, so I erred on the side of caution. "The sheriff's department found incriminating evidence at the man's cabin."

They stared at me for a moment, their eyes wide with anticipation, waiting for me to fill them in. When I didn't, Kyle said, "Is that all you can tell us?"

"For now, yes."

He gave me a nod. "Understood. I'm just glad this ordeal is over so we can enjoy what's left of our ski week."

As they turned to go, I decided to finally get a firm answer about that lift ticket. "Laurie?"

She turned back. "Yes?"

"When I was cleaning your room the day after you arrived, I noticed a lift ticket on your jacket. It had a logo on it with a mountain and a sun behind it. Where was it from?"

She looked up in thought, then turned to her husband. "Where's the last place we skied last season? It had to be Big Sky or Bottineau Winter Park."

He shrugged. "We skied both of them multiple times in the spring. The trips blend together in my mind."

She looked back to me. "It was one of those two. They're both about an eight-hour drive from Rapid City. Big Sky is just south of Bozeman, Montana, and Bottineau Winter Park is in North Dakota. Why?"

Yeah, Misty. Why? "Just curious how our local resort compares."

Laurie sucked air through her teeth as she considered the matter. "Hard to say. It's apples and oranges. Big Sky is much bigger than the resort here in Beech Mountain, so it's got a wider variety of runs. Bottineau Winter Park is smaller than the resort here, so you ski the same runs over and over, but it's less crowded than Big Sky and has a more relaxed atmosphere."

"It's a great place for families," Kyle added. "We took our kids there a lot when they were young."

With that, the two bade Rocky and me good night and went to their room.

Once they'd gone, Rocky turned to me, his eyes

squinty. "What was that about?" he asked, keeping his voice low.

I reminded him about my earlier suspicions, how the Jensens had claimed they'd never been to Banff, but that the logo on the lift ticket on Laurie's jacket resembled the Banff Sunshine resort logo. "With Tyson Pell in custody, I suppose it's a moot point anyway."

"You can relax now." Rocky reached out, took my shoulders gently in his hands, and kneaded them. "Woman, you are one big ball of knots. Just like those Christmas lights at the front desk."

It felt good to share a laugh. "Speaking of those lights, why don't we give them another try? Maybe we'll have more luck tonight." I walked back to my desk, circled around the back, and picked them up. The receipt Rocky had given me earlier remained under the mug on my desk, waiting for me to input it into my financial records. This receipt made me think of another—the one Rayan had shown to law enforcement. Though Tyson Pell was in custody and was presumably Goodwin's killer, the case had not yet been closed, of course. There was still a chance someone else had killed Goodwin. *Could that someone have been his assistant?* I couldn't shake the thought that there might be something significant about the pages he'd printed out Tuesday morning. Maybe they could provide a clue.

I handed the jumbled ball of lights to Rocky to work on, walked over to the computer, and sat down. I knew how to search a browser's history, but was there a way to search a printer's history? I brought up the browser and ran a search online to determine whether it was possible to see what documents had been printed from a printer. I discovered that there was, indeed, a way to see the names of documents that had been printed. In fact, depending on what variables had been chosen, it could even be possible to reprint a document. Rocky had set up the computers and printers for me, and I had no idea what options he had enabled, but I was about to find out.

I pulled up the completed print queue and took a look. Sure enough, on Tuesday morning, Rayan had printed two documents. One was titled "Invoice" followed by a series of numbers that seemed to represent the order date and account number. The second was titled "Resignation Letter."

Aha! I had been right about Rayan printing out more than one page. I clicked on the letter and sent it to print again. The device whirred to life and, seconds later, I held in my hands a letter postdated for the coming Saturday, when the Goodwins and Rayan had planned to leave the lodge and return to London. The letter was terse and brutal.

Nigel,

Working for you has been a bloody bore. Your repeated empty promises have left me with no choice but to resign. Don't be such an arse to your next assistant. While you're at it, be kinder to your wife as well. You don't deserve either of us.   —Rayan

Given the contents of the letter, it was no wonder Rayan hadn't shown it to law enforcement. Even so, the letter definitively exonerated him. If he'd known his boss was dead, there would have been no reason to spend time drafting and printing a resignation letter. He wasn't the killer.

I carried the page over to Rocky. "Take a look at this." He set the tangled lights down on his lap and took the paper from me. His brows rose as he read it. "Rayan was certainly going to burn his bridges with Nigel Goodwin. He must not have been planning to use Goodwin as a reference."

Rocky handed the letter back to me and I ran it through the shredder behind my desk, turning Rayan's insults into cross-cut confetti. The purpose of the letter was moot now, and I didn't want to risk someone else coming across it, especially Aileen. It would seem crass to speak ill of the dead, even if Rayan had been speaking the truth and been unaware of Goodwin's demise at the time.

Rocky and I spent the rest of the evening relaxing in front of the fire and, finally, untangling the troublesome lights. Maybe it was a sign that things were turning around.

Headlights flashed out front and, a couple of minutes later, my boys and Pebble came through the doors, jovially jostling each other as they carried their snowboards and gear.

I stood, put my hands on my hips, and stared my sons down. "Do you two ever check your phones?"

They stopped in their tracks, their expressions a mix of confusion and contrition.

Pebble wisely ducked away from them. "Later, bros."

Mitch and J.J. leaned their snowboards against the check-in counter, set their remaining gear down, and felt the pockets on their jackets and pants, giving themselves a pat down. Mitch pulled his phone from a pocket on his ski pants, while J.J. found his in his jacket. After looking at their own screens, they checked out each other's before looking back up at me. J.J. said, "We both missed a call from the same number."

"The *deputy's* number. She needs to know what you two were doing until the wee hours Monday night."

They both cringed. Mitch added a repentant "Uh-oh."

I bade Rocky good night and motioned for my boys to follow me back to my room. There, they called Deputy Highcloud together, putting the call on speaker so I could listen in. Lest anyone in the hall overhear, we kept the volume low. Yeti hopped up on the table next to the phone and tilted her head as if she, too, were listening to the conversation.

Highcloud's disembodied voice came through the device. "Did you two know you were playing against Amari Lott? Did he identify himself to you?"

"No, ma'am," my sons said in unison.

"We were playing mostly with friends from Raleigh," Mitch added, "but there was another player who joined in. He gave us some tips." He turned to look at me. "That's how we got to the higher levels Tuesday morning."

Highcloud asked, "Do you recall his screen name?"

"I do," J.J. said. "It was R I Am."

"Yeah," Mitch concurred. "I remember because it sounds like will.i.am from the Black Eyed Peas."

Though I'd heard of the popular hip-hop band, the name had instead made me think of Sam-I-Am, the star of the Dr. Seuss book *Green Eggs and Ham*. I must've read it to my sons a thousand times when they were young. I mulled over the name. If R I Am were rearranged, it would be Am R I, which was very similar to the name Amari.

The boys must have given the deputy Amari's correct screen name, because her next question was "How late did you three play?"

My boys' eyes darted my way. I raised my palms. "The cat's out of the bag. You're not in trouble." They were too old for me to punish anyway, young men really, though I'd forever think of them as my boys.

J.J. said, "We signed off around two in the morning. R I Am was still playing when we left the game."

How my sons could wake up just four hours later and be able to function was beyond me. Then again, when I'd been their age, I'd been capable of such feats myself.

Highcloud said, "And R I Am played continuously? He didn't take any breaks?"

Mitch said, "He was away from his keyboard a couple of times, but only for two or three minutes."

That must have been when he'd gone to get the ice from the ice machine. He'd apparently brought his laptop into his bathroom with him when he was icing his knee on the edge of the tub.

Satisfied that my sons had confirmed Amari Lott's alibi, Highcloud thanked them. "You've helped me clear a suspect. I appreciate that. But next time, do what your mother tells you. Hear me?"

"Yes, ma'am," they said.

With that, she ended the call. I felt glad to know that, while Amari might be a bit of an oddball, he wasn't a bad guy.

I hugged my boys good night. "Sleep tight and don't let the bedbugs bite."

"Ew," J.J. teased. "Your lodge has bedbugs?"

They disappeared through the adjoining door to their room, closing it behind them.

Though I was physically and mentally exhausted by that point, my curiosity about Laurie's lift ticket hadn't been entirely put to rest, and I knew I would never rest, either, until I did some research. I rounded up my laptop and pulled up the website for the Big Sky resort. Its logo had a semicircle in the back—representing the sun?—with two triangles in the foreground, a small one in front of a larger one. The logo appeared in black and white on the website. When I pulled up the website for Bottineau Winter Park, I found myself staring at the logo. It had a yellow sun with rays on the upper left and a snowflake on the bottom right, with a swoop of green, blue, and white through the center, representing a mountain slope. *Is this the logo I'd seen on the lift ticket?* It had the sun I remembered, and some blue on it like I recalled, but this logo was more colorful and more detailed, wasn't it? And I didn't remember a snowflake being on the logo at all. Then again, the tag had been torn and crinkled, and I'd taken only a cursory glance. Maybe part of the logo had been torn off. I was probably just getting confused. *What had Deputy Highcloud called it? Confirmation bias?*

I logged out of the site, climbed into bed, and turned off the lamp. Yeti curled up beside me. I closed my eyes to sleep, but all I could see were dented freezers and ski resort logos. I desperately needed some sleep. So why couldn't I stop thinking about that lift ticket?

CHAPTER 22

Misty

I woke Thursday morning, still obsessed with the lift ticket. With me being in the throes of menopause, admittedly my memory wasn't quite what it used to be. Still, I believed the logo I'd seen on the lift ticket attached to Laurie's jacket most closely resembled the one from Banff Sunshine. What's more, I couldn't shake the feeling that it hadn't been Goodwin's goggles that had caused the bruising around his nose. The shape of the bruises angled in the wrong direction, inward rather than outward. The collision with the skis could have caused it somehow, I supposed. After all, the front end of skis curved upward so that they'd glide over the snow rather than sink into it, but I had a hard time seeing exactly how the curved edge could simultaneously impact his face on both sides of his nose at once. It seemed highly unlikely.

Officer Hardy stopped by the lodge late Thursday morning after Pebble had taken the breakfast leftovers and dishes back to the diner and most of the guests had left the lodge for the day. "I just heard from Deputy Highcloud. Figured you'd want an update."

"You figured right." I offered him a cup of coffee, and we took seats at a table near the fire. Rocky was out back working on the water pipe for the hot tub. When he spotted Hardy through the window, he raised a hand in a *wait* gesture, and came inside to join us. He took a seat at the table as Molasses flopped down on the rug in front of the fire to warm up.

Hardy tossed back a big gulp of coffee. No doubt this murder case had kept him up late, perplexed and pondering, too. "Pell's claiming he's innocent, of course. He says he wasn't hiding out at all, that he'd gone on a deer hunting trip with a buddy."

More deer? The man not only had enough guns and ammunition to outfit an army, he had enough venison in his freezer to feed all the troops, too.

Rocky held his mug at his lips. "Is it true? Had he gone hunting?"

Hardy scoffed. "Who knows. His buddy backed him up, said they drove down to his deer lease near Maggie Valley in Pell's truck on Monday, and slept in their hunting blind Monday and Tuesday nights. They can't name anybody else who saw them down there, though, and Pell didn't have any game with him when he returned. He claims he didn't get a kill. Same for his hunting buddy."

Rocky appeared puzzled. "Maggie Valley is a two-hour drive. They didn't stop for gas or groceries or to use a men's room somewhere on the drive down or back?"

Hardy shook his head. "They say they didn't make a single stop."

It would be possible, of course, especially if Pell recently gassed up his truck before leaving for the trip. Even so, it was a convenient explanation for why he and his truck wouldn't appear on security camera footage at a grocery store or gas station. "Does his buddy have a wife or girlfriend who can account for his whereabouts?"

"No. He's just as charming as Pell. Easy to see why they're both unattached."

"What about his deep freezer?" I asked.

"Pell has an explanation for that, too," Hardy said. "He says the scrapes inside his freezer happened a while back when he used a screwdriver to remove the accumulated frost."

As impatient as Pell was, I could see him jabbing at the frost with the tool rather than taking a more patient, more methodical approach to dealing with the problem. Even so, it didn't explain the dents on the inside of the lid. "What about the dents?"

Hardy's face contorted in a sour frown. "From his fists, or so he says. He alleges that he banged on the inside of the lid to try to knock the frost off it, too."

My mind again coughed up an image of Goodwin trying to kick his way out of the deep freezer, and I sucked in a shuddering breath. I wanted to believe the dents hadn't happened that way, but was I just fooling myself? "You think it's really possible Pell damaged his own freezer?"

"Possible?" Officer Hardy repeated. "Maybe. Probable?" He raised his hands, unsure. "The guy's a loose cannon, that's all I know. The lab's still working on the hair sample. If it turns out to be Goodwin's, that'll be a key piece of evidence."

If only the lab could move faster! "The tech didn't find anything on the floor of the garage? No blood or other hair or anything?"

"No," Hardy said. "They examined his truck, too, but it was spotless. He took it down to the car wash down in Banner Elk before heading out on his hunting trip. He used their vacuums to clean the inside. He showed us the charge on his debit card."

Rocky's lip quirked. He was clearly dubious. "Why would he clean his truck *before* going on a hunting trip? If he and his friend planned to be marching around in the mud and muck, it would make more sense to clean it afterward. And how did he keep it so clean?"

"He says they tossed all their hunting gear in the bed. Clothing. Boots. Whatnot. The only things they kept in the truck were their guns, ammo, and a set of clean clothes to wear home. His dirty gear was in a duffle bag in the bed when he was arrested."

"His story held up, then." I bit my lip, frustrated to hear that Pell couldn't be pinned for the murder, and that the case had yet to be definitively concluded. "What about the other suspects?"

Hardy said, "Gus finally got in touch with me about his cameras. He said he was on his way to the police department after he left here when he got a call about a deer trapped in barbed wire off Highway 221 down in Linville. He drove down there to help get the deer loose. By the time he was finished, it was late and he decided he'd deal with the cameras later."

"What about the scratches on his wrists?" I asked.

"Allegedly, he got them wrangling a groundhog who'd holed up under a porch."

"Allegedly?" Rocky repeated. "You don't know if that's true?"

"He could prove he got a call asking for help removing the critter. But the folks who called him weren't home at the time he says he went to their house. I shined my flashlight around under their porch and nothing looked back at me, so either Gus managed to remove the groundhog or it decided to move out on its own.

Groundhogs have sharp claws and strong hind legs, so Gus could be telling the truth."

"I'd like to think so." I'd liked the guy, felt glad he was looking out for the area's animals. It dawned on me how ironic it was that an animal welfare advocate like Gus Bingenheimer and an avid trophy hunter like Tyson Pell had found common ground in opposing the new resort.

Hardy took another sip of his coffee. "I asked to see the photos and videos from his trail cameras, and he showed them to me voluntarily. Tyson Pell was in a good number of them. He tramped all over those woods on several different days, often with a gun in his hand. Paulette Frost was in several of them, too, but she only came by the property once and didn't venture far from the road. She just read over the sign, took a little look around, and left. I saw some of your guests in them, too. That French couple and Sebastian Cochrane."

Rocky leaned back and steepled his fingers in a studious stance. "The pictures give a time and date stamp, right?"

Hardy dipped his head affirmatively. "They do."

"When did the Fourniers and Sebastian go to the property?" Rocky asked.

"Sebastian was caught on the cams Sunday afternoon. He walked all over the property, end to end, just like Tyson Pell. That's when the Fourniers went by, too. In fact, they appeared to be speaking to each other in one of the photos. Sebastian went back on Monday shortly after noon."

"Monday at noon," I interjected. "That's when Nigel Goodwin had originally planned to take the group to the property to show it to them." I could certainly understand why the Fourniers would go out to the property.

They'd planned to buy a share in the resort. *But Sebastian?* "Why would Sebastian bother looking around the resort property if he had no intention to invest?"

"Hard to say." The officer scratched his chin. "Could just be idle curiosity."

A creepy thought crossed my mind. I recalled Highcloud telling me that Sebastian had invested in some parcels of raw land, and remembered what I'd overheard Aileen tell the Fourniers when I'd been eavesdropping—that Sebastian had made an offer on the resort property. *Had Sebastian wanted to snag the property for himself? Did he think that if he eliminated Goodwin, the resort project would be scrapped and the land would be put up for sale, maybe at a fire-sale price so that Goodwin's estate could be settled quickly?*

Before I could give the theory much thought, Hardy said, "Rayan Gandapur was in the last pictures on the trail cams and, boy, did he look pissed."

"I'd have been pissed, too," Rocky said, "if I'd had to trudge through all that deep snow."

"Me, too," Hardy agreed, before shifting gears. "The Beech Mountain Parkway webcam was iced over Monday night, just like your security cameras, but the webcam down in Banner Elk was operational. The footage showed Sebastian's Challenger driving by about fifteen minutes after he left your lodge, then heading back in this direction about fifteen minutes before he walked in here."

I mused aloud. "He might have told the truth about watching the hockey game with the guys he'd met in the taproom." Even so, it seemed odd he'd conveniently deleted the text he'd purportedly received. *Hmm.* I figured I'd run my newest theory by Hardy. "When you and Deputy Highcloud were here yesterday, she mentioned that Sebastian lives mostly off inheritance from his family's tobacco fortune. But she also said he's invested in parcels of undeveloped land. Is it possible he might have been hoping to get the resort property for himself? Could that be why he discouraged the others from investing in the resort, to keep them out of his way? If he killed Goodwin, the property would probably be put up for sale. When I was cleaning Rayan's room yesterday, I overheard Aileen say that Sebastian had approached her to make an offer on the property." I hadn't thought much of it at the time because I'd been more interested in the Fourniers as potential suspects, but maybe it meant something.

Officer Hardy's expression was both intrigued and doubtful. "It's an interesting theory, and I'm not saying you're wrong, but there's land for sale all over the mountain. If he wanted to own property here, he could just buy another parcel."

"That's true," I said. "There's other land available up here. But the resort property had access to the Elk River. Not many properties here do. Gus pointed out that the river access is one of the reasons the land is so critical for the wildlife. Being on a riverfront makes it special and more valuable, too, I'd guess."

After I'd expounded on the subject, Hardy's expression became less doubtful and more intrigued. "You know what? You may be on to something. I'll run the idea by Deputy Highcloud."

Turning to other persons of interest, I said, "Paulette Frost. What about her? Did her story check out?"

"She said she got a call from someone who couldn't turn on the gas fireplace in the unit they'd rented because the fireplace key was missing. The renters had supposedly called her from the ski resort and she'd gone there to meet them and turn over the key. She showed me her recent calls list and I got their phone number. I've left a voice mail for the renters, but they haven't returned my call yet."

Rocky's face clouded with skepticism. "Why wouldn't she just take the fireplace key directly to the unit and leave it there?"

"I asked her the same thing. She said she offered to do that, but the renters specifically asked her to bring it to the resort. She figured they didn't want her going to the unit because she'd see that they were violating the no-pets policy or that they had way more people staying there than they were supposed to. She said people do that all the time, especially young people who don't mind crashing on a couch or floor. Or maybe they didn't want her going there because they'd made a mess of the place and didn't want her getting worked up about it because they planned to clean things up before they checked out."

Again, the explanation was plausible.

Hardy finished his coffee and stood to go. "We'll be in touch."

Once he'd gone, I turned to Rocky and bit my lip. "The investors leave tomorrow. If one of them killed Nigel Goodwin, they might get away with it."

He reached out and gently cupped my chin. "You know it won't be your fault if that happens, don't you? You're not responsible for any of this."

In theory, I knew he was right. I didn't control my guests. They were responsible for their own actions. Still, it didn't sit well with me that one of them had perished while staying here, been dumped on the lodge property, and might have lost his life at the hands of another guest. Those facts put me right in the middle of things.

Besides, I wanted to prove to Nigel Goodwin, even if posthumously, that despite the modest appearance of my lodge—and the current lack of a hot tub—I did indeed provide five-star service in the form of solving his murder.

My sons and I completed our rounds, and they left midafternoon to spend a few hours snowboarding. Pebble was unable to join them today. One of the evening servers had called in sick and Pebble had volunteered to work a double shift. With the ball of Christmas lights now untangled, I decided to tackle some other tasks I'd put off, including ordering toothbrushes, toothpaste, and dental floss for the lodge.

I picked up the catalog and flipped through the pages, finding the toothbrushes and looking them over. If I opted for a single-color print and ordered a minimum of two hundred, it would add only seventeen cents per brush to have them personalized with my simple logo— The Mountaintop Lodge—printed in a rustic font, just like on the sign out front by the road. *I'll do it.*

I logged into my account online, uploaded my logo into the system, and approved the mockup. Before placing the order, I added a hundred small tubes of toothpaste, as well. People rarely asked for floss and I seemed to have enough on hand, so I'd forego floss for the time being.

When I completed the order, Rocky came in through the back door of the lodge on the far side of the great room. A gust of arctic wind came with him, riffling the pages of the catalog.

"I'm all done!" he called. "The electrical outlet has been upgraded and the water line is ready. Now all we have to do is wait for the hot tub to get here."

"Have you heard from the delivery guy?"

"He checked in with me earlier," Rocky replied. "The forecast tomorrow is for temperatures in the mid-forties. That'll help clear the roads. He should be able to get it up here on Saturday."

I could hardly wait. Every muscle in my body had been tight with anxiety for days, first because I wanted to ensure Nigel Goodwin was happy with my services, then because of his death and murder. Soaking in warm, bubbly water sounded like pure heaven. Of course, unless and until this murder was solved, I'd never be able to relax completely.

I went to pick up the catalog. The wind had turned the pages, landing on a two-page display of masks made for dentists to use when administering nitrous oxide to their patients. Because the dentist would need access to the patient's mouth, the masks were made to fit only over the patient's nose, with tubes to supply the laughing gas and an elastic band to hold the mask in place. As I looked at the mask, two thoughts crossed my mind. The first was merely a random musing. I recalled that Deputy Highcloud had pointed out that Aileen's CPAP mask covered both her mouth and nose because she was a mouth breather. I wondered how dentists administered nitrous oxide to mouth breathers like Aileen Goodwin, or if they even could. *Do they have to use some other type of anesthesia?* My second thought was much more imperative. *Could Kyle Jensen have used a nitrous oxide mask on Nigel Goodwin?*

Kyle was an orthodontist. He'd told me so when he and Laurie had checked in. *Brace yourself,* he'd said. *I'm an orthodontist. Get it?* I looked closely at the masks depicted on the page. The edges curved inward around the nose to form a tight seal. The light bruise on Goodwin's face had likewise curved inward.

Instant heat flowed through me as my heart rate ratcheted up. I recalled being surprised that the Jensens had driven all the way from Rapid City, South Dakota, to Beech Mountain, North Carolina. Even for people who enjoyed road trips, it was a long haul, and one fraught with potential problems this time of year. Weather could cause hazards or road closures. *Why not fly?*

I logged onto the website for the Transportation Safety Administration to run a search. Sure enough, while passengers could bring personal oxygen cylinders required for medical purposes onto an airplane, no compressed gases were allowed on board or in checked baggage. Only empty cylinders could be transported. In other words, TSA regulations would have prevented Dr. Jensen from bringing nitrous oxide with him on an airplane.

I sat back, my mind tossing thoughts about like the towels in the lodge's industrial-sized dryer. I thought back to Monday night. The Jensens had arrived back at the lodge late, after the ski resort had closed. Could they have offered Goodwin a ride back to the lodge, then doped him with the nitrous oxide and left him somewhere to freeze? They'd have had to sneak out through the window of their room to dump his body on the lodge grounds later, which posed the risk of getting caught red-handed or at least being seen by a witness. But maybe they'd thought doing so was less risky than maintaining possession of his body or dumping it elsewhere. Maybe they expected his death to be ruled an accident.

Am I nuts, thinking this?

I recalled Deputy Highcloud telling me to take deep breaths to calm myself when I was on the verge of freaking out, so I forced myself to do the same now. *In . . . out . . . in . . . out . . .*

Before I contacted law enforcement with this new theory, I had to make sure it didn't have any glaring holes. I didn't want to embarrass myself or, worse yet, waste their valuable time. I thought things over some more. While the sequence of events I'd constructed in my head could have taken place, there was indeed a glaring hole in this theory. As far as I knew, the Jensens had no motive for wanting to kill Nigel Goodwin. By all accounts, they'd hoped the man would help them feather their financial nest so they'd have security when they retired. They hadn't invested in the trouble-plagued Alberta resort, so seemingly had no score to settle there. Deputy Highcloud had seen the list of investors and their name wasn't on it. They hadn't even met Nigel Goodwin until they'd all convened here at my lodge.

Still, there was the pesky matter of that lift ticket . . .

CHAPTER 23

Misty

I spent some time online late Thursday afternoon, looking over Laurie Jensen's social media, desperately searching for some confirmation that she had, in fact, gone skiing in Banff. I don't know what I thought it would prove if I found evidence she'd once been to Banff, other than that she was a liar. Even if she'd gone to Banff, it didn't mean there was any connection between her and the failed resort or Goodwin's murder.

Laurie had a Facebook account, but she wasn't a regular poster. I got the impression that, because she had lived in the same small city all her life, she didn't have an extensive personal network outside Rapid City and didn't feel the need to constantly share about her life online. She probably saw her friends in person, met up for coffee or margaritas, maybe church or book club. Surely, they'd catch each other up on their lives then.

I noticed Joshua Wagner listed among her friends. *Wasn't that the name of her deceased brother?* I squinted at his tiny profile picture. With his blond hair and blue eyes, he resembled Laurie, though he had a close-trimmed beard covering the bottom of his face.

Having no luck with Laurie, I turned my attention to her husband. Kyle Jensen had no personal social media accounts, only ones for his orthodontics practice that included posts reminding people of the benefits of orthodontic treatment and good oral care in general. Many of the posts included corny jokes and dental-related puns. *What are dental X-rays called? Tooth pics. . . . Did you hear about the dentist who joined the army? He was a drill sergeant.*

I was about to log off when I decided to take a closer look at Laurie's brother. *How had he died so young?* I felt a little ashamed of my morbid curiosity, but it was only natural to wonder, wasn't it? I recalled that he'd been described as "an avid outdoorsman who loved the mountains" in his obituary and that he'd lived in Missoula, Montana, a state named after the very mountains he loved. I wondered if it was those mountains—the ones Emilio Salazar had deemed dangerous places—that had killed him.

I found his Facebook page and my heart squirmed in my chest. His header image was a photo of him with his arm around the shoulders of his pretty, petite blonde wife. She held an adorably chubby baby in her arms. Two young girls encircled them, the oldest looking to be around five or six years old, the other a toddler with her thumb in her mouth. Joshua looked so happy and full of life in his photos, much too young to have left the earth he so enjoyed.

The most recent posts had been made by family and friends in memoriam, saying what a great guy Joshua Wagner had been, full of boundless energy and enthusiasm, an eternal optimist, always there when you needed someone to lend a hand. Though several referenced the accident that had taken his life, none said exactly what type of accident he'd suffered. There were pics from hikes and camping trips with friends, his family in a canoe, on horseback, or riding on inflatable snow tubes. I scrolled down, down, down, to look at the posts he'd made himself before he'd passed on. Unlike his sister, he'd posted often, though he let the photos speak for him and used few words, if any, in his captions. There were several of him on skis or snowboards at unspecified ski resorts accompanied by captions like *Stoked! Nothing beats fresh powder!* and *Let's shred the gnar!*

But the photo that took my breath away was one of him in a reddish-orange jacket and pants with a logo on the left side of his chest. Though the logo was all in white on the jacket rather than in color, it was the logo of the Banff Sunshine resort I'd seen when searching online earlier, two snow-capped peaks with a semicircle behind them to represent the sun. The photo had been posted around this time last year. His caption read *Earning some extra bank north of the border. The Canadian Rockies Rock!*

My mind raced as I sat back to think. *Laurie's brother had worked as a ski instructor in Banff? Why hadn't she mentioned this to me when I'd inquired about the lift ticket on her jacket, whether it might have been from the Banff Sunshine Resort? Why hadn't she mentioned it to Sebastian when he'd asked if she'd ever been to Banff?* It would seem only natural to add this tidbit into the conversation. Then again, her brother had only been gone a matter of months. Maybe the pain was still raw and it was too hard for her to talk about him. Maybe she worried that mentioning her dead brother would make other people uncomfortable. That could certainly be the case. But between my thoughts about the nitrous oxide mask and knowing Laurie had a brother who'd worked in Banff, it felt like a connection was beginning to form, as loose as it might be.

My suspicions niggled at me and, at dinnertime that evening, I activated the system on the landline at the lodge's desk so that any incoming calls would be transferred to my cell phone. I also put out a note on the counter: "Gone to the diner. Back by 6:30. If urgent help needed, use desk phone to contact me."

I needed to get out of my lodge and get out of my head, and the best way to do that was to go over to the diner and get some of Patty's delicious food into my tummy. My sons were still off snowboarding, but Rocky came with me. With it being a weeknight, the diner wasn't overly busy, nothing Patty's staff couldn't handle on their own. I rounded her up to be a sounding board, along with Rocky.

Pebble came over and offered both a welcoming smile and two menus, one for me and one for her father. Unnecessary, really. Both Rocky and I had the menu memorized by now. "What can I get you to drink?"

We both opted for mugs of Patty's freshly pressed apple cider.

"Good choice," Pebble said. "I'll be right back with those drinks."

While Pebble headed off to round up the cider, Rocky and Patty sat side by side on the other side of the booth, listening intently as I told them my theory about the nitrous oxide mask and Laurie's loose connection to Alberta via her brother's short-term employment at the ski resort in Banff. They offered an occasional nod, squint, cocked head, or raised brow, sometimes simultaneously, sometimes at cross-purposes.

Pebble returned with our steaming cider and took our food order, stopping to check on customers at another table before turning in our order at the kitchen window. Though she'd been employed at the diner only a matter of days, she worked with proficiency, expertly balancing three plates of food on her arm as she went to deliver an order at a booth across the way.

Having finished filling in Rocky and Patty, I looked from one to the other. "What do you think? Am I crazy to suspect the Jensens?"

Patty was a straight shooter—one of her many admirable traits—and she gave me her honest assessment. "The case against them is weak. Just because they *could* have done something doesn't mean they *did*."

Rocky nodded in agreement.

Patty wasn't finished. In addition to being a straight shooter, she was also supportive—another trait of hers that I appreciated. "But a person's got to listen to their gut. They're a reflection of our instincts, our subconscious. Sometimes our guts know more than our brains. You'll feel burdened until you tell the deputy your theory. Maybe she can find evidence to support it."

Again, Rocky nodded in agreement. "What can it hurt?"

"My credibility," I said. "I don't want her thinking I'm making wild accusations."

Patty flung a dismissive hand. "You've already proved yourself to Deputy Highcloud. The local police, too. They know you've got a good head on your shoulders, that you're only trying to help. Besides, the accusations aren't wild. Even if you're wrong, you won't lose their respect."

I bit my lip. "I hope you're right."

"I know I am," Patty said.

Rocky agreed with her a third time. "I know she is, too."

"I'll do it, then," I said, feeling relieved already. "I'll call Deputy Highcloud." As soon as the words were out of my mouth, a loud growl came from my stomach.

Patty said, "See? I told you to listen to your gut. That's your gut telling you that you're doing the right thing."

Rocky disagreed this time. "I thought it was her gut saying she and I should order pie for dessert."

A grin tugged at Patty's lips. "A gut can say more than one thing at a time."

Rocky and I returned to the lodge a half hour later, our appetites satisfied and my mind a bit more at peace now that I'd made the decision to call the deputy. Rocky watched the front desk while I went to my room to place the call.

After I'd told Deputy Highcloud my suspicions, she said, "That lift ticket has become an obsession with you, hasn't it?" Though her words were harsh, her tone was gentle.

"It has. But don't you think it's odd that Laurie didn't mention her brother had worked in Banff?"

"Maybe," she said, "but it could simply be a difficult subject for her, especially if they were close. What did you say his name was?"

"Joshua Wagner."

"Wagner. Thanks. I'll come out there tonight and talk to the Jensens, too—see what they have to say for themselves. By the way, the lab got the results back on the hair found in Tyson Pell's freezer. It's his, not Goodwin's."

I groaned and put a hand over my eyes. "I was hoping the DNA would match and prove that Goodwin had been in Pell's freezer, that we could put this matter to rest."

"You and me both," the deputy said. "We're at a dead

end as far as Pell is concerned. He could still be our guy, and we're hoping to nail him on the charges for destruction of property, but that's only a class one misdemeanor. If he's convicted, he'd get a fine and one hundred and twenty days in jail at the most. He'll be arraigned tomorrow and the judge will set bail. Most likely, he'll make bail and we'll have to release him. I'll warn him to steer clear of your lodge. If you see him anywhere near your place, call the local police right away. I don't trust that man at all."

I didn't trust him, either.

"We've put Pell's hunting buddy through the wringer," Highcloud said, "but he's sticking to his guns. Either he's telling the truth, or the two of them worked hard to nail down their story. At least this new theory of yours gives me something else to consider."

"So, you think it's possible the Jensens killed Goodwin?"

"Yes," she said, "but *possible* is a low bar, you understand. I'm intrigued by this theory, but there's still the problem of the missing motive. I don't think either of us should get our hopes up. That said, I'll get in touch with the assistant medical examiner and have them check Goodwin's blood for nitrous oxide. I'm not sure it will show up in a tox screen, even if it was administered. I don't know a lot about medical stuff, but I've been in this business long enough to learn that if the effects of a drug wear off quickly, that means it leaves the system quickly, too. That's the problem with date-rape drugs. They're rapidly metabolized. Since nitrous oxide wears off fast at the dentist's office, my guess is that it's one of those substances that doesn't stay in the body long. But it can't hurt to have the M.E.'s office take a look."

"Thanks, Deputy."

"Thank you right back, Misty. You're no slouch. I'm glad we've got you on our side. By the way, I heard back from Amari Lott. He got the go-ahead from his client to reveal what he was working on, though only in general terms."

"What is it?"

"Virtual training programs for military pilots."

"Ah. That explains the secrecy." *As well as the mobile hotspot he'd brought with him to use instead of connecting to the lodge's Wi-Fi.*

"We've contacted the media to ask for the public's help," Highcloud added. "Maybe someone saw something, and they'll come forward. People often don't realize they've witnessed something important until they see a plea for information on the news."

I'd keep my fingers crossed that a witness would come out of the woodwork.

As we wrapped up our call, Deputy Highcloud asked me to shoot her a text when the Jensens returned to the lodge that evening.

Rocky and I kept a constant eye on the front door for the rest of the day. The Jensens came into the lobby at half past eight. I gave them a smile in greeting. "Decided not to close the resort down tonight?"

Laurie said, "Wish we could have, but we've got a lot of packing to do before we get on the road in the morning."

I feared they might hit the road at daybreak, before the results came back from the lab regarding the nitrous oxide. Some guests even checked out in the wee hours while I was still in bed, leaving their room keys in the drop box at the desk. "You've got a long way to go," I said. "Don't get on the road without eating a big breakfast first."

"Don't worry about us," Laurie said. "We wouldn't miss a last chance at those biscuits for anything."

Kyle leaned on the counter, a grin tugging at his lips just like when they'd checked in on Sunday. "You know what it takes to make a good Southern breakfast?"

"What?"

"Hard work, grits, and determination." He chuckled and raised his brows. "Get it? Grits?"

"Good one," I said. "I'll have to tell it to the staff at the diner."

As they headed off to their room, I whipped out my cell phone and texted the deputy.

Highcloud arrived twenty minutes later and came up to the desk. She glanced into the great room, where Celeste and Emilio relaxed by the fire, engaged in a game of cards.

She came up close to the counter and spoke softly. "Remember when I told you that Rayan had given me a list of the investors in the Alberta resort?"

"Yes?"

"Joshua Wagner's name is on it. He invested a hundred thousand dollars in January of this year."

Oh my gosh! The floor seemed to shift under me. *Could we finally have found the elusive motive, a reason why the Jensens would have wanted to kill Nigel Goodwin?* "Laurie's brother passed away in late March." An offhand comment Sebastian had made came back to me, that one of the investors had taken his own life after losing everything. I told Highcloud what he'd said. "But that couldn't have been Laurie Jensen's brother, could it?" I mused aloud. "Sebastian said the lawsuit to stop the Alberta project wasn't filed until July. Would Joshua Wagner have even known when he died in March that there was a chance the resort wouldn't go through?"

Highcloud said, "If I had to guess, the potential problems with the resort were probably simmering for months before the suit was filed."

I rounded up the dental supply catalog and opened it to the dog-eared page that depicted the company's inventory of masks for delivering nitrous oxide, along with details and pricing for each option. I pointed to the one that most resembled the shape of the bruise on Goodwin's face. "That's the one that caught my eye."

She looked from the catalog to me. "I can see why." She asked me for the Jensens' room number and I told her, pointing to the west wing.

As the deputy walked quietly to the hallway, Celeste looked up from the cards in her hands. She tapped Emilio on the arm and jutted her chin, silently signaling her husband to take a look. He turned, spotted the deputy just before she disappeared into the hall, and turned back to his wife. From this distance, I couldn't hear what he whispered to her, but the two wrapped up their card game, slid the deck back into the box, and rolled off to their room.

I remained on my stool, but had a hard time sitting still. I rested my heels on the cross bar, my knees bouncing like pistons. Would Deputy Highcloud bring Laurie and Kyle Jensen out in handcuffs? Would Kyle be cracking corny jokes all the way to the cruiser? *Did you hear about the duck that got arrested? He was selling quack*. He had better keep the jokes to himself if he went to jail, or his puns might get him punched in the face.

Even though I'd been the one to suggest their possible guilt to Deputy Highcloud, it was hard for me to imagine the Jensens doing something so horrifying. They seemed like such nice, down-to-earth people. But grief could make people act out of character. My sons shared a deep bond and, though I didn't see my siblings often, we too shared a strong familial attachment. I'd be out of my mind with grief and rage if I thought someone had caused their death.

To my surprise, Highcloud was back at my desk a mere five minutes after she'd left. "The Jensens told me that the very reason they came here and considered investing in the proposed resort in Beech Mountain was because their brother had sung Goodwin's praises. He'd met Goodwin when he gave the man a private ski lesson in Canada. That's when Wagner found out about the proposed Alberta resort. He invested right away. He believed it would be a sure thing. Laurie said that, after her brother passed away, they hadn't kept up with the progress of the Alberta resort. When her brother had invested, he knew it would be a long game, so it didn't seem necessary to follow the day-to-day developments."

It was a plausible explanation. I didn't regularly keep tabs on the value of my investments either, though my retirement account was relatively meager. Most of my money was in the lodge. A shameful blush warmed my cheeks. I felt foolish. "Did you ask how her brother died?"

"I did. He'd been partying with friends at a bar and drank himself to death. He was found dead in his car in the bar's parking lot the next morning."

"That's terrible!" Still, the guy seemed like the type who seized life by the horns, did everything to the fullest. I supposed it wasn't entirely surprising someone with that type of personality would inadvertently overindulge and perish from alcohol poisoning.

Highcloud nodded solemnly and continued. "The Jensens hadn't been aware of the problems with the

Alberta resort until Sebastian mentioned them here, but Laurie said it was a moot point anyway. Her brother was young and had plenty of life insurance when he passed, so even if he lost the hundred grand he'd invested in the Alberta resort, it wouldn't put his widow in a financial bind."

"In other words," I said, "his investment in the failed Canadian resort doesn't appear to be a viable motive."

"No," the deputy concurred, "but I'm not totally writing them off yet, not until we hear from the lab whether there was any nitrous oxide in Goodwin's system. I'll be in touch once we get the results."

I reminded her that the Jensens would be checking out the following morning. "They've got a long drive ahead of them back to Rapid City. I don't know what time they're planning on leaving, but it could be daybreak." I told her how I'd checked with them earlier regarding whether they planned to stay long enough for breakfast. "We start serving at six thirty. They could be first in line."

"Understood," Highcloud said. "We'll move as fast as we can."

CHAPTER 24

Yeti

There was an unusual amount of activity and noise inside the lodge Friday morning. Yeti heard the sounds of doors slamming, footsteps, suitcases being rolled down the hall, chatter and conversations.

From her spot on the side windowsill, she could see guests packing up their cars. Though her breath caused a small fog to form on the cold glass, she could tell it was much warmer outside today than it had been. The sun shone brightly and the icicles that hung from the edge of the lodge were melting away in a steady *drip-drip-drip* that turned the snow below them into slush. The sleds sat idle against the side of the lodge or leaned on the snow pile, nobody having time to play this morning.

Rocky walked past the window on his way to the tool shed. She wondered what he might be planning to work on. She'd seen him out back earlier in the week, and watched from the rear window as he'd installed a long pipe that led to nothing. She saw J.J. and Mitch helping guests with their luggage, rolling them outside on trolleys and placing them in their trunks or cargo bays. She hoped they'd come by later to give her some attention. Maybe they'd even play the game where she got to chase the bright red dot. They spent entirely too much time away from the lodge, in the cat's opinion. She could smell the sweat and musty melted snow on them when they returned, and she could tell from their animated voices and expressions that they'd had a good time, but she'd like it better if they stayed at the lodge more and spent more time with her. Maybe she'd hide under the bed in their room and grab their ankles the next time they tried to leave. That could work, couldn't it?

CHAPTER 25

Misty

The medical examiner's lab was moving as fast as it could, but things still took time. Deputy Highcloud had yet to call me Friday morning when Laurie and Kyle Jensen came to eat their breakfast at seven o'clock. I found myself staring at the two, wondering about them, wondering about Laurie's brother, whether they'd been truthful about what had happened to him, whether they'd had anything to do with Nigel Goodwin's death.

An *ahem* snapped me out of my thoughts. I looked up to see Amari at the desk, his room key lying on the countertop in front of me where he'd placed it.

I forced a smile at him. "Sorry, I was lost in thought."

He glanced at the Jensens before turning back to me, a puzzled look on his face. "What were you thinking about?"

Does he realize I suspect them? That my suspicions were why I'd been unwittingly staring at them? He might, but it was doubtful he'd call me a liar right to my face. I wondered whether he might suspect them, too. "Our new hot tub. It arrives tomorrow." I gestured to the back windows on the far wall of the great room, past the Jensens. "We plan to install it out back. I was wondering how much it will increase the water bill." Though not technically what I'd been thinking about, it was still true: it wasn't easy or cheap to get water up a mountain, and the lodge's monthly water bill was one of my largest expenses.

Amari either believed me or chose to let it go, and I checked him out. He'd had trouble rolling his suitcase in when he'd arrived, and he had trouble rolling it away now. I said, "I know you declined assistance when you checked in, but my boys would be happy to help. That looks heavy."

Amari again declined help. "It's not heavy. It's just got a stuck wheel."

Rocky was drinking coffee by the front window and happened to overhear. "Want me to take a look?"

I sang my handyman's praises. "Rocky can fix nearly anything."

To my surprise, Amari agreed. "That would be great. Thanks."

Rocky rounded up his toolbox, performed some magic on the wheel assembly, and had Amari's suitcase rolling smoothly in no time.

"Wow," Amari said. "It's like new."

Amari tried to offer Rocky a tip, but Rocky held up a hand. "Just happy I could help."

The Jensens came to my desk at 9:30 to check out. I had my suspicions that the couple could have killed Nigel Goodwin, but I hadn't completely ruled out the Fourniers or Sebastian yet, either, and Tyson Pell was still on my list, too.

I stared the Jensens down as I checked them out, but they seemed oblivious to my attempts to look into their minds. *Did you do it? Or was it someone else?*

As they stepped away from the counter, Laurie said, "I know it's premature, but I'm going to say it anyway. Have a merry Christmas, Misty."

"Thanks. You, too!"

Once they were out the door, I went to the front windows and watched as they rolled their bags across the cold, wet asphalt to their blue Subaru Outback. As they stowed their bags in the cargo bay, I spotted the trailer hitch, the one I'd slammed my shin against when I'd been helping Pebble wrangle the catering cart. The huge knot on my shin began to throb again in response, or maybe it had been throbbing all along and the reminder simply made me aware of it.

The couple climbed into their car and backed out of their space. They drove to the exit and waited as the usual long line of Friday ski traffic rolled by. Kyle hadn't turned on his blinker, though they'd surely be turning left to leave town. To my surprise, when there was a break in the traffic and they were able to move forward, they turned right instead of left.

Something's going on. I knew it in my gut.

If the Jensens killed Goodwin, the motive had to be Laurie's brother, didn't it? That seemed to be the most plausible explanation. The story they'd told Deputy Highcloud had made sense, but was it true or had they put their own spin on it? How could I learn more and find out? Again, my mind went back to the lift ticket on Laurie's jacket, and the next thing I knew I found myself calling the ski resort in Banff, asking to speak to someone about a private lesson. It was two hours earlier there, and I was lucky that the resort opened early. "I'm calling about Joshua Wagner," I said. "He was an instructor there last season? He gave my son a lesson and I was wondering if we could schedule another with him."

"Sore-ee," the woman said in the way that Canadians pronounced the word *sorry.* "He's not with the resort anymore."

"He's not? Why?"

"He passed away," the woman said. "Such a shame what happened to him. He was a great guy. Very friendly, as I'm sure you noticed."

I might have, had I actually met him. "He was so young. What happened? If you don't mind me asking." I felt uncomfortable posing the question, and I hoped she wouldn't consider my inquiry to be rude.

Fortunately, she was forthcoming. "From what I hear, he and his wife had an argument and he went out drinking. He passed out in his car. They found him the next morning frozen to death."

Frozen to death. Oh my gosh! Could this be the missing motive? I also suspected that Joshua Wagner might be the investor Sebastian had mentioned, the one rumored to have taken his own life. Of course, it appeared the rumor mill hadn't quite gotten the facts right. "Do you know what the argument was about?"

"Same thing all couples fight about—money. That's all I know."

I'd bet the money they'd argued about was the money Joshua had invested in Goodwin's Alberta resort. The loose connections of the case were weaving themselves together. I thanked the woman, hung up, and immediately placed a call to Deputy Highcloud. "I've got a motive." I told her what I'd learned. "The Jensens might have killed Goodwin in retribution for the death of Laurie's brother."

"We make a good team," she said. "You got the motive and I got the hard evidence."

"The lab results?"

"Yes. I just heard from them. They found traces of nitrous oxide in Goodwin's system."

"So, we've got them. Sled to rights." *Uh-oh*. Looked like I'd come down with a case of corniness. *I must've caught it from Kyle Jensen*. Even though it felt good to know that the case would soon be closed, given the sad circumstances, this didn't feel entirely like a victory. Justice could be a surprisingly elusive and complicated concept. But at least we'd get to the truth.

The deputy said, "The assistant M.E. speculates that Goodwin had the heart attack and died while the laughing gas was being administered, and that's why it didn't all get metabolized out of his system. I'm on my way to your lodge now to arrest the Jensens. If they try to check out, do your best to delay them."

"Too late." I bit my lip. "They just left, not two minutes ago. They turned right onto Beech Mountain Parkway from my lodge."

"Right? That's not the way out of town. They must be making a stop somewhere first. That could buy us some time. I'm on my way. I'll call the local police from my car."

I slipped my cell phone into my pocket and turned to J.J., who was sweeping the great room. "You're in charge of the lodge until I get back." With that, I ran out of the inn, slipping and sliding on the asphalt, wet with snowmelt.

Rocky was outside on a ladder, rehanging Christmas lights that had been weighted down with icicles and pulled loose from the building. His toolbox rested on the ground beside him. He called out as I slid and scrambled past him. "You all right, Misty? What's going on?"

It would take too long to explain. I continued my

precarious slipping, sliding sprint until I reached the exit. The traffic inched along in front of the lodge. The Jensens' car had already disappeared around a curve, though I caught a glimpse of it through the leafless trees as it negotiated another turn below. *Where are they going? Did they realize we might be on to them?*

I sprinted back to the lodge, nearly sliding into Rocky's ladder. I looked up at him, panting from the exertion. "The Jensens killed Goodwin! He had nitrous oxide in his system. That proves it! They turned right out of the parking lot."

"They did?" Two deep lines formed at the bridge of his nose. He knew what that right turn meant. They weren't leaving town—at least not yet or not via the primary route. *Are they trying to sneak out via a back road into Tennessee?* He climbed down his ladder. "Should we try to follow them?"

"Yes. Let's go!" With all of my guests checking out of the lodge and no new guests arriving until later this afternoon, I could leave my sons in charge for a short time. Problem was, the Jensens had a two-minute lead on us already, which would be even longer by the time we got into a vehicle and drove after them. If they'd turned off the parkway, it might be a lost cause. We might not be able to find them. But I had to feel that I'd done everything in my power to resolve the murder case—even if it meant nabbing two otherwise nice people.

"Let's take my truck." Leaving his open toolbox behind, Rocky hurried to his pickup, using his key fob to unlock the doors.

We climbed in, buckling ourselves into our seats in record time. He backed out of the space as fast as he dared and jammed on the gas, his tires spinning for a moment on the wet pavement before gaining traction. He braked at the exit. Vehicle after vehicle after vehicle drove past in front of us, all of them too close together for him to force his way in and the drivers too eager to hit the slopes to let us cut into the line.

My insides squirmed themselves into a tangled web of nerves. "Oh, come on!" I cried. "Someone let us in!"

A lone buck ventured out of the woods on the far side of the parking lot and, luckily for us, the oncoming traffic slowed lest the deer step out onto the road. Rocky punched the gas and we squeezed into the break in the line of cars. As the road wound back and forth, I scanned the side streets for a blue Subaru Outback with a trailer hitch. There was none to be seen.

Traffic came to a halt as we neared the ski resort. Most in line intended to turn left into the resort's parking lot, but the cars in the lot had backed up as it filled. An occasional car coming from the other direction stalled our progress, too, as those in our line had to wait for it to pass by before they could turn. I groaned. "This is a lost cause, isn't it?"

No sooner had I said those words than a blue Outback with Kyle Jensen at the wheel approached from the opposite direction, pulling a teardrop camper. Laurie sat in the passenger seat. They didn't notice Rocky and me in the long lineup of cars as they drove past.

"That's them!"

CHAPTER 26

Misty

My head whipped around so fast that I bumped my cheekbone on the headrest behind me. I eyed the trailer. What reason would the Jensens have to bring a camper up to the mountains when they had accommodations in my lodge all week? If they'd camped along their drive to North Carolina, why not park the camper in my lot? Clearly, they'd wanted to keep it a secret, out of sight. The built-in freezer in the small camper's kitchen wouldn't be big enough to fit a human body. They'd be lucky to fit a couple of ice-cube trays in it. *But the floorspace between the built-in benches just might be big enough to hold a deep freezer.*

"Turn around!" I cried. "Follow them!"

With an SUV right in front of us and another on our rear, Rocky had little room to maneuver. As he executed a time-consuming ten-point turn on the narrow road, I pulled out my cell phone and called Deputy Highcloud. I told her what I'd seen. "They're on the parkway heading down the mountain right now!"

"We'll try to intercept them," she said. "Stay on them

in case I need an update, but keep back until they're cuffed. Don't put yourselves at risk."

As I ended the call, Rocky pulled into the outbound lane. We followed the Jensens at a reasonable distance, behind two of the few cars headed out of town. My heart pounded as hard as if I'd just climbed Beech Mountain, and my ears pulsed with a warm throb. The Outback and camper eased around a curve to the right. We eased around the same curve twenty seconds later. Kyle Jensen slowed to wind around a bend to the left. We slowed and rounded the same bend a few loud heartbeats later.

They drove past the Mountaintop Lodge. So did we. Mitch was out front with a broom, cleaning snow from the sign so arriving guests could read it. He did a double take as Rocky and I drove past. A few seconds later, my phone pinged with a text from him. *What's going on?*

I texted back. *Capturing killers.*

He replied with a selfie. His eyes were round and his mouth gaped. *Be careful. I still need my mother.*

Awww. It was the sweetest thing he'd said to me in a long time. I commented with the kissy face emoji and, for once, he didn't text me the barfing emoji in return.

The two cars between us and the Jensens turned off at the road to the sledding hill, and we found ourselves directly behind the trailer. Rocky kept back, giving them space as Highcloud had instructed. The brake lights flashed on the trailer, then came on again, this time remaining illuminated. The camper came to a stop and so, presumably, did the car towing it though we couldn't see it from our position on the road directly behind them. Rocky braked, coming to a stop twenty yards or so behind the camper. Flashing blue lights lit up the bare trees head of us. No cars approached in the inbound lane. For safety purposes, law enforcement had blocked the parkway in both directions.

We watched as Officer Hardy walked up to speak to Kyle at the driver's window. Another Beech Mountain police officer came up on the passenger side of the Jensens' car to address Laurie.

The officers opened the doors and Kyle and Laurie climbed out, their hands in the air. Hardy directed the couple to stand at the edge of the road. The cops cuffed their wrists behind their backs and instructed them to kneel on the asphalt beside their car. Without snow pants on, they'd no doubt suffer wet, cold knees. The officers kept a watchful eye on the couple until a large SUV with the Watauga County Sheriff's Department logo came from the other direction. It pulled into our lane, facing us, its light bar flashing. Deputy Highcloud sat at the wheel. She raised her fingers in a subtle wave to Rocky and me, shifted the SUV into park, and opened her door, sliding down from the driver's seat.

With law enforcement on site now, Rocky pulled closer to the action. We climbed out and walked over, standing next to Deputy Highcloud as she read the Jensens their rights. The Jensens, suspected murderers yet also mannerly Midwesterners, looked up and gave us a nod in greeting. Both had tears in their eyes, appearing equally remorseful and resolute as they kneeled side by side, their shoulders touching in mutual support and solidarity.

Highcloud looked to Laurie. "We know your brother froze to death." Turning to Kyle, she said, "We also found nitrous oxide in Goodwin's system." Shifting her gaze between them now, Highcloud added, "You two want to come clean?"

The Jensens seemed to realize their best bet at this point was to cooperate. Or maybe they simply needed to get things off their chest to relieve their guilt.

After casting an apologetic glance at her husband, Laurie took most of the blame. "It was all my idea. I just couldn't let my baby brother die like that without making Nigel Goodwin pay for it." She gulped a sob and swayed on her knees, her voice raspy when she spoke again. "If not for Goodwin's greed, my brother would still be alive."

Noting the woman appeared on the brink of collapsing, Highcloud took her arm and helped her stand. She led her over to a boulder, brushing the snow from the stone before helping to settle her on it. "You admit that you killed Nigel Goodwin, then?"

"Yes." Laurie turned her head to wipe her tears on the shoulder of her coat. "We came here without a concrete plan other than to make Goodwin suffer the same fate as my brother. We brought a deep freezer in the camper. We figured the camper would be less suspicious than a U-Haul." She went on to say that they'd parked the camper in the driveway of a cabin they'd rented not far from the ski resort. They'd run an extension cord from the freezer in the camper to an outdoor electrical outlet.

Kyle sat back on his heels in the road, as if settling in to his fate. "We knew we'd have to look for an opportunity to get Goodwin away from the lodge." Instead, an opportunity had fallen into their laps.

Laurie picked up the story. "We spoke with Nigel Goodwin at the ski resort late Monday evening. He was having trouble getting in touch with his wife and Rayan about picking him up. We realized it was our chance. We offered him a ride back to the lodge. He sat in the front passenger seat, and I sat behind him."

Laurie looked down at the pink infinity scarf around her neck and gulped again. "I slipped my scarf over him and the seat like a lasso, and pulled back on it to hold his arms in place while Kyle forced the nitrous mask on him. He struggled for a few seconds before he went limp, but with his arms restrained there wasn't much he could do."

Her constant toying with the scarf made sense now. It was a major clue in the murder, an instrument of death. She must have felt as if she were wearing a noose around her neck.

Kyle explained that, at the time, they'd thought Goodwin had temporarily succumbed to the nitrous oxide as they'd planned, so he'd be easier to handle. They'd expected the effects to wear off shortly. It wasn't until after they'd put Goodwin in the freezer and he never regained consciousness and yelled or tried to fight his way out that they realized he had already died. "We didn't know what to do at that point, so we left him in the freezer and hurried back to the lodge. Later that night, I noticed that the window in our room had a latch on it, and we realized we could get in and out of our room that way. We'd seen the monitor in the lobby on our way in earlier. We knew the outside security cameras were covered in ice and snow, and that we could dump Goodwin's body outside without the camera recording it. We left his gear there, too. Nobody saw us leave the ski resort with him. We figured it would just look like he had a heart attack after walking back up the mountain from the resort. We didn't think the situation would raise any suspicions of foul play."

I now knew how they'd used up an entire box of tissues in a single day. They'd used them to wipe up the snow from the floor after climbing in and out of the window. It would have been a dead giveaway.

Laurie looked over at Kyle from her perch on the boulder, and the two exchanged a pitiful look. They hadn't been quite as crafty as they'd thought.

Kyle looked up at the deputy. "How did you know there was more to it? That he hadn't died of a heart attack?"

"Two things," Highcloud said, counting on her fingers. "First, his body temperature was lower than the ambient temperature. The only explanation was that he'd somehow been frozen. Second, the shape of the bruise on his face didn't quite correlate with skis or ski goggles."

I tossed in a question of my own for Laurie. "Did you actually see Goodwin get hit in the face with skis?"

Laurie looked my way, but there was no malice in her eyes. Only shame and sorrow. She shook her head. "No. That was a ruse. I thought it would explain the bruising."

"You did all of this to avenge your brother?" I asked.

Fresh tears welled up in Laurie's eyes as she nodded, and a dam within suddenly seemed to break. Her shoulders heaved as she sobbed, and I felt my heart break a little, too. After a moment or two, she was finally able to collect herself. "We were all dirt poor growing up, and we didn't want the same for our own families. Kyle and I got scholarships and were able to go to college, but Josh wasn't the college type. He became a brick mason. It was backbreaking work. Long hours, too. He and his wife lived on a shoestring to save up a down payment, and they were finally able to buy a modest house a few years back. But they always struggled to make ends meet, especially after the girls came along. When Joshua met Nigel Goodwin and found out about the Alberta resort, he was sure their ship had finally come in. It took a lot of convincing, but his wife finally agreed to investing the five grand they had in savings in the resort. It was all they had, but Goodwin wouldn't accept such a small amount. Josh went behind his wife's back and took out a second mortgage on their house."

I found myself wiping a tear from my cheek, too. "Is that what they argued about the night he died? The second mortgage?"

Laurie looked a little surprised by my question, not knowing I'd learned the details of her brother's death, but said, "Yes. She was so upset that she kicked him out. She would've come around eventually and forgiven him. We know that. I'm sure he knew it, too. But he went out drinking, had too much, and passed out in his car outside the bar. The bartenders noticed his car was still in the lot when they left, but he was slumped over so they didn't see he was inside. They figured he'd called an Uber or gotten a ride from one of the guys he'd been drinking with. By the time his wife found him the next morning, he'd frozen to death."

I couldn't imagine the horror, and I didn't even want to try.

Laurie burst into sobs again. "His wife has felt guilty ever since, that if she hadn't gotten so angry with him and kicked him out, he'd still be with us. The grief and guilt are eating her alive. We didn't blame her, though. We blamed Nigel Goodwin. He claims he only takes money from wealthy investors who can afford to lose it, but that's an outright lie! He had to know a ski instructor wouldn't have a hundred thousand dollars to lose, but he took our brother's money anyway. When his wife first got upset, Josh asked Goodwin for his money back, but Goodwin wouldn't return it. That's when my brother and his wife had the big fight that sent him to the bar." Laurie stopped her story there, though she did send a glance of regret my way. "Sorry for any damage we've done to your lodge's reputation. It's a nice place, and you're a gracious host."

Though I couldn't imagine the pain Laurie and her family had gone through, they'd dealt with that grief in the worst possible way. I prayed she wouldn't write a Yelp review from prison. The last thing I needed was my lodge becoming a destination for people looking for a nice place to dump a corpse.

I wasn't sure what to say in response. My emotions were all over the place. I figured I couldn't go wrong with "I'm sorry about your brother."

Highcloud appeared overcome with feelings, too. She swallowed hard and did a slow blink. I suspected she might have sent up a quick prayer while her eyes were closed.

Their confession made, the couple was gently loaded into Highcloud's SUV. After tipping her campaign hat at Rocky and me, the deputy slid into the driver's seat, and off they went to face justice.

CHAPTER 27

Misty

We followed Officer Hardy's patrol car as he drove back to the lodge to update Aileen that an arrest had been made. When we stepped inside, the remaining guests in the great room clamored around the officer, asking for details, but he raised a hand to put them off. "I need to speak with Aileen Goodwin first."

After discreetly updating my sons, Rocky and I sat at the desk, waiting to see if we could be of any assistance. Hardy had been in Aileen's room for a few minutes when we heard him emerge and knock on another door. "Rayan? Could you join us in Mrs. Goodwin's room, please?"

A quarter hour later, Hardy emerged and returned to the great room. The guests gathered around him and listened eagerly as he filled them in. "The Jensens have confessed to killing Nigel Goodwin."

Celeste's mouth dropped open. "The Jensens? I can hardly believe it!"

"Me, neither," Sebastian said. "Kyle was such a corn-pone. Are you for real, dude?"

Hardy sent my guest a long-suffering look. "Yeah. I'm for real."

The officer offered them an abbreviated version of the story, after which they appeared as conflicted as I felt. *It would be so much easier if the bad guys were entirely bad.* Even so, except in the case of immediate self-defense or defense of another, it was never right to take another person's life.

After Hardy left the lodge, the guests dispersed, returning to their rooms to pack for their departure. Thinking Aileen might need extra time to collect both her things and herself, I called her room and told her that she was welcome to a late checkout at no additional charge. "Rayan, too."

"Thanks, Misty," she said softly. "We'll take you up on that."

All of the other guests had gone when Rayan and Aileen came to the counter early that afternoon. Though Aileen's eyes were red and puffy from crying, her shoulders were square and she stood up straight. I sensed she had mustered some resolve to move forward now that she'd gotten some closure on her husband's murder. Even her clothing appeared less drab.

"I've spoken with the solicitors back in London," she said. "I'll take over as the chairman of the board of Adventure Capital. Rayan has agreed to stay on in a new role as the CEO. Nigel was primarily a front man, anyway. Rayan's done the bulk of the work for years now." She looked over at him. "I have no doubt he's up to the task."

I was glad Rayan's loyalty and patience had finally paid off for him. I was also glad I hadn't shown anyone his resignation later.

Rayan gave Aileen a grateful nod before turning back to Rocky and me. "My first order of business is to ensure the Fourniers' funds are returned."

"You don't plan to move ahead with the resort here, then?" I asked.

"No," Rayan said. "Aileen and I discussed it. We think it's best to focus on the resorts that are already in operation before expanding further."

Rocky asked, "What do you plan to do with the land? Are you going to sell it to Sebastian Cochrane?"

"We considered it," Aileen said. "Rayan even discussed the matter with him. But Sebastian had already moved on."

Rayan said, "He's looking into building a regulation-size indoor ice rink in the area instead. He found a relatively flat property near Banner Elk that would be suitable. The land is already cleared, as well."

A full-size indoor rink was a viable idea, a good one, even. An indoor rink could be open year-round, regardless of outdoor temperatures. He could maybe even host hockey tournaments or figure-skating competitions. And maybe some of the competitors or fans would stay at my lodge.

Aileen asked, "Any chance you have contact information for the wildlife man? Gus, I believe his name was?"

"I'm sure I could get it for you. Why?"

Rayan said, "We plan to turn the land over to him— or to the nonprofit he volunteers with, at any rate. Gus was right. The land should remain undeveloped."

My hands reflexively clasped in glee at my chest. I was thrilled to hear that the bears and deer and groundhogs would retain their riverside home. The locals who'd opposed the lodge would no doubt be happy, too, to hear that the land would remain untouched. *At least one good thing will come out of this tragedy.* I logged into my computer, typed Gus's full name into my browser, and found a phone number for his wildlife photography business. I jotted the number on a sticky note and handed it over the counter. "Here you go."

Rocky and I stood outside as my boys helped Aileen and Rayan load the SUV and the van. As the two drove away, I felt a sense of relief. Still, I wondered if it would be a good idea to burn some sage, like Brynn did to cleanse the lodge. I had only a second or two to ponder the matter before a flatbed truck turned into the parking lot, loaded with our brand-new hot tub.

"Hot damn!" Rocky said, slapping his knee. "Now we're in business!"

CHAPTER 28

Yeti

Humans were ridiculous creatures. They bring a tree inside, and when she tried to climb it, kept pulling her away. What did they think trees were for if not climbing? They also got annoyed when she batted at the balls hanging from the tree, or used her teeth to pull on the ribbons attached to the gifts below.

At least Misty had given her a new soft cat bed to nap in. Rocky had built her a cat tree out of logs, too. It was the perfect gift. She could sharpen her claws on the bark and watch the activity outside from atop the flat surfaces he'd sanded smooth. J.J. and Mitch had given her several new toys, including a catnip-filled mouse and a battery-operated snake that wiggled and slithered all over the floor. All in all, it was a wonderful Christmas for the cat, just what she deserved.

CHAPTER 29

Misty

Christmas Day was relaxing, festive, and perfect, with just a handful of guests to tend to. Jack drove up from Raleigh again. J.J., Mitch, and Pebble were already at the lodge, and Rocky's other two daughters came up from Boone, along with his son-in-law, bringing Rocky's granddaughter with them, too. *What a cutie!*

We pushed tables together and ate a fantastic holiday feast in front of the fire in the great room, catered by the Greasy Griddle, of course. We topped it off with wine from the local wineries.

Afterward, we gathered around the fire pit out back to roast marshmallows, drink hot spiced cider, and sing Christmas carols. When Jack launched into the first verse of "Rudolph the Red-nosed Reindeer," I cried, "no songs about noses!"

Rocky cocked his head. "So, no 'chestnuts roasting on an open fire, Jack Frost nipping at your nose'?"

"No! And I don't want to hear "'twas the night before Christmas,' either. No 'laying his finger aside of his nose . . .'"

Thankfully, there were plenty of other carols we could sing, and we could forego the old poem entirely.

All in all, my first Christmas in the lodge was a wonderful holiday.

New Year's Eve was quite festive, too, though a bit more demure. We spent it with Patty and her husband Eli, a long-haul trucker who was off the road and home for the holidays. After a delicious dinner of diner take-out at the lodge, we soaked in the hot tub, grateful for the relief the warm, bubbling water and powerful jets provided to our tired, achy muscles.

"Aaaah," Eli said, a look of ecstasy on his face as he leaned his head back against the edge. "This jet is doing wonders for my sciatica."

The water was doing wonders for me as well, making me feel renewed, washing away the worries that had recently plagued me. I was grateful for the fresh start the new year represented.

On January second, I'd just checked in a nice couple from Nashville, a carpenter and a police detective, when Brynn's Prius pulled up in front of the lodge. I walked out to help her with her bags. She climbed out and gave me a hug. "It's so good to see you, Misty!"

"You, too, Brynn. I'm glad you're back. I've missed you. How was the trip?"

"Fantastic!" she cried. "The solstice celebration was everything I'd hoped it would be."

"Thanks for the postcards," I told her, "and that beautiful Moravian star you sent."

"My pleasure."

We went around to the back of her car and she opened the trunk. She grabbed one of her bags, and I grabbed the other.

As we headed toward the lodge with her luggage, Brynn turned my way and asked, "Did I miss anything exciting here?"

Did you ever! "Meet me at the hot tub out back in ten minutes. We can soak our legs while I fill you in."

"Hold the phone." She stopped in her tracks as her face lit up in surprise. "We've got a hot tub now?"

"Yep," I said. "Rocky installed it just in time. We've booked a group for the Highland Games this summer. The guy who called asked whether we had a hot tub. We wouldn't have landed the booking otherwise. He said his shoulders get real sore after the caber-toss competition."

Brynn wagged her brows. "A bunch of men in kilts running around the lodge? Sounds fun."

I certainly expected it would be. I slid my assistant a mischievous grin. "We'd better order some tartans and stock up on the scotch whiskey."